Critical Acclaim

"There is nobody like he[r] ... in her original way"—*A. ...*

"Completely alive in its ... ... humour ... Miss Brophy manages her plot gaily, and her novel is fresh and full of the unexpected"—*Guardian*

"Brigid Brophy has talent, and something more than talent ... originality ... Her book has many things: colour, gaiety, neat dialogue, well-aimed satire, moments of deep insight"—*Daily Telegraph*

"Totally successful in its delicate and compassionate handling of a series of difficult relationships ... Miss Brophy writes with increasing power ... a most interesting writer to watch"—*Sunday Times*

"Talent, odd but abundant: Miss Brophy gets better and better"—*Evening Standard*

"*The King of a Rainy Country* is well written indeed"—*The Times*

BRIGID BROPHY

was born in London in 1929, daughter of the novelist John Brophy. She was educated at St. Paul's Girls' School and St. Hugh's College, Oxford. In 1954 she married Michael Levey, who was the Director of the National Gallery from 1973 to 1986. He was knighted in 1981. They have a daughter and three grandchildren. In 1984 Brigid Brophy developed multiple sclerosis, a progressive and disabling neurological affliction.

Her first novel, *Hackenfeller's Ape* (forthcoming from Virago), was published in 1953, and *The King of a Rainy Country* in 1956. They were followed by *Flesh* (1962), *The Finishing Touch* (1963), *The Snow Ball* (1964), *In Transit* (1969), *The Adventures of God in His Search for the Black Girl* (1973) and *Palace Without Chairs* (1978).

In addition to her series of brilliant fictions, Brigid Brophy has written plays and many non-fiction works, of which perhaps her most famous is *Mozart the Dramatist*. This first appeared in 1964, and a revised edition was issued in 1988 to wide acclaim. She was one of the founders of Writers Action Group, which successfully campaigned for the establishment in Britain of Public Lending Right for authors. She is a member of the Labour Party and of the National Secular Society. She has held office in the Writers' Guild of Great Britain, a non-party-political trade union affiliated to the T.U.C., and in the British Copyright Council. She is a vice-president of the National Anti-Vivisection Society and is known for her abiding and impassioned championing of animal rights.

Awards include the Cheltenham Festival Prize, 1954, for a first novel; the *London Magazine* prize for prose (1962); and the 1985 Tony Godwin award. A loyal urbanite, Brigid Brophy lives between Earls Court and South Kensington.

VIRAGO
MODERN
CLASSIC

NUMBER
353

BRIGID BROPHY

✰

THE KING
OF A
RAINY COUNTRY

With a New Afterword by the Author

✰

But these are all lies:
men have died from time to
time and worms have eaten them,
but not for love.

✰

Published by VIRAGO PRESS Limited 1990
20–23 Mandela Street, Camden Town, London NW1 0HQ

First published in Great Britain by Martin Secker & Warburg Ltd 1956
Copyright Brigid Brophy 1956
Afterword copyright © Brigid Brophy 1990

The right of Brigid Brophy to be identified as the Author of this
work has been asserted in accordance with the Copyright, Designs
and Patents Act 1988

All rights reserved

A CIP Catalogue record for this book
is available from the British Library

Printed in Great Britain by Cox & Wyman

For
MICHAEL LEVEY
my husband

CONTENTS

		PAGE
PART ONE	. . .	9
PART TWO	. .	105
PART THREE.	.	203

PART ONE

✷ I ✷

I HAD been scared for a fortnight. Concentrating on my fear, I became dogged and literal. At once another fear seized me: fear that I might bore Neale.

I recognized the day, the moment I woke, as the day of the interview. Only secondly did I remember I was moving house. About nine, earlier than I had appointed, I took a taxi to Neale's flat.

He came to the front door carrying a plate of cornflakes and helped with one hand as I lifted my cases into the bedroom. While I made a pile of them, embarrassedly, he relaxed against the wall and went on eating.

"Want some?"

"No, I've had breakfast."

"Well, I expect you want to get off. You can unpack later."

"There's no point in my arriving too soon," I said.

"Why not? The sooner you go, the sooner it'll be over."

I looked up at him; he was taking a mouthful. Nevertheless I assumed he meant me to know he had read my cowardice. What he did not mean to shew was his reaction.

He led me to the front door, carrying his plate affectedly at shoulder level because the corridor was narrow, and saw me off without lingering.

I walked to Oxford Street and took a bus. My mouth

was so dry that it caused me a palpable pain to ask for my ticket. I got off at Marble Arch and began to walk down Park Lane, listening to the compact sound of my footsteps. It was the very last of summer or the very first of autumn. Without my noticing when, the pavements had contracted and toughened under the early cold. All summer they had felt hard, dry and brittle like a dog's paws; this morning they suddenly offered a surface crisp and resistant. Between traffic I glimpsed that the trees on the other side were autumnal; patches of mist hung above the hollows of the park. But for the moment it could not sadden me.

To my surprise the orange sunlight still contained warmth. On my face I hardly felt it, but where it struck my arms and shoulders I was warmed through the wool of my suit. It reminded me of some comfort that had been applied to me in my childhood, perhaps the feeling of a hot-water bottle, in its cover, being held to my ear.

Something of the morning's poignancy penetrated my concentration; and it was followed by a sorrowful quickening, a resigned sense of adventure. I walked faster. With interviews in mind, I felt compelled to define my attitude to the time of year: I told some imprecisely imagined interlocutor that each year I hoped to have outgrown being moved by the autumn and each year I hadn't. Oblivious in autobiographical fantasy I carried myself down the road and turned left. I brought myself to a stop outside a modern portico, beside which a brass plate read: d'Arcy Appointments Bureau. Cowardice tightened its screw on my stomach.

I took out my compact and comb, but the whole neighbourhood, with its expensive false pride, vetoed my using them. Knowing I had been blown untidy by an autumn wind and melted shiny by a summer sun, I pushed the glass door. I was nineteen and this was the first time I had looked for a job.

Inside, I found the correct door and knocked on it. A girl's voice called "Come in."

My fear vanished and I never thought of it again.

I had fallen in love with Neale two years before at a coffee party. He sat on the floor cross-legged, holding a golliwog. I sat on the bed, facing him. Next to me was a man I had been interested in. That afternoon, however, when he spoke to me I scarcely answered, and when he moved closer to me I moved away. After half an hour I was near the top of the bed. Looking for something to play with, I turned back the counterpane and pulled out my hostess's pillow, which I took on to my knee and began pummelling and weighing in my hands. "Tanya," I called to her, "a new occult practice. You hold someone's pillow and let their personality seep through. Or else it's a branch of phrenology. One feels the bumps."

"I should have thought the rest of the bed would be more informative," said the man next to me.

Camouflaged by our playthings, Neale and I watched each other. I studied him in a peculiar way, rather as my eye might have run over a beloved building, feeling its way into the shape and the stone: I surveyed Neale not for curiosity's sake, nor as a possible conquest, but imagining what it was like to be him.

For each of us there was the question: was the other equally interested? We believed so; we could not trust our own belief. We looked again. Our looks met, and retired, Neale's into the golliwog, mine into the pillow I held.

Neale's gesture of retirement was a pained angular turn of the head, sideways and down, and as my eye caught it I recognized that I was understanding it, or

13

rather following it like a map or a musical score: it was as meaningful to me as a gesture of my own.

One or two people left the party. The man next to me asked me to go out to tea with him. He was ten years older than Neale and me, and had served in the war: he was big, brutal to look at, very gentle in speech. I knew his rule was bed or no bed with no shades of indecision or persuasion between.

He stood up, and asked me to tea again. I refused. I was unflattered by his complaisance. I had hoped he would protest and that Neale would see. Emotionally opportunist, I felt half regretful to see him go unexploited. The wintry afternoon darkened and Tanya did not switch on the lights, perhaps hoping to speed her guests; and at last none of them was left except Neale and myself.

We spoke to one another through Tanya. The conversation became lazy and full of pauses, almost immobile under the memory of the party that was past. Even Tanya stopped chattering, although her vitality did not cease: she curled girlishly on the window-ledge, to catch the last light, and painted her nails. Her long face, yellow and bumpy like a walnut, nodded on a body too spindly for it. She looked older than she was, but she always had done: she was unchangeable: when we were all eighty she would have the comfort of looking—still—forty. Childishly she held out her hands for us to admire; then, slipping down from the window, said:

"Now, young man. You must take this young lady out to tea."

My excitement was cut off: I knew that if Neale had any spirit he must object.

I did not know, at that time, his curious obedience. He stood up; picked his coat off the floor and his leather gloves off Tanya's dressing-table, and said: "Very well."

14

I felt I should protest; instead I said to Neale, "Thank you," and to Tanya, "Thank you very much." I added: "For the party," in case Neale should think me beholden for her good offices.

Neale said to her: "About the golliwog——"

"O I'm sure it would love to have tea."

"It would be easier if I knew which sex it is."

"It's a boy, surely?"

He put it down on the dressing-table. "Then I don't want it."

"O my poor Neale!" Tanya picked it up. "I don't mean to be coarse, but now I look at it more closely"— she thrust it at him—"I think it's a girl."

"I don't want it in·that case, either."

Tanya halted, baffled at having failed to be obliging. She repeated, wailingly: "But I'm sure it would love to have tea."

"Very well." Neale took it. "I'll give it tea, but I've no use for it."

"How cruel you are!"

"Nonsense," he said, putting the toy in his pocket. "Does it good. Teaches it its proper place." He added to me, as we went down the stairs: "You see, I'm afraid of disappointing it."

We went out into the half-dark. Neale asked me, "Are you good at marbles?"

"Yes, very."

"Bet you're not as good as I am."

From time to time I looked at him in the light of the few early lamps to be switched on. He was of a manageable height; his clothes were rather shabby and predominantly brown and his way of wearing them was, like his whole way of moving, neat, self-contained, precisely defined. His topcoat was too tight and gave him a pouter-pigeon chest which seemed to be leading us on

15

our journey; only just behind it came his napoleonic nose. His colouring and the whole cast of his face were napoleonic and the skin was easily ruffled or furrowed.

"Isn't it cold? Let's walk faster." He set off and out-distanced me. I halted.

"What are you waiting for?"

"A reasonable pace."

"All right. Here you are." We started again; but at once he began to go faster. I clenched my teeth, determined not to pant, and kept up with him. He looked at me, and giggled. "You mustn't run. That's a cheat. It must be strictly walking." We reached the teashop panting openly and both laughing.

He put the golliwog on a seat by itself and ordered tea for three.

"Three?"

"One is for him"—Neale pointed—"or her."

For the next few days I waited either for some sign to come to me casually that Neale had never thought of me again or for him to sweep me away, perhaps literally and to some exotic country. When we did meet again, I had imagined a million meetings in advance, each more romantic than the real one; and yet, because my fantasy had failed to capture Neale as he was and had been unable to answer my questions about him, the real meeting was more exciting than the invented. I thought I should remember it inflexion by inflexion but it merged into later meetings, and they merged into our knowing one another well. Even then our understanding surprised us. We would light on consonances which stabbed us both like poetry, and Neale would say "O yes, yes, yes", each word spoken on an indrawn breath so that it was no more than a noise, a warning cry or mating call. Once when we spoke of this mannerism he said he had learnt it from me, but I thought it was the other way round.

We lent each other money without keeping account; we spoke of what *we* could afford; sometimes we discussed a house *we* would own. Our relationship was verbal: allusive and entangled. Deviating further and further into obliquity, we often lost track. "I don't think I think you know what I mean." "We'd better say it openly." "Much better. But I'm not going to be the first to say it." "Neither am I."

Between confidence and the luxury of giving up we veered, straddled or fell. Sometimes Neale warned me to expect nothing of him. At other times it was he who accused me of not trying. "All that matters is to try and try. We've got to keep on searching for it." Once, a third person who was with us demanded:

"What is this it?"

"O, just it," Neale said.

"I never know what you two are talking about."

We were pleased at being coupled as *you two*, but also afraid lest, in the unspokenness of our understanding, neither of us really understood.

In the d'Arcy Appointments Bureau it was confidence that ruled me, but I did not have to supply it myself. The woman who received me—I thought it unlikely she was actually Miss d'Arcy—had a gift for setting people at ease; evidently this was why she had been chosen for her job, and the job had in turn developed the gift. Cleanly but quietly dressed; pleasant-looking without making a bid for beauty; personal but without personality: she reminded me at once of the ideal air hostess and of the ideal aeroplane—pressurized and thermostatically controlled, perpetually in living-room condition. Even while I observed it, the temperature made its effect. I recognized that a natural friendliness was here prostituted, but I could feel no indignation; I might have been in the control of an excellent hypnotist, and while I was

17

thinking that the passes were meant only to put me in a trance I began slipping into it.

I sat back and told her more about myself than I had meant to. I said I was not looking for a career; I expected to have to work only for a year or two and wanted a job I could live on meanwhile.

"Now, what speed is your shorthand?"

"Slow," I said. "But supplemented by a quick intelligence."

"I see." She made a note. "And your typing?"

"Much better than my shorthand."

"About what speed?"

I found I could not remember what range typing speeds came into. I was afraid that if I named a speed I might accidentally claim a world record. "Quite honestly, I can't remember. But I'm competent."

She nodded, and made another note. "Your shorthand is Pitman's?"

"Basically. That is, I use it as the basis of my system."

"*Your* system?"

I was pleased at wringing a little surprise from her. "I have my own system, rather as Bernard Shaw did."

"O yes?"

"Fundamentally," I said, "my interests are literary— or at least concerned with the arts. I'd like a job, if possible, on the literary side."

"Yes. I see."

"Is that crying for the moon? Does everyone ask for it?"

"Well, a lot of people do seem to think they'd like to be an author's secretary."

"And you can't do anything for them?"

"I wouldn't say that. We like to get the right person fixed up with the right job. We like our clients to be suited."

18

"Then——?"

"I've got a bookseller here," she said, pulling a box towards her and taking out a card. "Would that suit you, do you think?"

"Perfectly, I imagine."

"It's only five pounds a week."

"Well, I suppose—if it really suited me——"

She smiled. She pushed away the box, pulled up a typewriter, rolled in a sheet of paper and began to type rhythmically and fast. "What do you think of the weather we're having?"

"It's heavenly, isn't it?"

"Isn't it? I couldn't have believed the summer would last so long." She pulled out the paper. "There you are. You can go and see him any time in business hours."

I thanked her and folded the paper.

Outside on the landing I looked at it. The bookseller's name was Finkelheim: the address was in the same street as Neale's flat. I burst back into the office. "This address you've just given me—it's the street I live in. The number should be just opposite. Not that I've ever noticed a bookseller there, but I only moved in today."

"Really?" The woman smiled friendlily, unsurprised, not even amused by my enthusiasm. "Well in that case you simply must get the job, mustn't you? No trouble about arriving in time in the mornings."

"No. It will be ideal."

"It's somewhere off the Tottenham Court Road, isn't it?"

"Yes."

"Well, I do hope you get it. And that it suits you."

I took the bus back the way I had come; and then, as I passed Neale's front door, smiled as if I was keeping from it a secret to my advantage. There was no book-shop opposite; at the number I was looking for I found only a grubby hallway, which seemed to be open to the public. I went in; it smelt, like the entrance to Neale's, of cats. There was a threadbare staircase. I started up it. On the first floor I stopped to comb my hair, but I did not like to powder because it was too dark to see the result. I went on; and at the fourth or fifth landing found a door marked Finkelheim.

He was a bonily handsome man of about thirty-five, with a heavy black stubble on a white skin. His office was infinitesimal and piled with books; he could hardly open the door to me and I could hardly squeeze in. In the far corner was a table where I assumed I should work, but for the moment I sat on a kitchen chair beside his desk.

He spoke with a strong lisp such as I had never heard before from a real person.

He asked me my name, my first name and whether I had a nickname; how old I was; where I lived.

"Just opposite, as a matter of fact."

He leered quickly. "Alone?"

"No. No, with a friend."

He told me he would not test my shorthand as I might be nervous. "Mostly it will be only writing letters. I am mostly wholesale, you see?"

"Yes, I see."

"They told you five pounds a week?"

"Yes."

"That all right?"

"Yes."

"When can you start?"

"When would you like?"

"Now? Have you got something to do? Won't you start right now?"

"I suppose I could."

"Thank God. I have got two months' letters."

20

"Shall I move over there, then?"

"That's right." He paused suddenly. "You said you have got a good education? I mean you are really all right with educated things?"

"Hopelessly intellectual."

"Thank God again."

He dictated me four letters. "Right. You do those, then we have some more."

"Right."

"There's one other thing. This d'Arcy Employment Bureau. You know I have to give them your first week's salary? I mean, I give it to you, then I have to give the same to them all over again. That makes ten pounds."

"Yes."

"Well, what if we tell them I only give you four. I really give you five, but I only have to give them four. Making nine pounds. That all right? You trust me?"

"I suppose it's all right, if you really want to do it."

"It's better that way. You go ahead and type it. Type 'I have taken employment with Mr. Finkelheim at four pounds a week', and you sign it, see."

I rolled the paper into the machine. He got up and came across the books to my table. "One other thing. Those letters I gave you—I dictate rough. You put them into educated English, see."

After I had typed the affidavit for the employment bureau, I read back my shorthand of Finkelheim's first letter. It ran: "Dear Sirs: Your order for thirty of the Irish book is underhand we thank you for same and forward." I typed: "Thank you for your order for thirty copies of the Irish book, which we are sending you."

I treated the other letters in the same way and took them to Finkelheim's desk.

"You go to lunch now," he said.

I rang Neale, but there was no answer. I lunched at the Indian restaurant in the next street.

When I got back to the office, Finkelheim said: "Look, what you give me is maybe the real class, but I don't want it. I want what my business colleagues will recognize as class."

"I'll try," I said. It seemed to me that his accent was now cockney.

I re-typed the first letter: "We are in receipt of your order for thirty (30) copies of the Irish book. We have pleasure in forwarding you the same."

Finkelheim read the letter twice. Then he said: "By God, you're quite a girl!"

When I got home that night, Neale opened the door and began: "Which reminds me, I've had you a key cut. It's in the bedroom."

"Thank you." Squeezing past him in the corridor, I noticed he was wearing a floppy cravat made of black ribbon. "I've not seen that before."

"It's my tie for reading Baudelaire in."

"Is tonight your night for reading Baudelaire on?"

"Well, isn't it?" he said. "Isn't it that sort of evening? Hasn't it been that sort of day?"

I went into the bedroom. "I suppose so. My French is very bad."

I began to unpack. From the kitchen Neale called through: "You can have the two bottom drawers. Throw out anything of mine."

However, there was nothing of his in them except some lemon-yellow newspaper and a pair of canvas shoes.

Presently he came and stood in the bedroom door. "Not every girl can boast of two bottom drawers."

"I don't know that it's a boasting matter."

"Mm. Did you get a job?"

"Yes. With a man who sells books."

"The English for that is a bookseller."

"That's just where you're wrong." I told him about Finkelheim; in particular about the changes of accent. "When he answers the phone, he uses the lisp. Sometimes he keeps it up, but sometimes, if it's someone he seems to know well, he relapses into cockney. He's not sure which to use with me."

"Do you think he's schizoid?"

"Almost certainly."

"I'd better keep an eye on you, if you're to work for him."

I was pleased.

"Where is this place?" Neale said.

"Just opposite. Number thirty-eight."

I could see he admired me for having kept the secret until I was asked. He paid me the compliment of his catch-phrase for surprise: "Well, bugger me backwards!"

"Not in *those* trousers," I answered ritually.

"I should think supper's ready," he said.

We went through—the kitchen was the only other room. He had set the table with a cloth and cut some bread. In the middle of the table stood a jar of marmalade; on the window-sill, which was next to the table, a melon and a camembert.

"What's in the frying-pan?"

"The pudding. I invented it tonight."

"What's it made of?"

"Cornflakes and syrup."

We ate it, out of the pan, after the rest of the food. Neale made coffee. Finally I began to clear up.

"O, leave it. Leave it tonight. My life has enough washing up. We could go into the other room and look at the sky."

We stood at the window side by side, not looking at

one another. "Isn't it sad?" Neale said; then, in a moment: "O, how I wish it would die."

I said nothing.

"Why is it so sad? Why *is* this time of year? Why won't it give up?"

"I don't know."

"What are we to do?"

"Every year," I said, "I hope the autumn won't move me. But every year it does."

"Yes, that's it. Yes, yes."

Presently in the dark I sat down in the wing chair, my back half-turned to Neale and the window.

"Poor Baudelaire," he said.

"Why?"

"It's too dark to read."

After a moment I asked: "Do you want the lights on?"

"No."

Later, Neale stirred; the curtain jerked. "No," he repeated. "It's not as if one didn't know."

"If you know anything, don't withold it."

"What do I know? I only know that—or, rather, I only know: Je suis comme le roi d'un pays pluvieux, Riche mais impuissant. . . ."

"Yes."

"Isn't that sad?"

"Yes." I rested my head on the wing of the chair. "I can bear anything except a status quo."

"Ah, but if one can't bear either of the alternatives?"

"I suppose if that were really so," I said, "then . . ."

"Is it true there are only two alternatives? There ought to be a third."

"Perhaps there is a third."

"Perhaps there is. Do you think it's likely?"

I said after a moment: "Yes, I think so." I couldn't tell quite where Neale was, or if he was on the point of moving: but I knew he was no longer looking through the window; he was turned towards me, and he was tensed.

I moved, intending perhaps to stand up; but I only fitted myself better into the chair.

"Neale?"

"Yes."

"I want to know something."

"Well?"

"Will you tell me?"

"Probably, I should think."

I paused, selecting which of the questions. "Why did you invite me to come and live here?"

"O, that," he said. He felt his way abruptly across the room. "Tell you tomorrow." I heard him lift his topcoat off the back of the door and put it on. "No time now. I've got to go to work."

"O, of course," I said.

"Had you forgotten?"

"Almost."

"Ha! What does that indicate? That you wanted——? Anyway, there's no time now."

Still without putting the lights on, we went to the front door. As we opened it, a blast of frostiness and a yellowish dazzle of street lighting fell on us. Neale stood for a moment hunched in a wizened attitude.

"It seems terrible to let you go out."

"Nonsense. I love it. Don't you be sorry for me." He went without farewells.

I put on the light in the kitchen and blinded myself for a moment. Then I washed up, thinking of the squalid restaurant—he had once taken me there to eat—where Neale did the washing up all night. He was aggressive in his refusal to be fastidious.

I tidied the kitchen a little and tried to divide the

draining-board into two regions, one for the pan scourers and one for Neale's shaving material.

Sitting at the kitchen table I wrote a letter to the d'Arcy Employment Bureau explaining I had cheated them. However, it seemed unfair to incriminate Finkelheim, so I tore the letter up. Instead I wrote on a blank sheet CONSCIENCE MONEY and folded a pound note into it, wondering if it would provoke Miss d'Arcy to surprise.

I undressed, washed at the sink and walked through to the bedroom, where I got into Neale's bed.

✳ II ✳

AUTUMN settled on us. Neale seemed to wear his great-coat perpetually, wherever he was. He would clench his hands in the pockets, tighten his shoulders and seem to sharpen his nose: time and again he would quote— it was like a tune going round our heads—"Bientôt nous plongerons dans les froides ténèbres; Adieu, vive clarté de nos étés trop courts."

"I don't know why you go on saying nous plongerons. It seems to me we have plunged."

"Ha. But one can go on saying adieu."

In the mornings the sun was red and frosty behind mist. In the evenings the mist was slight, little more than a rough feeling as one drew breath; it hung from street lamp to street lamp like a sad triumphal swag; and sometimes as we opened the front door we could see it puff into the flat. I worked all day for Finkelheim, and Neale at the restaurant all night.

Often we had people to supper, and we used to play gramophone records afterwards. When no one came Neale would hurl me out into the dark as soon as we had eaten, and we would walk down the road to the pub. "Isn't it worth coming out into the cold—to enter this warmth?" At first we played shove-halfpenny; but I became so good that I could be sure of beating Neale, and we gave it up. We were seldom alone. Occasionally, instead of parting from me outside the pub, Neale would

27

walk back with me before he went to work. More rarely still, as I was going to work in the morning, he would say: "I'm not sleepy yet. Walk you round the block once, before you go in to Finkelheim's."

Finkelheim got through his arrears and we had less to do. He took to going out, after dictating me some letters to get on with—I imagined he found the office too cold for him. In so small a place, it should have been possible to work up a fug, but its rawness protruded. Everything was new except the black gasfire which had never been connected. The books themselves, still in their dust jackets, were publishers' remainders; most of them were printed on thick paper which weighed incongruously light. A few were piled into bookshelves unseasoned and unpainted, which I imagined Finkelheim had had made on the cheap only just before I came; the dust that lay on them was blond, more like sawdust than the deposit of real books. Where I had cleared a track to my table I had revealed the floor covering as equally new and cheap: yellow-ochre linoleum, with a pattern of orange ivy leaves. There was a small dormer window, but the office was lit by a mauve strip on the ceiling.

Confined together, Finkelheim and I were bound to observe one another and to think what we saw important. We kneaded our relationship for a day or two, and then it took shape: small, lumpish, putty-coloured but reassuring because defined; it created the atmosphere the place lacked. The leer he had given me at our first interview grew into a game. He would say:

"You still sharing with a friend?"

"Yes."

"You let me know when the friend moves out."

However, I felt perfectly safe. The game could not grow beyond a certain intensity for lack of material.

Had we been set down in a place where work did not provide a common convention and our proximity was not enforced, we should have been dizzy with freedom; we should have misunderstood one another, stumbled over one another verbally and finally, awakening to the strangeness of the context, seen one another as strange.

Our acquaintance expanded by jumps: but we were on an island and its outer limits were fixed.

One of the jumps happened when Finkelheim had been out in the morning. A man had called and left a circular begging for a Jewish charity. I gave it to Finkelheim on his return, and he seemed to study it for a long time. I had the impression he was wondering whether to say something to me. I went on working.

"You think I'm a Jew?" he suddenly said.

"It's none of my business. But I assumed so."

"You assumed—good."

"Why good?"

"Because that's what I wanted you to assume."

"But actually you're not?"

"No. No more than you. You keep this under your hat."

"Of course."

He took a piece of paper out of his wallet and passed it to me. It was a Home Office document recording that someone named Gilchrist had changed his name to Finkelheim.

"Do you mean you're really Gilchrist?"

"I used to be."

"I don't quite see why you changed it."

He took the document back and folded it away. "A man I know gave me the tip when I first came into this business. 'You want to save yourself a lot of trouble?' he said to me. 'Then you change your name so it looks you're a Jew. That way nobody will expect any easy

29

terms from you. You won't get asked any favours.' It seemed pretty sensible to me. What I didn't reckon on was the real Jews would ask the favours." He picked up the circular and crumpled it. "I can't stand Jews."

I felt obliged to demur.

"You don't know what you're talking about," said Finkelheim. "I tell you—Jews. They're soft-hearted, sentimental—that's Jews."

From then on he never used the Jewish lisp to me; and when he picked up the telephone and lisped there was a complicity between us.

In the office it was easy to talk to Finkelheim, easy to find him attractive, easy to control what I felt. In that world I was on a simple, shapely planet: but outside and all round it lay a far more important world: the cosmos of my relationship to Neale, shifting rather than noticeably expanding, frightening in its infinity. Crossing the road to and from work, I changed the scale of my thoughts. I wondered, as a problem in probability, if the inner and outer universes would ever touch.

One starry night Neale and I walked home from the pub past Finkelheim's. The contrast struck me between Neale's elusiveness and my easy advances into knowing Finkelheim. I felt impatient.

"Neale, do you remember what I asked you the night I first came?"

"You mean, why . . . ?"

"Yes. You never told me."

"I must go. I shall be late. I'll tell you tomorrow."

"You said that last time," I called.

He stopped beneath a tree and shouted: "But this time I really will."

However, the next night we had a guest. I went into the kitchen and found him sitting alone with his back to me. He looked round and then stood up. He was a fair, thin young man, facially rather like Michelangelo's David.

"Hullo. Who are you? Where's Neale?"

"Est-ce que vous parlez français, mademoiselle?"

"O *Lord*. Un tout petit, petit peu, monsieur."

He bowed a little. "François Dulappe."

I told him my name. "You've no idea how foolish English people feel at having to say their own name aloud."

"Excusez-moi?"

"N'importe. C'est trop difficile à traduire."

We sat down facing one another at the kitchen table.

"Où est Neale?"

François alluded with his head towards the bedroom.

I said, "Il dort? Encore? C'est longtemps qu'il dort aujourd'hui."

"Il doit être très fatigué."

"Ou très paresseux." After a moment I went to the bedroom. The door was shut, and Neale had pinned on it: Do Not Wake. Ne Pas Reveiller.

I went back to François, who said: "Il dort?"

"Oui, il dort."

François asked, "Vous connaissez bien la France?"

"Non, pas très. Un peu. Ceci est votre première visite à Londres?"

"Oui."

"Ah! Votre première visite. Où habitez-vous?"

"En France?"

"Oui, en France."

"À Paris," he said.

"Ah. À Paris." I looked at my watch.

He asked. "Vous êtes pressée?"

"Pressée? Non. Je demeure ici."

"O. Mois aussi."

31

"Vous aussi?"

"Moi aussi je demeure ici."

"Neale vous a invité?"

"Oui."

"O. Bienvenu."

"Merci."

"Je vous en prie." I looked round the kitchen. "Il faut que je prépare quelquechose à manger."

"Puis-je vous aider?"

"Non, merci."

I chopped some onions, put them on to fry, and began to do the washing up from breakfast. In the middle, Neale whirled into the kitchen wearing his topcoat over his pyjamas, bustling, blowing into his hands. "Ah, so you two have met. Isn't it cold? Comment allez-vous, François? And you. How are you?"

"Furious," I said.

"You'll recover. Qu'il fait froid. On a l'hiver à Londres, n'est-ce pas? Some winter. C'est la mélancolie du nord. Ah, des oignons. J'adore les oignons. Mais! Il faut réchauffer les mains." He held his hands out to the flame on the gas stove. "Je n'osais pas me lever. Il faisait trop froid. Brrr! Still, one mustn't give in. No point standing about. Commençons. À l'attaque." He cast off his top-coat and left it in a pile by the gas stove. Stepping forward to the sink, he took off his pyjama jacket and let his pyjama trousers crumple to the floor. As he stood washing I worked round him, getting supper. I was embarrassed by François's presence, and he by mine.

"Dépêche-toi," I said to Neale. "C'est presque prêt."

"Un moment!" He gathered his clothes, pressed them in a pile against his stomach and, stooping, ran from the room. We heard him crooning Brrr along the passage. "Il a froid," said François.

I finished cooking and served the meal. Neale came

back, dressed. "Que j'ai faim." However, the impetus with which he began to eat was forced; presently it began to run down, without carrying us beyond the first course.

"La jeunesse anglaise," François said, "est-ce qu'elle est—pour la plupart—socialiste?"

"Je ne sais pas, moi," Neale said.

None of us wanted cheese; Neale made coffee. François took a bottle out of his pocket. "Du cognac?"

We had half a tumblerful each.

"Parmi les jeunes anglais—la religion—est-elle importante?"

"C'est une question très difficile. Qui peut dire?"

François nodded. After a moment he said: "Et la sexualité?"

"I wouldn't know," said Neale. "Demandez à elle."

"Ni moi non plus. Je ne sais point."

François gave us more brandy. Neale felt the side of the coffee pot: it had gone cold.

We sat silent under the strong unshaded electric light. Outside it began to rain. The drenching sound was the loudest in the room. After we had listened to it for several minutes, François said:

"Il pleut."

Neale began to sing, loud and melancholy, "And it shall rain for ever and e—e—ver."

François turned to me. "Qu'est-ce que c'est que ca? C'est un chanson des étudiants?"

Neale himself answered. "Non. C'est de la musique de ce grand maître Handel—le premier des musiciens anglais."

"Sans blague?" François asked me.

"Sans blague," I confirmed.

We sat on.

At last Neale stood up. "Bon. Je sors." He went through to the bedroom for his coat, and I began to follow him. François said:

33

"Il sort? Maintenant?"

"Il ne vous a pas dit?"

"Quoi? Non."

"Il fait le vashing-up."

"Comment?"

"Il lave les assiettes—à un restaurant—toute la nuit."

"Pourquoi?" François demanded.

"Pour l'argent. Et aussi—dans ce métier il n'y a rien de responsibilité."

Without waiting to see if François had understood, I followed Neale. I shut the bedroom door behind me. "Neale, what are you playing at?"

"I thought it would be good for your French."

"For God's sake——"

"I've left everything ready for you." He had taken the undermattress off the bed and made it up into a couch on the floor.

"Put it in the kitchen," I said.

"There isn't room."

"Where on earth did you find him? And what on earth made you ask him here?"

"I found him in the restaurant early this morning, looking for coffee. He had nowhere to go. I always ask people here if I—or, rather, if they like me." He smiled.

"It seems a little unfair to him. Do you realize he didn't even know you were going out?"

"I can't help it if he doesn't understand English. I don't see how he'll ever learn if he won't make the effort. He's here to learn English, you know."

"How long is he going to stay?"

"Till he's learnt it, I suppose." Neale pushed past me. I heard him open the kitchen door and wish François Bonne nuit. I caught him again at the front door. "Neale."

"I shall be late. You teach him English. Bonne nuit."

Embarrassedly, François and I made an arrangement. He went to wait in the bedroom while I washed and undressed in the kitchen. Then I went through, in pyjamas and dressing-gown, and left him in the kitchen.

By the time he came back, undressed, I was in bed. He looked at the mattress on the floor. "Vous permettez?"

"Je permets quoi?"

He said something, making a smoothing gesture above the mattress. I asked:

"Voulez-vous bien parler en les mots les plus simples que possibles?"

"Oui, oui, d'accord. J'ai dit—vous permettez que je couche seul?"

"Naturellement je le permets."

"Mais—vous comprenez—ce n'est pas parceque vous n'êtes pas très charmante. C'est parceque moi, je . . ."

I made a pout of sympathy. François interrupted at once. "Ah—non, non, non, non, non. Pas impuissant, non. Pas impuissant mais—comment dit-on en anglais? C'est un des mots que je connais—*quair*."

"I should say that was the Irish for it. The English is queer."

"S'il vous plâit?"

"En irlandais on dit quair. En anglais queer."

"Mais c'est pareil? Ça veut dire la même chose?"

"Oui, oui, la même chose—par tout le monde."

François got on to the mattress. I pointed. He put his head on one side. "La lumière," I said.

"Ah, oui." He got up, bowed to me slightly and switched off the light.

Next morning I saw Neale in the kitchen before François was awake. "What's he going to do all day?"

"I don't know. See London, I expect."

"How can he, without a word of English?"

"He has a few words, I think."

"Yes, one of them is queer. You must have disappointed him rather badly. Did you realize he was?"

Neale grinned. "But you'll protect me, won't you?"

From time to time Finkelheim and I were irked by the restriction of our acquaintance, and we bore one another a grudge. He would speak to me abruptly. I would find myself pouting as I worked. I felt that he underpaid and undervalued me; I resented his leaving it to me to shift the books out of my way, as if I was an unskilled labourer; for a few days after François came I even believed fantastically that Finkelheim ought to pay me proficiency money for my improved French. I supposed that his resentment of me arose about exactly that sort of point. Perhaps he objected to my having, through my education, a supererogatory value which he could think of no way to capitalize. For a day or two we each carried round a swelling of resentment. However, we feuded silently; and because nothing had been said, it was easy for the whole nexus to melt away. Then, as a reconciliation, Finkelheim would show me one of his strokes of non-financial generosity. "You wrap up warm this weather," he advised me one day. "I don't mind if you don't look very attractive during the winter months."

Since I was so often left alone with little to do, I began to take a book to the office to read. The first time Finkelheim saw me bring one in he said: "Coals to Newcastle, eh?"

I smiled but said nothing, suspecting he was worried about my wasting time he had paid for.

Next day he attacked more gravely. "What do you want to spend your money on books for when you can read all the books here for free?"

I pretended to take it for a joke.

36

"No, seriously," he said. "You ought to familiarize yourself with the stock."

He continued to watch me. I put down my own book and pulled a few out of the bookcase beside me. I had taken them out before and tried them; they were all of a curiously immaterial type, never telling a story or stating a set of facts that gripped the mind. I turned the pages. There were two American uplift books, belonging to a series: *How To Be Happy Though Middle-Aged* and *How To Be Happy Though Fat*. The third book I had taken down was called *Mud In My Mascara*, the memoirs of a ballerina I had never heard of. Presently I put them all back in the bookcase and reopened my own book.

"I suppose you have very highbrow tastes," said Finkelheim.

"Yes, very." I didn't look up.

"Funny, I haven't. In fact, I don't read much. Odd, isn't it—me being in the business."

I made no answer.

"Of course I'm not educated," he pursued. "The only long word I know is pornography."

Momentarily I glanced at him; and he pounced. "That's what I sell, you know. That's what I make money out of. Did you know?"

"No," I said. I reached out to the bookcase, to look at the books more carefully.

"Not in that bookcase," Finkelheim said. "Those are just a sideline. I'm not particular—I make money any way I can. But the real stock is over there." He pointed to a bookcase beside the window, one I had never examined. "You look at it one day when I'm not here."

I looked briefly before I left that evening. Mostly they were volumes of photographs of nudes, sometimes with coy captions. None of it seemed interesting. I discovered the Irish book which Finkelheim had referred to in the first letter I had typed for him. It was called *A Thousand And One Irish Beauties*: there were perhaps a hundred photographs in it, of dark-haired girls, all rather sad, lumpish and peasant-like.

Neale was delighted when I told him at supper. "Ha. A pornbroker."

"Qu'est-ce que vous dîtes?" said François.

"Elle travaille dans la rue Montpornosse."

"Mont*pornosse*? Comment?"

"Figurativement," said Neale.

"Je ne comprends pas."

"C'est un calembour affreux," I said.

After supper we went round to the pub; Neale had promised to give François an English evening. There was a small group in the bar. François listened for a moment and then said: "Italiens."

"I'm afraid so. Yes."

We bought our beer and sat down in the corner with the shove-halfpenny board. Neale explained the game and lent François some coppers. François beat us both twice before the Italians borrowed the board.

Another wave of visitors rolled in. "Grecs," said François. "Ou Turques."

He took a pipe out of his pocket. Neale and I tried to tease him about how English he looked. We each borrowed the pipe and smoked it for a minute.

Finally some English friends of Neale came in. Neale introduced us and explained that François did not speak English. The conversation began in French. After a moment it lapsed. "Pardon," somebody said to François.

"Je vous en prie."

The new group were drinking gin, and we switched to keep them company. We started off in French again. I found myself talking stupidly to a stupid man with

38

a moustache. Presently he said to François: "Quand il y a quelquechose compliqué à dire il faut parler en anglais." François nodded politely. Everyone was careful to keep him drinking. Sometimes he got two to everyone else's one. Once or twice I heard Neale's voice raised: "Parlez français. Parlez français"; but a second afterwards he would break his own rule. François sat silent, gin drinking and pipe smoking, but he seemed not to get drunk.

"And what do you do for a living?" the stupid man asked me.

"I work for a pornographer."

"No! Really?"

"Yes, really. Sans blague."

Understanding two words, François looked up.

The stupid man whistled. "Well, bugger me backwards."

From all round us, as if from an obedient congregation, came the response. "Not in *those* trousers."

François asked me sardonically: "Et ça, c'est aussi un morceau de ce grand maître, Handel?"

"Non." I shook my head. "Cette fois, c'est un chanson des étudiants."

As I walked home with him, François asked me if Neale worked the whole of every night. "Même le dimanche?"

"Oui."

He nodded.

"Your girl friend out all day?" Finkelheim asked me. "Or does she stay at home?"

"My girl friend?"

"The one you share with."

"O her. No, as a matter of fact she's at home most days."

"Well, I'm going out now," Finkelheim said. "Shan't

be back till tomorrow. I thought you might ask your friend over to keep you company."

"I suppose I might."

"Go ahead, go ahead. You use the phone. You can leave threepence on my desk."

"Thank you."

About three, when I guessed he would be up, I rang Neale. "Hullo."

"Hullo."

"I wondered what you were doing."

"Having coffee. What are you doing?"

"Longing for coffee."

"Is Finkelheim there?" Neale asked.

"No, he's out for the day. Is François there?"

"No. He's gone."

"Where?"

"Back to Paris."

"Poor François. We didn't give him much of a time."

"Ah well," said Neale. "He's served his turn."

"I wonder what his turn was. Was he your answer to my question?"

"I suppose so, in a way."

"And was I to protect you against him, or was he to protect you against me?"

"It's much too difficult a problem. I'm eating corn-flakes out of the packet. Can you hear?"

"I wondered what the crunch was. It increases my appetite. You'd better come over here."

"No. You sound so cannibalistic."

"I assure you I'm not interested in you from that point of view. Now are you coming?"

"I don't think. . . ."

"O don't be silly," I said. "Make some more coffee and bring it across."

"Very well. Will you meet me half-way?"

"I'll come down to the entrance hall. In five minutes' time."

"Very well," Neale said.

As I got near the bottom of the stairs, the light was strange and I felt suddenly excited. I came down into the hall and looked out: it was as I had half expected. The sky was muffled black, opaquely tinged with green and pink; and snow was falling, silently and delicately, into the street.

I stood in the lee of the hall, watching, feeling an unnatural warmth; it was only when I examined my sensation that I found it to be the invigoration of cold.

Most of the road was covered already. Only at the height of its camber did patches show through, dark grey and wet like the back of a hippopotamus.

Presently the front door at the other side of the street opened. Neale came out and across, bearing a cup full of coffee in each hand, and scarcely able to hurry. There was no sound of footsteps. He joined me in the hall, breathing hard, grinning, twitching his face. "Snow-flakes on my eyebrows. A few in my eyes. One or two fell into the coffee."

We smiled at one another, and I took one cup from him. "All right," I said. "Come upstairs."

III ✫

I LOOKED at him as he sat cross-legged on the floor, his back to Finkelheim's desk, warming his hands round his coffee cup. All autumn long my two worlds had spun hummingly on their separate axes. Now, on the first day of snow, they had touched. Both, it seemed to me, gave a jerk and stopped whirring.

Now that I possessed it, I could think of nothing to do with my happiness. I felt as if I had brought Neale to some revel, persuading him to disguise himself in order to get in; and once he was in, there was nothing to amuse him. More than ever the office was empty of atmosphere; and I was afraid, as Neale set his cup down, that he would say he had to go.

I decided to make another demand on his obedience. "Put threepence on the desk, Neale. It's for my phoning you."

He stood up to get at the money in his pocket. "All right. What now?"

"What do you want?"

"You'd better show me round."

"There's nothing much."

"Where's the pornography section?"

I pointed to it. He took a book out and stood turning the pages. I picked my way across and looked over his shoulder.

"I see what you mean. It is depressing." He squatted

42

down, put the book back and ran his finger along the other books, now and then taking one out. I looked down on nude after nude. Some of them had been photographed with their hands loosely tied above their heads, and they looked embarrassed. "It's very mild. And not much variety."

"How could there be?"

Neale stood up with another book. "I wonder how this got in with the rest." He showed me the stainproof, waterproof orange cover: it was a manual of sex technique by a doctor. Neale began skimming through it. The manner was proselytising: the faith, it implied, was morally worthy but uncomfortable to practise. Towards the end there was a chapter called 'Marital Harmony', which we read in full. Not looking up from the book, Neale said:

"Do you still want me to marry you?"

"Why are you asking?"

"I was just thinking. What hope is there for us"—he tapped the open chapter—"who can't even get into the bed at the same time of day."

"O, isn't there anything gay in the whole place," I said. I knelt down and began pulling the books out on to the floor: twenty or thirty copies of the Irish nudes, twenty or thirty copies of Finnish nudes. "What about this?" It was a tall thin volume which we had only one copy of. I took it back to my table and sat down with it; Neale came and stood behind me.

The title page read: "The Lady Revealed. Turn the pages one by one."

"Instructions for people who've never seen a book before," said Neale.

I turned the first page.

Facing us was a line drawing in three colours, green red and black, showing a girl in a longish skirt, with frilly trousers below, holding a black fan in front of her face. It was a costume extracted and stylized from a mixture of Victorian pantomime, ballet of the Taglioni period and the traditional dress of Spanish dancers. The drawing was elongated to the point of affectation but still classic and elegant. The colour lay bold but matt on a background of slightly frosted white, as if the paper was almost transparent. It would have made a pleasant, expensive Christmas card.

"Isn't it good, in a way," Neale said.

I took a hank of pages and turned it over, expecting to see a new drawing. Instead, there was the same drawing, but modified. The fan had gone, but there was a black mask covering the whole face. The skirt was shorter. The trousers had been replaced by white stockings, embroidered in green.

Neale said: "Don't skip. You'll spoil it. Don't you see the principle?"

I turned back to the beginning. The paper was in fact transparent, but when one looked at the whole thickness of the book it seemed solid. On each transparent leaf was printed a single part of the drawing, a single item of the girl's dress. As one turned the pages, one undressed the girl.

"Isn't it ingenious," Neale whispered.

I began turning the pages.

As each one went over we could see, from its underside, the small piece of clothing depicted on it, alienated and almost unrecognizable when it appeared alone on the page.

The fan gave way to the mask; the skirt vanished, the all-over mask was replaced by a black strip, with eye and nose holes, across the centre of the face; the legs became visible; eventually the girl stood before us in short modern underclothes.

I turned the last transparency but one. We could see right through now. All the art had gone into the dressing: the end of the book was a photograph, merely another nude. The remaining transparent page kept her mask on.

"Disappointing," Neale said. "That's all there is to it. But isn't it brilliant to keep the mask till the end."

I turned the last page and watched the mask, now a meaningless black shape with slots, fall.

I looked at the nude.

Affronted, my mind would not grip for a moment. I saw dots printed on the page and would not let them compose into a face. Even when they did, I would not at first allow for the slight alterations of seven years. Eventually, however, I made the admission. I was filled with the same excitement of coincidence which had possessed me when I was handed Finkelheim's address. I recognized the nude's face.

"O my God, that's funny."

"What is?"

"I used to know her."

Neale waited while I laughed. I looked through the little dormer window at the peculiar-coloured sky. I felt suddenly shocked. More worlds had met than I had intended, and into their collision they had drawn the sickening dimension of time. Each of my spheres had been set spinning again, and I scrambled to get a hold on any of them. My mind had slipped out of the knack of it, and for a moment I could not adjust it to comprehending that things once present had become things past.

"I'm sorry. I feel rather sick now."

"I don't mind. But I thought you had a good head for pornography."

"I have. It's only this." I turned back to the book open on the table. "I was at school with her. I haven't seen her for seven years." I told Neale her name, Cynthia Bewly. As I pointed, to draw his attention, my finger touched the photographed flesh and I flinched.

"You're having a very snobbish reaction," Neale said.

"Snobbish?"

"As if you didn't believe the girls you were at school with had bodies."

I pushed the book away, folded my arms on the table and laid my head down. Neale switched off the light; the mauve strip flickered and faded. He came and sat on the floor beside me. Dimly the bizarre light from outside coloured the office. Neale put his head in my lap. "There ought to be somewhere that would take in people like us. They ought to start a home for incurable romantics."

The memory was quite sharp, but distant. It was like a small photograph in which, if I tried to enlarge it, the detail blurred outwards into nothing. The four of us were there in the sunlight, miniature figures in school blazers: myself a short, compact child, with a fringe of dark hair across my forehead, large eyes and a tiny, very white-skinned nose; my satellite, Gill, a still smaller girl, monkey-like in her way of moving and her sense of humour; Annette, tall, thin, unsuitably named, colourless in hair, face and personality, who accompanied Cynthia everywhere; and Cynthia herself.

I had a special place on the bank above the tennis courts, which ran along the sun-struck wall of the main building. As I lay there in the grass, my gaze would descend the wall, slip round the gothic windows, slide down the paint-thick drainpipe; it would outline the statelier lower windows, peering for a moment into the hall inside; then down, over the last few feet of grainy brick; across the path, which was bumpy with flints; up, like a sparrow's hop, on to the grass verge; proceed for a foot or two level, until the lawn took its sudden roll down the bank—then my gaze would plunge too, would roll too, until it fetched up short and expanded away without interest over the kempt, flat tennis courts.

This process I could not communicate to anyone, not even to Gill who lay comically, tossing her head, by my side. It was my method of apprehending everything. Relationships, the fact of Latin words, my appreciation of the warm early afternoon—I took them all in as if they had been shapes. I did not think or feel my thoughts: I travelled them. Without a defending layer of words, I was at the mercy of every fact. Facts and events, the warmth itself, lapped me like waves lapping a helpless body on the shore; and the feelings which from time to time plunged up about me were quite involuntary.

The afternoon stirred, split and became brilliant. The mist was shattered from the tennis courts: only a few strands lay low, like superstition, about the bushes at the edge. Like strips of tinsel, the mist ornamented the day, reminding me, in its prettiness, of the idea of fairies; it seemed to have degenerated from something once powerful and still malevolent, its danger pagan, disquieting but alluring.

A few strangers arrived. A girl panicked and ran, calling, across the lawns.

For an interval nothing had begun. I knew this was the last day of term, but it meant nothing to me. I could not remember the beginning of summer, nor of the summer term, and could not imagine their end: July lapped me immortally on either side. The approach of the school fête, which had taken up so much of Cynthia's and Annette's time, had not troubled me. The fête was organized by their form, the form above ours. Gill and I had been told we should have to play some part in it next year, but we had taken no notice.

47

Presently the grounds were full. Strange voices shouted; familiar ones were raised to solicit custom. A crowd moved to the swimming bath where there was a display: splashes and inarticulate names lay on the air above the bath, half trapped by the surrounding walls. The dismantled courts were trodden from stall to stall; and at one stall, in front of a screen labelled Garden Produce, stood Annette, with another girl I paid no attention to, and Cynthia.

My gaze crossed Cynthia's forehead; it descended her nose; then, moving methodically outwards in each direction in turn, it traced her thin mouth. It was a face where the flesh seemed pared away. Planes, spines and the declivities my gaze lingered in almost with agony, were all as bare as an archaic statue or the blanched breast-bone of a bird.

Her gestures were leanly angular. Talking to Annette, her hands inside her blazer pockets flat against her hips, drawing the clothes taut across her back, she would slightly and not unintentionally overbalance; and the angles made by her elbows would sharpen suddenly. As she served a customer, her head would plunge, sideways and down, while she searched the stall: or she would disappear behind it, leaving her hand stretched fine against the wooden screen. Each gesture created, for me, a shape of poignancy; I would move in the grass, drawing breath, as if a glance had been deflected or a subject impetuously changed.

The grounds were warm, now, with people as well as sun; and the air, vibrating in the July afternoon, was alive with opportunity. Gill urged me to go and explore. She was excited by the mystery of the occasion: the possibility of meeting somebody's parents; perhaps of being rude to them, or even, in this atmosphere of licence and no time for revenge, to one of the staff. However,

I lay still, pinned where I was by the sight of Cynthia. Out of temper, Gill stayed with me.

Then Cynthia moved. Leaving their stall to the third girl, she and Annette wandered away over the lawn into the people. I followed them. Gill followed me; but she made a show of independence by stopping on her own at various stalls.

Cynthia stopped at the lemonade booth. I waited, separated from her by only one or two people, knowing she was aware of my presence.

A raucous noise sounded behind me. I turned. Gill was holding up a klaxon horn.

"Where did you get that?"

"White elephant stall."

"Give it me." I took it and approached Cynthia. She asked:

"What's that?"

Instead of saying a klaxon horn, I sounded the answer on it: short-long, short-long.

Cynthia giggled.

I made the horn imitate her, in a phrase of squeaks.

Over the rim of her lemonade Cynthia giggled again, even as she said: "It's a revolting noise. How can you be so *young*?"

I made the horn grunt.

She handed her lemonade to Annette and began to droop with laughter. I had not myself thought the horn so funny as that. I began to dread a punishment that might follow my receiving kudos undeserved: either there was some vacuity in Cynthia or I did not understand quite what she was laughing at. I found myself precipitated, out of my uneasiness, into daring. "Cynthia, will you walk round the grounds with me?"

"Silly, I've got my stall to look after."

"O, of course. I didn't mean now," I said disingenuously.

"When did you mean?"

"At break. Or in the dinner hour."

"You *are* funny," Cynthia said, turning away. "I suppose you mean next term."

I caught at her. "All right then. Next term. Every day of next term."

"I couldn't possibly say now." She put her arm through Annette's. "We must get back to our stall."

As they went, Gill touched my shoulder. "Can I have my klaxon back?"

I gave it her.

"Come and look round the fête," she said. I followed, unwilling and half embarrassed, as she ran from stall to stall sounding her horn in each stallholder's face. "Shall I honk one of the staff?" "If you like." She waylaid the English mistress, who smiled and brushed her aside. The whole enterprise, indeed everything connected with Gill, had for me a curious prosaicness. As soon as I could I led her back to my place on the bank. Cynthia and Annette had disappeared.

I stood in disorientated misery, like a child missing its mother in a public place. Although I knew what was going on, I failed to recognize it: I wondered what all these strange people were doing. The blue, the green, the bright summer frocks, were all violent enough in colour but not vivid, like a painting that had not succeeded in representing light.

Annette came along the path. I ran to her and asked where Cynthia was.

"Gone."

"Where?"

"To catch her train. She has special permission to go early, you know."

"I didn't know."

"I've been helping her get her things in the cloak-room. She left you a message. She says we will walk round the grounds with you next term."

"O."

Annette began to walk towards the Vegetable Produce stall. "Tell me something about Cynthia," I said.

"What do you want to know?"

I could think of nothing to ask. "She has special permission?"

"Yes. A lot of girls have in our form. Haven't they in yours?"

"O yes. Several."

I no longer watched the stall; I did not even follow my course down the side of the building. Stretched out on the grass bank I laid my head on the ground between my arms, letting the diminishing sun beat the back of my neck while I cherished the afterglow. I rehearsed my conversation with Cynthia, and even my conversation with Annette, which I could remember more coherently. I blushed for the errors I had made. I tried to summon Cynthia's face and found that Annette's, much clearer, obtruded. From time to time Gill poked her hand, her smiling face or her klaxon horn over the wall of my arms, and I drew closer into myself to preserve my happiness from her.

The warmth dropped out of the day. I sat up; Gill was glad, but I paid no attention to her. Up against the rhododendrons a little mist was collecting like re-formed battalions. The sunlight was still at its splendour, but there were hints of cold, of dark, like a crack developing on the surface of the afternoon.

I realized the sentence of next year, which I had precipitately agreed to; I recognized it meant an interval of eight weeks before my excitement would be taken up.

I was being kept waiting by another person's deliberate wish. The autumn must advance, fighting its way up the hill; slowly the summer must yield ground, slipping down the damp slope, sliding anyhow, turning back the blades of the grass in its reluctance to descend into the dangers, the dark, the swirling ground-level winds, the dry, smothering drifts of leaves. I knew I could keep my excitement waiting. With an adult patience I contemplated the dangers not only of this particular descent but of the descent of a whole lifetime. Now I had realized time, I surrendered totally to Cynthia; in her conviction that I would wait she had shown me the immensity of her confidence. Yet for the same reason I had less to surrender; my plunge down any slope would be, from now on, less involuntary.

★ IV ★

I SPENT Christmas with my parents and Neale with his. We began our quest for Cynthia, not particularly seriously, in the New Year. We sat in the kitchen with the oven lit and its door open to keep us warm. Neale picked up the A-D directory and looked for Bewly. "There are about fifteen of them. Have you any idea where she lives?"

"I don't even know she's still in town."

"If she is, she doesn't keep an establishment of her own. You can't remember her parents' initials?"

I shook my head.

"We'll just have to work through the list."

He dialled the first number. He rested the receiver on his knee, and we heard the ringing burr. "Do you imagine she'll want to be rescued?"

"I couldn't guess," I said. "She may love posing in the nude."

"I suppose she may. Still, that's not really the point. It'll do if we just find her."

The burr went on.

"She seems to be out on a job," Neale said. He moved to put the receiver down. Just before it touched the cradle there was a click, and a ticking, far-off voice said: "Hullo."

Neale pushed the receiver to his ear. "Does Miss Cynthia Bewly live there?" Swiftly he took the receiver

53

round to his other ear and gestured to me. I set my cheek against his, the bowl of the receiver separating our ears. At the other end there was a silence.

At last a slow, Irish voice said: "Who were you asking for? I didn't quite catch."

"Miss Cynthia Bewly."

"O. I was wondering if you'd said Miss Sheila Bewly."

"No, Cynthia."

"There's no one of that name here. I'm sorry, if you wanted to speak to her."

Both sides rang off.

Neale took out his pen. Reaching forward to the directory, he drew a line through the first Bewly in the list. "We'll do one a night. It'll help us through the winter."

The next night we tried the next number. There was no answer then or the night after. The following afternoon Finkelheim left me alone in the office. I put threepence on his desk, rang Neale and asked him to come over. Together we sat in the office, silent in the cold. At last Neale said:

"We may as well try that number again. If they're not there in the evenings they may be in the afternoons." He got through and asked for Cynthia Bewly. A voice said: "Speaking."

Neale passed the receiver to me. "Cynthia?"

"Yes?"

"Do you remember me?" I gave my name. "From school."

The voice was unsure. "It's a long time ago."

"I think you must be the wrong Cynthia Bewly," I said. "Your voice doesn't sound right."

"What did you want?"

"I saw your picture in that book."

"What book? What picture?"

"The one with no clothes on."

The voice said: "Now look here. I shall have this call traced and get the police to stop you."

After that, we made our calls from a public box, turning ourselves out each night in the numbing cold. If one box was occupied, sooner than wait we tramped to the next: along small dark streets where inadequate lighting cast plastic shadows on the rows of short square houses, grimily stuccoed, all looking as if they backed on to railway stations. Perhaps because the Tottenham Court Road neons turned the sky pink, our part of London always gave an impression that snow was coming. Our evenings were pierced by mechanical noises striking into silence: our footsteps playing fugues as we marched down the middle of empty roads; our footsteps grating on the concrete of the phone box; the coins dropping; the burr; Neale's fingernails tapping the bakelite receiver as we waited, gripped by cold. Often there was no answer. Often the person who answered would ask us to hold on. We would hear footsteps going away; then coming; then going again. Always they sounded like metal-studded boots on concrete steps. To our own life there was added a world of images: institution-like buildings, with concrete and iron staircases, as big and empty as the backstairs of a theatre, where a single caretaker laboured up and down; or packed, slummy communities with a single telephone, to which neighbours summoned one another by running out into the paved area and shouting. Sometimes when we were asked to hold on, nothing, except the footsteps, ever came. We would ring off in the end and go to the pub.

It seemed strange to me that we should be trying to trace Cynthia at this time of year; it was at this time that I had first realized and mourned the loss of her. The autumn term, for which she had made me wait, carried my happiness to agonising height. My incredulity and my complete security trembled together. When, however, we went back to school on a dead January day to begin the spring term, Cynthia refused to speak to me. I struggled for a little and only provoked her temper. I tried to talk to Gill for consolation, but she would hear nothing on the subject of Cynthia, and everything else bored me. In the end I turned Gill off and stalked round the school alone staring at my brick wall or at my slope, now shiny with mud. Each night I took home my realization. The autumn term, the first period of time to take precise shape in my mind, assumed also the poignant quality of time: it had become irrevocable. Night after night, through the winter and the bitter spring, I lay face down in bed, and at the sharp thought I turned sideways into my pillow and cried.

The year came right round: our form began to prepare the summer fête. The dull, routine girls planned stalls. One or two athletic and musical girls proposed to hold country dancing in the gym; any visitor who paid sixpence would be taught the figures and allowed to dance. A small group, which included Gill and me, wanted to devise something new. I had several ideas: a roundabout, a grotto, a display of fat women. I was overruled, and we made our plans to turn our classroom into a haunted house. I painted big signs to pin up all round the grounds with an arrow pointing the direction and the words Adults Only.

When the fête came we spent the bright afternoon in artificial darkness, half scared by our own fabrications: the melons with torches burning inside them; the skeleton, outlined in phosphorescent paint, clawing its way up a sheet of black paper; the spider's web with the pale green papier-mâché spider. We had emptied the room of desks and made a twisting route, walled by screens, which our victims were to follow. Some of the horrors were pinned or propped on the screens; sometimes there was a gap through which the visitors glimpsed a tableau. Behind the screens we sat breathless, preserving the atmosphere. One of us clanked a chain. Another dropped pebbles into water. Gill was a part of the grand tableau at the end of the route: a refectory table was laid for a medieval dinner, with tankards and kitchen knives. The presence of a number of diners was to be inferred: some tankards and one knife were suspended in the air above the table; but only the head of the feast was visible, a vague shape covered entirely by a sheet, sitting in a high seignorial chair. From time to time she groaned beneath the sheet.

My own job was to wait behind a screen near the start of the course, where the visitors were still blinded by having plunged into the dark. At this point nothing frightening had happened to them. The inaction and the silence—apart from the screams of people farther in, which we sometimes simulated ourselves—was supposed to work on their nerves. Across the path, at head height, we had stretched a few threads of black cotton. Harmlessly but unexpectedly these brushed against all but the shortest of our visitors. Most of them shrieked; and often a hat would roll off. It was my business to dart out invisibly and collect the hats, and then double round behind the screens to the exit and leave them for their owners to recover.

On my way I had to pass Gill in her sheet. I ducked down and crept by in the shelter of her chair. I would pinch her and whisper "Groan!" Usually she gave a jerk, because she could have little idea of when I was there. I would whisper "Excellent " and creep on.

Late in the afternoon it became hard to hold the atmosphere. Fewer strangers came through and more members of the school. Some of them made exaggerated clanks and groans to compete with ours and which sometimes, because we did not expect them, frightened us. We tried to drive the other girls out, but it was difficult to find where they were in the dark.

A woman's hat fell at the foot of my screen. I reached round and grabbed it, and set off for the door. As I passed Gill she was giggling. I said: "Shh." The giggles began to choke. "Gill, shut up. You'll spoil everything." The whole sheet twitched. Hiding as well as I could behind her chair, I tackled her. I found one arm through the sheet, and held it while I pinned the other. The outline of a third arm struggled and tried to push me away.

I said: "O Lord!" After a moment I whispered: "Gill, what is it? Have you got someone under there with you?"

Cynthia's voice said: "Must you follow me *everywhere*?"

I ran out of our form-room, dropping the hat on the threshold, and across the yard where the sunshine pierced my eyes, to the gym. The piano was banging away. I joined a group and began to dance Haste To The Wedding. Set after set, dance after dance; I performed all the mocking running steps and the ludicrous jumping up and down, until I knew I was red in the face, my breath hurt and I could hear my heart louder than my feet.

Neale and I rang all the Bewlys. Some we had to try several times before somebody answered and told us Cynthia did not live there. At the end our telephone directory had fifteen lines drawn through its text; and Neale said, as he drew the last: "We'll have to think of something else."

Finkelheim was on the phone. As I came into the office, he waved me good morning with his free hand, and then, because he was lisping, winked at me. As I passed his desk I looked down at the book whose pages

58

he was turning to and fro as he talked. It was *The Lady Revealed*. He was undressing and dressing Cynthia.

I took the cover off my typewriter and sat down with nothing to do. I pretended to be brushing the type faces.

"Ten shillings?" Finkelheim was saying. "Don't be funny. Well, of course, it's only one copy. It's a rare book. It's a collector's piece. I tell you, the very least, the absolute minimum, I can let you have this book for is—wait a minute and I'll quote you." He turned to the back of the book where he had made, as he did in all our books, a small pencil code-mark which I presumed told him how much he had paid for it. "One guinea. And that's robbing myself. All right, all right, all right, I make it twenty shillings. No, I am not, and you've no right to say I am. I tell you it's a very artistic production. A lot of art's gone into this book. No, I said twenty. Tell you what, I'll let you have it on appro. When you see it, you won't be able to part with it. I'll send it you on appro, one shilling packing and postage, no deposit because I trust you. Okay?"

He rang off, reached into his desk for paper and string, and made *The Lady Revealed* into a parcel, which he handed to me. "You don't mind taking it to the post? A little exercise will warm you up." He gave me a sixpence.

I carried the parcel downstairs and across the road into our flat. Finkelheim's office was at the back of the building; he could not possibly see or suspect; but I felt fearful until I had let myself in.

Neale was in bed. He opened his eyes. I explained.

"Are you going to steal it?"

"Don't be silly." I sat down on the bed and began undoing the parcel.

Neale yawned. "Couldn't you have made Finkelheim a counter-offer?"

"He wants a pound for it. Anyway, I'd have no use for the book. I just want to know who publishes it, so we can ring them up. Perhaps they'll know where Cynthia is." I found the publishers' name, a firm I had never heard of, somewhere in E.C.4, and made a note of it. Neale sat up and helped me to rewrap the parcel. Finkelheim had used the smallest piece of brown paper he could; it was hard to get the folds exactly as he had had them, and if we didn't the address slipped off the front of the parcel. As soon as we had managed it, I hurried out to the post office. The day had by now revealed itself; it was almost warm, almost spring.

"You took a long time," Finkelheim said when I got back. "Post office full?"

"Quite a queue."

"Civil servants. Parasites. They don't produce anything —just a burden to the nation's economy."

I said: "The parcel cost eightpence. You gave me sixpence."

He put his hand into his pocket, then stopped. "Tell you what. Next time you use the phone here, you only leave a penny. Then we'll be square."

I used the telephone that afternoon, when Finkelheim had gone out and Neale had come across to join me. I no longer bothered to summon Neale. If he had nothing else to do when he woke in the afternoons he came up to the office and listened outside the door. We had an arrangement that if, by mistake, he should enter while Finkelheim was there, I should pretend not to know him; and he, simply as a member of the public, should say he was looking for a copy of *Les Fleurs Du Mal*, a book I knew Finkelheim did not have in stock and which, because he had never heard of it, he would not offer to obtain specially. However, Neale was cautious. On afternoons when Finkelheim had failed to go out, I would hear Neale's footsteps at his usual time; then silence. I would suspend my typing and do something less noisy so that I could listen to Neale listening. At first he always held his breath as he tried to make out if the sounds inside came from one person or two. After a bit he had to exhale in a rush, and I would hear a noise like snuffling outside the door. I was always afraid that Finkelheim, who was nearer the door than I, would hear it too. Then Neale would control his breath again. I became hysterical with knowing he was there. I would invent something to ask Finkelheim, timing my words to drown the new exhalation of Neale's breath but trying to stop talking in time to catch the sad sound of Neale's footsteps descending the stairs. Often the questions I put to Finkelheim were stupid, and he treated them as such; then, for an hour or two, we would carry resentment against one another.

This afternoon, as soon as I heard Neale coming, I opened the office door to him.

"Ah, good. We'll ring those publishers."

A little to my surprise, they were listed in the directory. We got through. "You speak," Neale whispered. "It'll sound better if it's a woman."

I began: "I believe you publish *The Lady Revealed*?"

"Yes."

"I wanted to make an enquiry about the young lady in it."

"I'll put you through to Editorial."

We waited. "Sounded quite unperturbed," Neale said. "Perhaps they get a lot of enquiries about her."

The editorial department came through. I explained again. "As it happens, I was at school with her. I've lost touch and would rather like to trace her."

A priggish voice said: "I'm afraid we couldn't possibly answer an enquiry of that sort."

"Would you forward a letter, if I sent it care of you?"

"We couldn't undertake to do that."

"This is perfectly bona fide," I said. I gave my name. "What's more, I know her name."

"Do you?"

"Cynthia Bewly. It is, isn't it?" I challenged.

"I'm afraid we couldn't say. I'm afraid there's nothing we can do for you."

"As a matter of fact," I said, "I wanted to get in touch with Cynthia to ask her how to get her sort of work. I was thinking of going in for the same line myself."

"What line?" the voice said. It had changed: I couldn't tell if it was more interested or more guarded.

"Posing. Perhaps you can help me. Do you know anyone who might have work to offer?"

"Are you experienced?"

"Not exactly. I could learn."

"Are you prepared to do artistic poses?"

"Yes." A pause. "Should I come and see you?"

"You might."

Neale took my hand. I said into the phone: "You wouldn't like two of us?"

"Would you work together?"

"Certainly, if you wanted."

"Two girls?"

"Well, actually, no. A man and a girl."

"That's not so much in demand. It's not so rare."

"O."

Neale whispered to me: "You go. I'll come and wait outside. You can whistle if you need me."

"What's that?" the voice said.

"Nothing."

"I heard a man."

"My fiancé," I said. "The one whose services you've just refused."

"Where are you speaking from?"

"An office."

"A post office?"

"No. My office."

"Do you run an office?"

"No, I work here."

"And your fiancé, too?"

"Sometimes. In the afternoons."

"This office of yours—it wouldn't be a police station, would it?"

"No, of course not."

The voice laughed. "What did your fiancé say about a whistle?"

"No, honestly——"

The voice rang off.

"At least it's a change," Neale said, "to be taken for the right side of the law."

"I suppose so. That other Cynthia Bewly never did put the police on us."

"Not yet. It may take them some time to trace the call." Neale sat down on Finkelheim's chair. Presently I asked:

"What should we do if we did find Cynthia?"

He shrugged. "Ask her if she's happy in her work. What should we *do* if we found anything we're looking for?"

"It's not as if I'd still be fond of her."

"No. I expect she's horrible."

"Not so much horrible as dull."

"Yes, dull's the most likely. Still, a butterfly's dull once you get it in your net."

"We'd better give up," I said.

"Give up the search? Why?"

"Because you can't get time back. I ought to have learnt that after Cynthia left me. There's nothing to do about time except bear it."

63

"There's always something to do."

I shook my head.

Neale brought his knees together, rested his hands on them, and stood up neatly, almost bouncing on the ball of his feet. "What about the others? Can't you get in touch with them? Annette, Gill?"

"Even if I could——"

"Have you got addresses for them?"

I took my address book out of my handbag. I had an old note of Annette's address; nothing for Gill. "I suppose I could write to Annette and put Please Forward in case she's moved. Gill went up to Oxford."

"Can you remember which college?"

"Yes. But she's probably been sent down by now."

"You can put Please Forward on hers, too."

"But neither she nor Annette kept up with Cynthia. I'm pretty sure. It's most unlikely they'd know anything. Cynthia more or less dropped Annette when she took up with me. Gill's friendship with Cynthia only lasted a week or two. It was probably only done to annoy me. And I haven't kept up with either of them."

"They'll be all the more touched to hear from you."

I took out two sheets of typing paper. Neale picked up a book from the floor.

"Neale?"

"Yes?"

"Suppose they really were touched? I don't want to see either of them again. I mean, I quite actively don't. And I don't want them snooping round our flat."

Neale asked: "Are you afraid they'll think we go to bed together?"

"No. I'm afraid they'll guess we don't."

After a moment Neale said: "Well, give your address as Poste Restante. You can explain your plans are rather unsettled."

"I suppose that's true enough." I couldn't remember which street our local post office was in, so I named the one in Great Portland Street. I wrote the same letter twice, almost word for word: I asked after the recipient first, and then after any old friends, particularly Cynthia. I added that I was working for a bookseller. 　　　.

I sealed the letters into brown envelopes, the kind Finkelheim used for transactions worth less than five pounds, and set them out side by side on my table.

Neale looked up from his book. "This is new stock."

"Oh, the male nudes, yes. They quite interested me when they first came in, but I seem to have got through them now." They were like the photographs in body-building advertisements, but without the bathing trunks, and often photographed from the back or the side.

"I was looking," Neale said, "to see if any of *my* old school friends were here."

"And were they?"

"Not a soul I know." He closed the book and took my letters. "I'll post these for you."

The Lady Revealed came back to the office. Finkelheim undid the parcel, took out the covering letter, and handed me the volume to put away. "They wouldn't meet my price." He looked at the brown paper carefully. It was his own, turned inside out. "At least we've got our brown paper back." He put it into his drawer.

"You've made fourpence," I said.

"Fourpence?"

"You charged a shilling packing and postage. The postage was eightpence, and you've got the packing back."

"So I have." He laid his finger down the side of his nose. "You're quite a girl. Make you a partner one day."

I went back to my table. In a minute Finkelheim said:

"You've forgotten to take into account the cost of your labour. You took the parcel to the post—all that time you were gone. The way you were reckoning, anyone would think I didn't pay you."

I said nothing. We had begun another small feud.

★ V ★

FOUR lunch-hours running I took the bus to Oxford Circus and enquired at the Great Portland Street post office. The fifth time I went it was my twentieth birthday. The morning greyness was trembling, about to break apart into an afternoon that would certainly be spring, or even summer. The moment's walk from the bus-stop made me hot. I enquired again, and was given a letter. I could tell nothing from the handwriting; and the post-mark was Bangor. I crossed to the other side of the post office, took a telegram form out of the box and pretended to compose something. Then I opened the letter and saw it was from Annette.

> It was nice to get your letter and hear how you are getting on. Your job sounds most interesting, and just the sort of thing that would suit you. You must tell me more about it. I am living up here in the wilds of Wales, working as a nursery teacher, believe it or not. I quite enjoy the work, but the little dears do get a bit wearing at times! I visit London in the holidays, and it would be nice to see you if you were ever free.
> I have hardly seen anyone from "the good old days" and don't expect I have any news you won't know already. Gill won a scholarship to Oxford, you know—she always was "brainy"—unlike me! I have not heard from Cynthia since we left, and I don't know what she is doing, but someone

told me she was making some extra money by posing at an art school for the evening classes. I think they said it was the South-East London school.

I went into one of the phone booths and put through a call to Neale. He took some time to answer; I re-read Annette's second paragraph while I waited. When he came through, I told him about it.

"Right. We'll go there tonight. I'll give you supper out, for your birthday. I must go now. I was in bed."

All afternoon, as I sat in Finkelheim's—Neale did not come over—I was consciously but not voluntarily reconstructing life at school. Cross-fertilized by Annette's letter, my memory was stronger. Names I had never hoped to recover came floating up like fragments of shattered tooth appearing in the gum socket. As I recalled the tenor of that life, I was amused by its incongruities: in all the relationships between the four of us, we had always seen one another unmade-up; we had never offered one another a drink or a cigarette; and every school morning except in summer I had performed what was to my present mind the masculine action of putting on my tie in front of the mirror. These, however, were only the quirks of school life. The essence was its restriction. Even imagination was restricted, by ignorance. What went on behind the closed door of Cynthia's form-room was mysterious to me. We moved in our fixed time-tables like separate planets.

At first I accepted that Cynthia was loosed on me at given times of day for short intervals. At the beginning of the autumn term I claimed her promise of walking with me, and discovered Annette was coming too. It did not occur to me that I could prevent it. But Cynthia, higher up the spiral, was more free. She contrived, the first time, to walk next to me. The second time, Annette

68

did not appear at all. I was dazzled by Cynthia's contrivance, but also afraid; and I did not ask how she had excluded Annette.

Cynthia shewed me ways of swerving out of my course into hers. I took up art: and this meant that in free lessons Cynthia and I would draw from the life—from a girl in a gym tunic posed on a desk—while Annette worked at fancy lettering in another part of the studio. I discovered for myself that if I slipped into the wrong queue at dinner time I could sit next to Cynthia. I would watch her profile: I felt unable to eat. Presently this became her feeling too. We would each crumble a slice of bread, each worked on by asceticism.

On Fridays Cynthia forwent her privilege of taking an early train and went to the after-school meeting of the French club. Annette did not belong to it. I joined it. We had a book of stories in French about various parts of the world. At the end there were questions which we dealt with orally. The question came to me "Qu'est-ce que c'est qu'un bonze?" I had no idea; the question went on to Cynthia, who answered as the book had taught: "Un bonze est un prêtre japonais". In the margin of my book I drew eleven rough figures, their hands clasped inside their kimono sleeves, and gave it the caption "Onze bonzes". I passed the book to Cynthia. She laughed, and then began to laugh loudly. She had to turn up the lid of her desk; and to keep the pretence going she took out a notebook and began writing in it. A minute later, however, the notebook was passed to me. Cynthia had written: "A code message. – – – – – – – –."

I stared down at it, knowing what I wanted it to mean.

Cynthia whispered: "Can you work it out?"

I whispered back, not daring to look: "I don't know. I'm not quite sure."

That night I walked with her to catch her late train.

It was a glowing evening and already almost dark. We walked slowly, looking down at the pavements. I kicked through a drift of leaves that had blown up against a wooden fence, and turned over a horse chestnut. I picked it up and gave it to Cynthia, who put it away in her satchel. "Haven't you any gloves?" she said. "Aren't your hands cold?"

"Not very."

"Put your right hand in my pocket."

I did and for a moment walked along awkwardly.

"Do you mind if my hand comes in too?" Cynthia said.

It lay inert in her pocket alongside my hand, each separately clenched; and then, as we went round a corner, both hands opened with the same convulsion and pressed each other palm to palm.

The next day I ran upstairs to Cynthia's classroom between lessons, stood in front of her desk and threw down a piece of paper. I had written: "A code message in French. — — —'— — — —." Cynthia opened the paper and read it, and then looked up at me direct for a moment. She folded the paper away carefully, and the smile she gave me seemed to be similarly folded away, carefully, into herself.

While I was shut off from Cynthia, I used Gill for amusement. In dull lessons in our own form-room I would repeat to her jokes that had made Cynthia laugh. Because repeated, they did not detonate; yet I did not care if I won no success with Gill. All was dross that was not Cynthia, and Gill especially, because she was the most familiar to me of my own familiar form. In spite of this, Gill had changed, but not enough to win my interest: she was like a thoroughly known tree which in the spring shewed a number of new whippy shoots. She had suddenly grown tall; she was leggy. Her face had settled into a shape, the curly gold and pink prettiness of a painted wooden statue of an angel.

What had been Gill's childish truculence had changed into power to lash. In my own sphere I was no longer secure. I escaped from it to Cynthia, and forgot to be afraid of Gill; Cynthia became arbitress of my safety. We marched round the big field, happy when the weather was bitter because we should be completely alone. Long delayed, but always some time before the bell rang that summoned us inside, Cynthia's hand would take mine. When it rained, we were confined to the main hall. I would run for a place under the windows, up against the radiator; and there as we stood side by side, Cynthia's hand would move towards mine over the radiator's undulations and we would gaze out at the rain drenching the tennis courts and running in streams down the grass bank. Sometimes in the dinner hour I went to the chapel with Cynthia, for a meeting of the Young Christians. Sharing a song-sheet we would stand with our hands touching while I kept silence for shame and Cynthia sang:

> *No need to cry, no need to whine.*
> *Jesus is a friend of mine.*
> *No need to wonder who I am.*
> *He's the shepherd, I the lamb.*

Kneeling in silent prayer we held hands beneath the pew. Sitting, we gazed at one another while everyone else was embarrassed to look anywhere, as one or other of the girls made a public confession, usually of thought-crimes against the staff. Cynthia and I never confessed to anything. Once Gill came to a meeting. I saw her edge in at the back of the chapel, and was afraid for what she might do when she heard the hymn. However, she made no demonstration until confession time, when she was the first to speak. "I wish to confess to the meeting that I

71

smoke marijuana." The gesture was not successful because I was the only person there who knew what marijuana was, and I was not prepared to help her make her effect.

Towards the end of the autumn term the rigidity of our courses began to disintegrate under an impetus that came from outside, not from Cynthia and me. The classes became less formal; girls would be sent for and taken out of lessons, unsettling those who were left; for some lessons classes were amalgamated, for some they were dismissed unexpectedly; there was a sound of hammering in the main hall. At each tremor the first thought of Cynthia and myself was for each other. If my lesson was declared closed I would leap out through the confusion and upstairs to see if Cynthia was free too. The whole structure of school life trembled under small shock after small shock, like a stage set about to be struck. In fact, however, a stage set was going up. The platform in the main hall was under requisition; and there the head-mistress conducted morning prayers beneath a cardboard arch, a bowery ornament of the forest of Arden. I wrote a play of my own, a farce set in the small French village of Mise-en-Seine, which I showed to the English mistress: she gave it me back, saying it had amused her; I was at the depth of my mind disappointed, having had some fantasy that she would drop the play of her choice and put mine into rehearsal instead.

Neither Cynthia nor I was cast. We enrolled ourselves in the studio to paint scenery and sew silk roses, and then enrolled ourselves with Miss Falconbridge as scene shifters in the main hall. Night after night Cynthia caught the later train. We would stand at the foot of the stage, hands clasped behind a painted bush, threatened with dismissal if we so much as whispered.

"Why, cousin! Why, Rosalind! Cupid have mercy! not a word?"

"Not one to throw at a dog."

Elegant, gap-toothed and flexed like a greyhound, Miss Falconbridge stood at the back of the hall, her arms crossed, one hand holding her paper-bound copy of the play, calling on her players to speak up.

The Celia asked: "But is all this for your father?"

"No, some of it for my child's father: O, how full of briers is this working-day world!"

The Celia was a pretty, dark-haired girl, the Rosalind a pretty, red-haired girl, both of whom I disliked. Yet even they were touched by the colour of the lines they spoke. Cynthia and I moved closer to one another as we crouched behind the bush, getting a grip on it and preparing to rush it into place for the second act. But Miss Falconbridge loped to the other side of the hall and called for the first act again. The players scrambled on to the stage again, amongst them Gill, in a gym tunic now too short for her, the length of her legs conspicuous since she was standing above our level of vision. It was prefigured for her that her fair skin should be browned with grease-paint, that she should wear a pointed brown beard and a single gold ear-ring and her long legs should be covered by a wrestler's black tights. Her eyes gleamed already, as if out of the depths of grease-paint; her bare legs straddled the stage; and she roared magnificently:

"Come, where is this young gallant that is so desirous to lie with his mother earth?"

The Orlando complained to Miss Falconbridge that although Gill was technically the loser of the bout she never let herself be thrown without first twisting Orlando's arm or squeezing her ribs in realistic contention.

Neale gave me a birthday supper of fried eggs in an aquamarine snack-bar in the Waterloo Road. Afterwards we set out into south London. We sat in the lighted trolleybus; lurching and humming, it carried us through neighbourhoods which lacked the characteristics of London and yet obviously, to anyone suddenly set down there, were London, if only because they could be nowhere else. Through the windows we could make out wide streets and pavements; the tall buildings were granite-grey. We got out where the conductor told us to, and found we were at an enormous road junction, at the centre of which someone was changing the points on the tram lines, and someone else, just visible in the weak lamplight, was manipulating a pole to lift the arm of a trolleybus on to a new wire. Apart from an occasional clashing noise, and the whirr as an electric motor started, the place was almost silent. Very few people were on the pavements, and those there were seemed dwarfed and formally dressed; they had an old-fashioned respectability, like figures from a pre-1914 film. We asked one of them the way, but he didn't know. We wandered round, trying to remember the directions the bus conductor had given us, and presently we found the art school. It had a dark green notice-board outside, which we read with difficulty. We went through a wooden door and crossed what seemed to be an asphalt playground towards another door above which there was a dim light. Just before we reached it, I started: there was a fruit tree, quite tall, in full blossom, standing near the building, cemented into the asphalt; the light lay on its white upper branches gently, like light on a girl's head. We rang the door-bell; no one came. The door was unlocked. We went in, to a vestibule whose walls were painted olive-green below, yellow above, with a band of chocolate between. Neale stamped to and fro to attract attention, but no one responded. We walked along the corridor, found a door marked Office, went in and explained ourselves to the girl inside.

"I don't know, really," she said. "You'd better go up to the life class and ask Mr. Bingley."

We followed her directions: up concrete steps with an iron hand-rail, along unpolished wooden corridors; the building seemed to embody those institutions we had imagined in our quest by telephone. We passed doors labelled after technical processes of printing or dyeing, from behind which came a hum either of study or of light machinery; at last we reached a door marked Life Room.

We opened it, went in and found we were staring at a blank, black screen.

Gently, Neale moved one side of the screen and we stepped round it.

A woman's voice said: "I can feel that draught from the door again."

Neale moved the screen back behind us. I looked quickly at the model; but she was middle-aged and plump. She was standing with both arms raised like an Andromeda, and as she spoke she was at pains to shew that she was not moving from her pose.

No one took any notice of Neale and me.

Above the dais in the centre hung a big, black-enamelled light, shaped like a darning mushroom. It threw a magic circle of brightness, round whose edges sat the students. We were beyond its pale; so was the screen in front of the door, the screens in front of each window and the little cubicle of screens at the far end of the room. On the dais next to the model an oil-stove was burning and her left flank had become pink and spotted.

Moving round the outside of the circle, in the shadows, and coming forward behind each student to look over his head at the drawing-board he held, was a man in a tweed suit, with a peppery beard, whom we took to be

75

Mr. Bingley. He came closer to us; I heard him say, to a girl he was leaning over: "Your buttocks are wrong." He bent forward further still and made a mark with his pencil on her drawing. He passed us. Neale signalled to me. But I said nothing.

When he had completed the circle, Bingley ordered a rest. Someone drew chalk marks round the model's feet; then she clambered off the dais, emphasizing her stiffness, and went into the cubicle of screens. Bingley lit a pipe and sat down next to one of the students. The model came out of the cubicle, wearing a tarnished kimono, and sat down on the other side of the circle. She lit a cigarette and her kimono lapsed open over her body.

We picked our way awkwardly round the outside, introduced ourselves to Bingley and told him what we wanted.

"The name is familiar," he said. "She's not here now. But I think she was here."

"When?"

"Last year?" he wondered.

We would not let him off; we stared at him. Gesturing for help, he called: "Tom!" A pale-faced young man came up.

"Tom, do you remember Cynthia Bewly?"

"She used to be one of the models, didn't she?"

"Yes, but when?"

"Last year," Tom said.

"These people are trying to trace her." Bingley waved us into Tom's care. Tom asked:

"Would you recognize her?"

"Yes."

"I've got my portfolio from last year." He brought it and untied it. We began to look through a stack of prissy, academic drawings.

"You mightn't be able to tell from these," Tom said.

"They're figure studies, really. Mostly five-minute sketches. I didn't do the faces in much detail—they're rather abstract in a way."

"I think we'd recognize her without the face," Neale said. He looked sideways at Tom, but Tom shewed no impression.

We picked on one; the face was detailed enough to make us sure. We took the drawing out, and held it up. Bingley came and stood behind us. "Got what you wanted?"

"I remember now," Tom said. "She was a good model. There are more of her farther on." He took out the other sketches to shew us. One of them was dated.

"So she was here last year," Neale said. "Is that all you can tell us? Don't you know where she went?"

Tom shook his head.

Bingley said loudly, to the whole room: "Does anyone know what became of Cynthia Bewly?"

No one answered; no one moved; no one interrupted the background noise of conversation. The question, and Cynthia's name spoken so publicly, merely rose above the room, and hung on the air like the cloud of smoke which had collected beneath the mushroom light.

I said to Tom: "What was she like? What sort of person was she?"

He held his drawing out at arm's length and concentrated on it. "It's curious. I can't remember. I can't get any clear idea of her at all." He slotted the drawing back into his portfolio.

As we went home, Neale said: "It'll be fun to see Cynthia dressed, one day." He came with me only as far as Leicester Square, where we parted, and he went off to work; but as I turned towards the Northern Line he came running back. "I forgot to tell you. I made you a cake for your birthday. It's on top of the kitchen cupboard."

I thanked him.

"It's the first time I've ever made a cake." He grinned at me. "Any man can give a girl his virginity, but one's first cake . . ."

It turned out to be a sponge, lightly iced, with a few slivers of angelica on the top. It was a little doughy but not unpleasant. I lay in bed propped on my elbow and ate half of it.

The next day Finkelheim went out soon after luncheon and told me he would not be back. I sat listening for Neale. I had one or two false alarms and ran out on to the landing, but he was not there. His usual time passed. I sat on until it was within half an hour of my time to go home and I knew he would not bother to come now.

I could feel rather than see that the afternoon outside was early summer. Passages of sunshine fled past the dormer window; the sky was blue, tossed by streaks of white cloud and pools of grey. I felt sure the day would have exhausted its effort by the time I was free to go.

I surveyed our quest and decided it had got us either nowhere or into trouble. I revolted from what I now considered bungling; the real method, it seemed to me, would have been to go back to school, find Miss Falconbridge who, I knew, organized an old girls' society and tried to keep track of past pupils, and ask her where Cynthia was. At first I saw this as something I might have done; then, inspired by the gusty beginnings of summer, I saw I still could do it. I found myself possessed of enough moral energy, and of the stamina to endure seeing the place again. However, the plan was crippled: I should have to go on a weekday and within school hours, and I could think of no truthful way of making Finkelheim give me a day off. I felt impatient that Neale was not there to prompt me.

I stood in the middle of the office, too full of energy, annoyed by the prospect of the day's falling off without being enjoyed, and suspecting that Neale was keeping away to compensate for any advance he felt himself to have made in baking me a cake. I picked up the receiver and began to dial our number. Someone knocked at the office door.

I called Come in; the door opened; I put down the receiver.

There were two men, amusingly alike. Each was about thirty-five, tall, broad, dressed in a putty-coloured trench coat over a dark suit. The lapels were open, showing a blue soft collar of thick cotton and a tie striped in dull reds, golds and gunmetal: the work of some inexpensive but safe, even dingy, outfitter. Both men had unusually large faces, rather flat, with big features; health saved them from being ugly. The one who spoke—slightly the broader, older and healthier—had a deep voice and an accent not quite educated. He opened the door again behind him and swung it so that he could read the lettering on the outside, and then, closing it again, asked me:

"This is Finkelheim's? A bookseller's?"

"Yes."

"You were making a phone call?"

"Yes."

"Go ahead."

"No, it's quite all right. I'll wait."

We all three stared for a moment at the telephone.

"Mr. Finkelheim not here?"

"No."

"When do you expect him back?"

"Tomorrow."

"Morning?"

"Yes."

"You work for him?"

"Yes."

"Just the two of you work here?"

"Yes."

"You're his secretary?"

"More or less." I could not quite bring myself to ask who they were.

"Letters, do you do? Keep the books?" He added: "Or do you mostly work by phone?"

I said nothing.

"We'll come back tomorrow."

As they were at the door, I asked: "Who shall I say called?"

"We're police officers."

I listened to the stairs creaking as they descended; once I was sure they were out of the building I began for a second time, and much more urgently, to ring Neale. As I dialled the last number, it occurred to me not to trust the phone. I rang off, gathered my handbag and, careless of the ten minutes I still owed to Finkelheim, ran downstairs and across the road. As I opened the front door I shouted: "Neale! That woman did get the police!" Neale was out. I found a note from him on the kitchen table: "What a pig you were with the cake. I've gone out for the evening. See you tomorrow."

We had made the telephone call to the wrong Cynthia Bewly from Finkelheim's. Now it struck me that if the police officers had watched the outside of the building after leaving it they would have learnt my home address from my flight across the road. I began to listen for them, expecting them to knock at each flat unhurriedly until they discovered me. I began to tidy the kitchen.

When they did not come, I decided to eat; but we had hardly anything in. I was afraid that the men were still in the road. I dared not go out. I poured myself a plate of cornflakes, and then found I did not want it.

I could think of no way to get in touch with Neale. His absence made me furious.

I found I could not read. At about half-past nine I went to bed.

I could not prevent my mind turning at an unnatural rate, and unproductively, without gripping, like a bicycle wheel spun in the air, as I considered the alternatives of explaining or not explaining to the police. What confused me most, and threw me into tumult and hysteria, was my innocence. Of all the perversions in the world the compulsion to make obscene telephone calls was the one I least shared.

I felt myself dropping asleep: unhealthily, since I knew I was sleeping. Suddenly I jerked awake. The image left in my mind was that I had stopped, saving myself just in time, with one foot over a steep, slippery bank.

I dozed again, and woke again gripped by the thought that our telephone directory was evidence against us if anyone should find it with the fifteen Bewlys crossed out. I was terrified that I should have forgotten the point by morning. I forced myself to get out of bed, and wrote on a scrap of paper: N.B. Destroy phone book.

When I fell really asleep I dreamed I was giving birth to a child—or I was the child; and the process of birth seemed to be a nightmarish sliding down something in the dark.

★ VI ★

WHEN Neale came in next morning, I was still in bed. He stood over me. "You'll be late."

I shouted, falsetto with hysteria: "Get out!"

Presently I dragged myself up, put on my dressing-gown and went into the kitchen. Neale was eating corn-flakes. He asked: "You feeling bloody?" I told him what had happened the day before.

"It seems quite simple," Neale said. "If the police are going there this morning, you won't."

"What about Finkelheim?"

"He can cope. I'll ring him up and say you're ill."

"It's almost true."

"I'll say I'm your uncle. I doubt if that is."

I sat down and had some breakfast.

"Feeling better?"

"Yes. But rather heinous."

"Make the most of it. Enjoy it."

I left him alone to ring Finkelheim. "Look, Neale, could you tell him that if two men call he's not to worry —I'll deal with it?"

He came through into the bedroom, and I asked: "Was it all right?"

"Perfectly. He says he hopes you get better soon because he's got a lot of work."

While I dressed, Neale undressed. "Now you've got your free day, why don't you go to your school?"

"How can I? If I go out, if the police didn't see me Finkelheim might."

Neale got into bed. "Ring for a taxi," he suggested.

I hesitated.

"Go on. It's a lovely day. And I want to get some sleep."

I darted from our porch into the taxi, and as soon as I was inside I bent forward, as if to adjust my shoe, and kept my head low until we were round the corner.

I got out at Baker Street; if I had had the money I would have taken the cab all the way for the pure panache of arriving in it at school. Outside the station there were barrows of tulips, lilac and roses. I wondered for a moment whether I would not simply go and sit in Regent's Park. However, leaving sunlight outside, I went down into the station. At once I was bewildered. I could not quite remember which of the illuminated indicator boards to consult, or what the distinction was between the Watford and the Aylesbury line; I was certain only that there was a great distinction which I had once known so well that I scorned other people's ignorance. I felt as if I were being taken through a piece I was meant to have learnt by heart; I could not anticipate the next line, but when it was put to me I recognized it. So strong was my feeling that I ought to know, that I was ashamed to ask. I marched about the empty foyer, walking quickly to give the impression I was not lost. I moved from level to level, surprisedly coming on steps going down and steps going up to the street, with alleys of sunlight pouring down them. After perhaps ten minutes I discovered the right platform.

The chestnut trees in the front garden were in flower, both the grey-white one and the deep pink which I had used to hate because it seemed to me the colour of an artificial substance, perhaps marzipan. The drive had been altered in some way I could not make precise. The building did not, as I had expected it to, look smaller than I had remembered—if anything, larger. I had never really looked up at it before. What my memory had supplied as its gothicness turned out to be more debased than that: a matter of dutch gabling, of too much red roof, like a felt hat pulled too far on, of cream pebble-dash and dark green window frames. It was like part of an ideal farm; it was a suburban villa, or a suburban doll's house, built on a big scale; it suggested health as it might be depicted in an advertisement, on a red-cheeked yokel.

I walked up and hesitated. I did not know which way to go in. I felt it impossible to use the girls' entrance, which led to the locker rooms; but I had never in my life gone in by the main door, and had no idea what lay immediately inside it.

At last I went up the steps. The main door was open. Inside I found a small waiting-room, and an office, neither of which I had seen before. No one was in them. I went through. I was in the main hall.

So many details I had remembered; more I had forgotten: the exact yellow of the parquet; the shape of the headmistress's chair on the platform.

I realized this must be lesson time. There was no noise, except for a voice occasionally raised in the distance.

Then footsteps approached. Although I had wanted someone to come, I walked over to the windows and stood looking out, my hand resting on the cold radiator, pretending I was waiting by appointment. The footsteps passed through the hall, and I did not see whose they were.

84

Presently a bell rang. There was no immediate stir. At last a girl came into the hall, and I stopped her and asked if she would find Miss Falconbridge for me.

"Wouldn't you like to wait in the waiting-room? There are chairs there."

"No, I'd rather stay here, if you don't mind." I apologized: "I'm an old girl." I gave my name.

While I waited, I walked to the window again and looked out again at the tennis courts.

I recognized Miss Falconbridge's step. She came towards me across the hall, holding out her hand, smiling. "What a lovely surprise!"

I had forgotten how much I liked her.

She seemed now, as she had seemed when I was at school, a woman of perhaps forty. Beneath the plain cardigan, despite the plain chignon, she was elegant; her lean, yellowish face would have been beautiful were it not for her teeth and would, even so, have been attractive if she had believed it.

She asked me at once if I would stay and lunch with the staff; but I said I had to go.

"Then we must make the most of these few minutes."

"Am I keeping you?"

"Yes of course. But what does it matter?"

She led me into a corner by the far side of the platform where we were out of the way. The platform reached to shoulder height. She put her books up on it.

"Now tell me how you've been getting on."

I wondered if I should tell her about Neale, even about the police. The irony was clear in my mind of my coming back to my old school on the day when I was threatened with a criminal charge. I told her I was working for a bookseller.

"Yes, that would be the right line of country for you."

While she asked me about myself, I probed, without asking, at her. I remembered so well the tone of her voice, rather high, sounding many of the syllables clear and musical on the soft palate. Beneath her warmth of friendship, there was her old shyness, which forced her into giving this impression of enthusiasm straining on an unbreakable leash. While I turned my back on the side of the platform and leaned, she faced it, her wrists resting high on it; she looked down; she slipped her foot in and out of her black court shoe, turned it over sideways, swung it a little.

If I had told her about my life, she would never have gone beyond a conventional answer; she would never have said anything extraordinary that might have helped me. Yet in the ordinariness of all her conversation there was not bluntness but gentleness. I had always respected what seemed to me her unhappy control. My apprehension of her as a person who had given up took in the certainty that she had had something, I was never to guess what, which had been potential.

"My dear," she said at last, "I have a lesson to give."

"I've kept you far too long."

"I wish you'd stay to lunch."

"I wish I could. There's one thing. I wanted to ask you—do you know where Cynthia Bewly is now?"

"Cynthia Bewly. Yes, I know. Wait a moment and I'll get it straight."

"It's wonderful how you remember any of us."

"You're not so unmemorable. Cynthia is at the South-Eastern school of art."

"Yes," I said. "She was."

"Has she given it up?"

"Yes."

"I'm sorry, that was the last I heard."

86

I walked with her down the hall—she refused to let me carry her books—until she told me to come no further. She asked me to visit the school again and stay longer—at any rate to keep in touch. As she went, she said:

"I'm sorry to hear Cynthia's given up art. She had quite a talent for drawing."

I walked back to the corner at the side of the stage. I stooped down. There was the small, square door which led under the stage. It was locked.

In this corner Cynthia and I had stood in darkness on the last night of our autumn term. A black curtain cut us off from the audience in front. At our side another black curtain, forming the wings, divided us from the stage above us: sometimes the curtain moved; once the shape of an elbow was thrust through towards us; once or twice the hem of the curtain, just on our eye level, was caught up and we saw a frill of light. Occasionally a character made her exit on our side. There would be a rent of light, rapidly healed; we would realise someone was standing on the edge of the platform—we would see the gleam of a face sweating behind its grease-paint; the figure would leap off, into us, and scuttle away; but if she had landed too heavily we would hear Miss Falconbridge—from the other side, from our side, from somewhere in the wings, actually on the stage but behind the curtain—whisper "Shhh."

During the fourth act, Miss Falconbridge was next to us, listening; she hurried away; she came back urgent. "I want two volunteers. Is there anyone here? I can't see who you are."

We whispered our names.

"Hymen's lost her crown. She needs it for the next act."

"I don't know where——"

87

"It must have got in with the old props." Miss Falconbridge stooped, and unlocked the door.

"I never knew there was a door there," I said. "I never knew you could get under the stage."

"You weren't meant to know."

We hunched ourselves to enter; there seemed to be steps down.

"Here, take my torch."

There was a sort of half-ladder inside: four dusty, bare wooden steps. We began to peer our way down them. Miss Falconbridge pushed the door to behind us.

Outside sounds became muffled. We were enclosed.

I led, with the torch's beam. We advanced into an enchanted hush, as if snow had begun to fall; and in the torchlight we saw fractions of dust, and sometimes a sharp but weightless splinter, continually descending as the characters above us moved about on the stage. At first we stooped; but the floor of the stage was well clear of our heads. The footfalls came to us like heavy but far-distant bumpings, and the voices, pursuing lines so familiar, seemed to reach us a moment late, distinct but laden with reverberance.

The immense stone floor had been swept, long before, with a wide broom which had left orderly furrows of brownish fluff. There was no cluttering of the space, only a few separate piles of wreckage. A painted screen lay on its side, one of its panels pierced by a gilt stick that must have been a chair leg. Elsewhere there was a bundle of masks, all tied together; and tied to them was a balloon that had withered on its string. Another heap consisted of Spanish shawls. At the far end was an artificially rustic structure, stuck over with silk roses.

"To think we had to make so many new ones, when those are here."

"Those are faded," Cynthia whispered.

88

Hymen's crown lay tumbled alone in a clearing. I picked it up and slipped it, like a vast bracelet, over my wrist.

Overhead, the Rosalind chided her Orlando. "I will be more jealous of thee than a Barbary cock-pigeon over his hen, more clamorous than a parrot against rain; more new-fangled than an ape, more giddy in my desires than a monkey: I will weep for nothing, like Diana in the fountain . . ."

Cynthia tugged one of the roses out of its frame. The green ribbon which bound its stem had turned an acid yellow. She began to unpick it, exposing the wire.

I cast the torchlight round, on the dust.

Cynthia came up to me, faced me and pushed the wire stem through the flannel of my lapel, drawing it down on the other side so that I was wearing the flower.

I slipped the gilt cardboard crown off my wrist and held it above Cynthia's head. Gently I brought it down.

She brushed it off. "Don't be absurd." Suddenly we kissed each other.

"Oh coz, coz, coz, my pretty little coz, that thou didst know how many fathom deep I am in love!"

I stood in Cynthia's arms, with my arms round her, trying to see her face. The torch in my hand shed its light casually behind her back. I had known that people kissed, but I had never involved the fact with myself. I found I had no idea how I had come into Cynthia's arms, how that space had been leapt which had always seemed sacrosanct. I had been not only without anticipation but without desire; and now all the desire I had in the world had been fulfilled beyond its own horizons.

I found that the desire had formed to kiss again. I cast my mind back to find out how it had been done, and copy it; but I could not discover any means behind the act. As my memory played on the immediately past moment, it became irrevocable.

I was left with a new moment, and with desire. Plotting clumsily, I bent my head towards Cynthia, my lips bitterly closed together.

We heard the door open and Miss Falconbridge say: "Haven't you found it yet?"

As we convulsed apart I felt a kind of guilt I had never experienced before. We filed out, handing up the torch and the crown, and I was dissimulating in an entirely new way.

As I emerged, the Rosalind spoke her departing line. "I cannot be out of the sight of Orlando; I'll go find a shadow and sigh till he come."

She stepped into the wings above me.

The Celia finished: "And I'll sleep."

The curtain at the front of the stage was rushed rattling across by the girls whose duty it was.

The morning after my day off I crossed the road to Finkelheim's in possession of my courage again, determined to treat the whole thing as casually as Neale would have done, and to explain it to the police as the absurd accident it was.

⋆ VII ⋆

As I walked up the stairs I met Finkelheim running down them, with his arms full of books. "Thank God to see you. You're at least two minutes late. Come on, help me get the books down."

"What books?"

"What books—my books—what do you think my business is?"

"Where are they going?"

"Outside. Didn't you see my station wagon?"

"I didn't know it was yours."

"It's not. I just hired it. You get some books to bring."

He pushed past me, and one of the books slipped from the crook of his elbow and tumbled on the stairs. I picked it up and followed him into the street. He snatched the book and tossed it into the car with the others.

"What is going on?"

"Shhh. Wait till we're in the office."

I followed him silently up the stairs. "Now."

"Let's get the worst of them out before we talk." He gathered another armful. Reluctantly I did the same. He looked at my books and knocked them out of my arms. "Not those. Those!"

"Which?"

"The men." He was pointing to the male nudes.

"They're to go first?"

"Don't play so innocent," he said, standing up with a

new load. "Don't you know it's much worse to get caught with naked men on the premises than naked women?"

Gradually we got most of the books downstairs. I did my best to leave the heaviest part of the work to Finkelheim. As I followed him up the stairs for the last time I asked again for an explanation.

He threw down to me: "What was this funny joke about you'd deal with the two men?"

I waited to answer until we were in the office, now strange in its emptiness; Finkelheim closed the door.

"I thought they'd come for me," I said.

"O did you. And what had you done?"

"I made rather a foolish phone call. The woman threatened to put the police on to me."

"You don't want to pay attention to threats," Finkelheim said. "You won't get anywhere in this world if you do."

I looked round the room. "What about the furniture? Aren't you taking that?"

"No. It's all on hire, except the bookcases, and I've sold them already."

"You act quickly."

"Have to."

I asked: "Are they going to prosecute?"

"How do I know? They took some books away. About three pounds' worth gone down the drain."

"Surely they'll give them back if you win the case?"

"There won't be any case."

"Won't they trace you?"

"There won't be any Finkelheim. I'll change my name again."

"Have you a new name in mind?" I asked.

"Haven't had time to think. I'll look in the phone book. That's the best place to choose a name—wide area of choice. One thing: I won't be Jewish again."

We were silent.

"Know any good Armenian names?" he asked.

"Not off-hand."

"Well. I suppose you want to be paid? A week in lieu of notice?"

"Yes."

He took out his wallet and counted out the notes. "You don't want any of the books? I could get them out of the car again if you were interested. I could let you have them at a third off."

"Have you still got *The Lady Revealed*?"

"That was one the police took. I've got one quite like it."

"No, I don't think so, thanks."

"Well."

"Well."

"You better be going now. I got to be going myself."

We walked down the stairs.

"This so-called your uncle," Finkelheim said. "He the friend you share with?"

"As a matter of fact, yes."

Finkelheim got into the driving seat. He said through the window: "You want to be careful, you know. You don't want to trust men. You make him marry you."

"I'm doing my best."

"That's right." He winked at me. He switched on the ignition and started the motor. "Well, I don't suppose you want me to write you a testimonial?"

"I don't think so, thank you."

"No. You're a smart girl. You don't need any testimonials."

I crossed the road slowly and went into our flat. Neale was asleep. I sat down beside him and watched him. I remembered the last words Cynthia had spoken to me; on the day of the fête, after I had rushed into the gym and danced. Presently I had seen Cynthia come in with Gill and Annette. They stood up in a set at the far end, the three of them in a row with Cynthia in the middle. I left my own set and ran round to them. I seized Gill from behind, whirled her out of the way, and took her place. "Cynthia, you've got to talk to me. You've got to explain."

"*Must* you?" she said. "*Must* you."

"Yes! Why did you end it all? So suddenly?"

"I don't know what you're talking about. Stop making a fool of yourself."

"You stop it. You stop this beastly dancing." I snatched at her arm and pulled her out of the set. She giggled a little, but protested. I pushed her against the parallel bars. "Cynthia, why did you break it all off like that?"

She tried to twist away.

"Why?"

"Well! It was all pretty silly, wasn't it?"

Neale opened his eyes. "Back already? Or have I overslept?" He woke up a little further. "Or are you under house arrest?"

"It wasn't me they were after."

"Who was it then? Finkelheim? For selling obscene books? Did they get him?"

"Not they," I said. "Not him. He's flitted. As an employer, he's folded up."

Neale settled down into the bedclothes, and I thought he went to sleep again. Presently he asked: "Did he pay you?"

"Yes."

"You'd better take me out to lunch." He swung out of bed and put his socks on.

It was an uncertain day. We walked down the Tottenham Court Road after lunching at our Indian restaurant.

"Is it going to come out?" Neale said. "Or is it going to rain?"

"If it did come out we might go to Kew."

To my surprise he said: "Yes."

At once the sky darkened.

By accord we stopped outside a cinema and looked at the stills, themselves faded, in the fading light. It was a French film, with Annabella; there was a shot of an artificial-looking mountain village; of two people walking towards the Pont Neuf; of a short-haired girl in lamé giggling over a glass of champagne.

"We could go here," Neale said, "I suppose."

"I've seen it."

We walked on. The next cinema was showing a film of Tosca. It seemed to be an Italian production, but it starred Helena Buchan; there was a picture of her lying on the floor, propped on one elbow, singing Vissi D'arte.

"It'll be terribly old," Neale said. "Look how young she looks. The sound track will be awful."

The third cinema had a banner over the door: "Gala Festival of Silent Comedies."

"I hate feeling obliged to laugh," Neale said. We walked past. We reached the corner of Oxford Street, and paused, looking at the sky.

"We could take a seventy-three from here."

"Or should we see what's on at the Oxford Street cinemas?"

We walked to them, but we had seen the films they were shewing.

"I'm sure it is going to rain."

We continued to walk towards Oxford Circus. I said:

"I suppose I'll have to get another job."

"Yes, you will. I can't support you."

"I expect I shan't get a holiday this year."

"This is your holiday—today."

"A rainy one, I imagine."

As we passed the bottom of Great Portland Street, Neale pointed to the post office, and said: "Is it worth asking in there?"

"Hardly."

Nevertheless I wandered in. I was given a letter.

We crossed the road and I opened the envelope walking down Regent Street. Gill had written, without super-scription, and giving no address:

> *Christ how I hate voices from the past. I should certainly not have answered yours if I hadn't found this immediately after. Probably that sort of thing happens quite often if, as I do, one reads the gutter press line by line, but for the moment it looked like the sticky prod of providence.*
>
> *God knows why you want to know, but the answer to how am I is bloody. What did you expect. I was engaged to a medical student but it was no good because I couldn't stand loving a man who knew about my insides. And how has Cupid that was begot of thought, conceived of spleen and born of madness, been treating you, dear?*
>
> *As for other soi-disant friends from the so-called best years of our laughingly named lives, I hear from nobody. The enclosed is self-explanatory, so far as anything can be ex-plained. Whether the half change of name denotes marriage, rise in social caste, naturalisation among foreigners or goddam restlessness, I wouldn't know. Don't ever write to me again.*
>
> *Yours, Gill.*

I gave Neale the letter to read, while I felt in the envelope. I pushed two fingers into it, and then tore at it. "She's forgotten to put the enclosure in."

We stopped.

"Or it's dropped out."

We turned, and began to walk back up Regent Street. We took one side of the pavement each and tacked to and fro, meeting in the middle. All the time, the sky was getting blacker and blacker. We worked our way up the incline and reached the top of the road without finding anything.

"What about the island?" Neale said. "We came over that way, didn't we?" We waited for the traffic and then ran across.

The press-cutting, shiny and sepia, was lying flat in the middle of the island. A star print from a rubber heel had been stamped on the bottom corner; otherwise it was unharmed. As I bent to pick it up, the first drop of rain fell on to it.

We stood close together, peering at a picture of Cynthia in a bathing suit, with her legs crossed. The drop of rain had sunk into the paper soggily, blurring her face. The caption read: "Cynthia Beaulieu is one of the British starlets arriving in Venice next month—in time for filmdom's own international get-together (no connexion with the Film Festival at the same venue)."

"We've done it!" Neale said. "We've achieved the first stage." He pulled his plastic mackintosh out of his coat pocket and began to unfurl it.

"I don't see we've achieved anything."

He spread the mackintosh round us both, pulling it over our heads. "Don't you realize? I've seen her with at least some clothes on."

Holding the mack to us we ran across the road, meaning to shelter in the entrance to the tube, but a crowd of people had formed, pushing their way in.

"Come on." Neale pulled away from me. I followed the empty transparent wing of the mackintosh held out for me, and caught him up. We began to run down

Regent Street, which had emptied; we caught hold of one another by the waist, and hurried awkwardly as if we were in a three-legged race.

"Where are we going?"

"Anywhere!"

The rain was tumbling down the gutters of Regent Street.

"Venice," Neale added.

"What about it?" I could hear the rain beat on the plastic above me; but nothing kept it off my face; I could feel it like tears on my cheeks.

"Let's go there."

"You might as well say the moon. She might as well have gone to the moon for her publicity." I was out of breath.

"Don't stop! Well, why not the moon?"

"I must stop." We slowed down. Neale was panting too. After the run, I could hardly force my legs even to walk at a normal pace. The rain grew thicker.

"Wouldn't you like to go to Venice? Wouldn't you like a break between jobs?"

"O, of course I would," I said, exhausted, dropping behind, losing my place in the mackintosh.

"Come in here." Neale pulled me into a shop. As we went inside, we felt the cessation of the rain in our ears.

Neale shook his mackintosh over the doormat. We were in a travel agency, carpeted like a cinema, hung with airline posters. I tried to brush the rain off my face and to comb my hair through my fingers. Neale walked up to the counter. The clerk looked at him.

"Do you want any couriers," Neale said, "to escort parties to Italy?"

The clerk stared at us both, then said:

"You could try the manager. Through there."

The manager was a small man in a blue-striped suit;

pink-faced, fluffy haired. We went in, and Neale repeated his question.

"Do sit down," the manager said.

We each took an arm-chair. The manager lifted some papers off his desk, made a bundle of them, squared them off and put them into a folder. At last he said:

"Do you know Italy well?"

I answered, honestly describing my various visits. I knew Neale had been only once; but the manager seemed content to let my answers pass for us both.

"I take it you could supply testimonials? Or, if we had to fix things in a hurry, you could let me have the names of referees we could apply to?"

I thought of the testimonial I had refused from Finkelheim. However, we both answered: "Yes."

"Do you think you could take a party round? The transport's all laid on, you know, and the accommodation. It's a question of coping. Are you tactful?"

"Very."

The manager said nothing.

Neale asked: "Is there a vacancy?"

"I have a party of Americans," the manager said, "in France at the moment."

"We really wanted Italy."

"Yes, yes, I know. The French tour is perfectly all right, any way. They're being well looked after, by one of our French connexions. But they're due to go on to Italy."

We did not dare speak.

"The French agent," the manager went on, "deposits them at Nice. Our Italian agent meets them there and takes them over. Unfortunately, the Italian part of the arrangements has broken down."

"How soon," Neale asked, "are they due at Nice?"

"In two days' time."

"You're in rather a hole," Neale said.

The manager stood up and began to walk round the room. "I could fly out myself. I could send one of my people from here."

"But isn't your season," Neale said, "just working up to its busiest?"

"Yes. I really need everyone here." He walked a little longer; then sat down and passed us a blank sheet of paper over the desk. "Would you write the names of your referees there?"

Neale wrote down his headmaster. Underneath I named Miss Falconbridge.

The manager took the paper back, looked at it, then at us. "We don't, normally speaking, employ couriers by twos."

I asked: "But the party's mixed, isn't it? Men and women?"

"Yes."

"Two of us would really be more tactful."

"In the circumstances," the manager said, "you may be right. However"—I saw him look at my hand and perceive no wedding ring—"from our point of view, two couriers might make the whole proposition un-economic." I guessed he was weighing the loss to his prestige if he employed us against the loss to it if he supplied no courier at all.

"It's no good if we don't go together," Neale said. There was silence. Neale added: "We might accept one salary between the two of us. But we should need two sets of expenses."

Changing the subject, the manager described the Italian itinerary. "As far as the Italian part of the tour goes, it finishes in Venice. The party is handed over there to the Greek courier, who takes them on by sea."

I found myself smiling. I looked down, to conceal how

exactly this suited us. From Neale's voice I could tell that he too was concealing excitement. "We should require our fares home from Venice."

"I could arrange that."

"You might give us open tickets," Neale said. "In case we wanted to stay on in Venice for a little holiday."

"All right," the manager said. "You might need it." He opened his folder again. "Well. Are you prepared to be in Nice the day after tomorrow?"

"You'll fly us there?"

"You must realize—two couriers—I'll fly you to Paris. You can go on by train."

"All right."

"Cheap night flight," the manager said.

I was terrified Neale might insist and, perhaps, lose everything. But he nodded.

The manager wrote us a chit. "If you give that to the clerk in the front office, he'll fix you up."

The clerk received us unsurprisedly, holding out his hand for the chit. He gave us a cardboard wallet full of documents about the tour, and two badges. He made out our plane tickets, copying our different surnames on to them without reaction. "There you are. That's the lot."

Neale burst out: "Goodness, aren't we lucky."

The clerk opened his mouth, and then merely ran his tongue round his teeth. At last he decided to say: "I hope you like the party when you meet them. Bon voyage."

Outside the agency we stood breathless, and then began to laugh, bending, turning sideways away from one another, Neale drawing up his knees like a warhorse. "O Lord," he said, "O Lord, O Lord." The pavements were drying spasmodically; sun beat warm on us. "But this is nothing," Neale said. "Wait till we get to the South." He took my arm. "Have you got any summer clothes?"

"Yes, I must look them out." I gave a start. "Pretty quickly, I suppose."

"We'll have to do everything pretty quickly."

"What about your job?"

"I'll give notice. I'll give up the flat, too. We can't afford to keep it on while we're away. We'll have to find someone to take in our things. Who do you think would?"

"Tanya?" I suggested.

"Right, let's ring her up. And we'll have to let those people know we've named them as referees." We set off, but outside one of the big shops Neale stopped me. "Why don't you buy a new dress?"

We went in and stepped into the lift, where we began to giggle again. Neale sat down on the leather seat and doubled up; the women in the lift looked at him unkindly.

We emerged, let our laughter loose and then walked into one of the halls, where we began to pick through a rack of cotton dresses. Neale pulled one out. "This is heavenly." "It's hideous," I said. I took out one of my own choice. "My one is much better," Neale insisted; "what's wrong with it?" I shrugged. "In any case, I simply can't wear square necklines."

"Can I help you, madam?"

I asked if I might try the dress on. The assistant took the dress I was carrying, and said: "This way." I followed her. Neale followed me, carrying the dress he had chosen. As we reached the embrasure, the assistant turned and took the dress from him. "Would you like to wait over there, sir? There's a couch, if you'd care to sit down."

I followed her down a corridor and into a cubicle. She switched on the light, drew the curtain behind us, and hung the two dresses on a hook on the wall.

She waited for me to undress. I waited for her to leave.

She began to unzip the dresses. "Which will you try first?"

I pretended to examine the one Neale had picked. "I can't really wear yellow. Have you got it in other colours?"

"It does come in pink, madam."

"I wonder if you'd mind slipping out and fetching me a pink one?"

She sighed, forced a smile, and went out.

I pulled my own clothes off as quickly as I could, and got into the dress I liked. By the time the assistant came back I was doing it up in front of the mirror. "It suits madam very well."

We both stared at my reflection.

"And it fits you. You have a stock figure, madam, although you're short."

"I like it very much," I said.

"Would you just like to try the other? The pink or the yellow? Before you decide?"

"I don't really think so. I'm afraid I don't like it in pink after all."

"Perhaps you'd care to shew the gentleman the one you've got on."

I walked out self-consciously. Neale was sitting on the sofa, looking like Proust. He turned. "It's divine. I told you it would be."

"But this isn't the one you picked."

"Isn't it? Isn't it really?"

"No!"

We began to laugh again. I bought the dress with the money Finkelheim had given me. Neale took the paper carrier, and we went down again by lift, sitting side by side at the back. The square edges of the parcel poked at the knees of the people standing in front of us. As we left the shop, Neale asked me: "By the way. How's your Italian?"

"Minimal. How's yours?"

"O, not too bad. I should think I could get us round."

The sky was grey again as we hurried home.

We took our belongings by taxi to Tanya's. "Pile them in the bedroom," she said. "They'll be quite safe. Tanya will take care of them."

"There's just one thing I want to look out," I said. I opened my trunk and found the box where I kept old letters and mementoes. Neale leaned over my shoulder and looked at some of the letters. "You certainly did collect men," he said.

Tanya said: "Don't laugh at our little vanities."

I picked out a silk rose.

"Is that the one Cynthia gave you?" Neale asked. "Are we taking it with us?"

I handed it up to him. "Yes."

He took it. "It *has* faded." He folded it small and put it away in his wallet.

.

PART TWO

✶ VIII ✶

I<small>T</small> was the cold, sickening early hours. I stirred in my arm-chair. "Neale?"

"Yes?"

"What I don't understand is why you go so far—come so far—for something that belongs to my past, not yours."

He spread his hand, shewing me the open palm over the side of his chair. His plastic mackintosh, which he was wearing for warmth, gave a crack. "Your past, my past—what's the difference?" He added: "You and I are practically the same person, aren't we?"

I was pleased; but in a moment I asked: "Does that mean there could never be a relationship between us?"

"O, I don't know," Neale said. "I was almost asleep. We've got to keep hoping."

"For what?"

"That it will all be different when we get to the South."

We had not slept on the flight, although the passengers had been left alone so that they should. We landed in mist, but it was daylight; we gave up the cards we had filled in on the plane, and were virtually excused the Customs; we got into the bus. The seats at the back were almost derelict, the horsehair coming through the leather covers, but we chose to sit there for fear of the driver's horn. The bus started; we began to drive springlessly through a grey Paris. I dozed. We lurched and my cheek jarred on Neale's shoulder. I opened my eyes, recognized the Madeleine, and dozed again. We drew into the air terminal. A thin line of us was led out of the bus and silently upstairs. We waited; recognized our luggage coming down the moving belt; collected it; and stood in the vacant hall with it at our feet. "It's an unholy hour," Neale had said. "We'd better go down to the waiting-room and sleep a bit."

We sat in tweed-upholstered chairs; the pegs in the wooden frames gave an illusion they could be adjusted, but they could not. The low tables were the wrong height for the chairs and curiously placed towards them; however we moved our chairs, we were uncomfortable.

Occasionally we heard a bus rumble into the tunnel next door. The loudspeaker spoke once. The two bar-tenders behind the counter murmured. A tall air-hostess, wearing not quite a uniform, stepped into the building, which seemed almost too low-ceilinged for her; on high shabby heels she clacked round the floor, while she looked at the jewellery and scent bottles in the flat glass cases.

I opened my eyes. Neale was awake too. I felt something between hunger, cold, fear, nausea. I knew we were both suffering from thoughts that had raced out ahead of time; we wondered how long it could take for the day to mature; how long to get through the day; how long to be carried overnight to the South.

"Shall we go out for breakfast?"

"We might as well have it here."

We sat on stools at the bar; the coffee was milky and bitter. "I can make the traditional remark of the British housewife abroad," Neale said. "It's a change from the washing-up, anyway." He looked at his watch. "It's not quite such an unholy hour as it was."

"Let's walk round a bit. François won't be awake yet."

We strolled out of the air terminal towards the river. We ran into a crowd of office workers pouring out of the Gare des Invalides. Hesitating, endangered, we crossed the main road, and stood leaning on the stone wall looking at the river. Uncertainly the sun lay on the flat water; uncertainly it lit the plane trees. "O this terrible city," Neale said. "Am I in love with it, or do I hate it?"

We crossed the road again, less cautiously, and walked down the Rue de l'Université, looking in the windows of the bookshops.

"What is it about houses in Paris?"

I looked up at the long façade of them. "The shutters. Simply and solely the shutters."

We wandered on till we were almost lost, and then sat down in the cold outside a café. We drank black coffee. It came through the filter an auburn colour tinged with gold; it tasted bitter. We finished, tipped heavily and made our way into the inside of the café. In a gold-and-crimson recess, ruled by a sharp-faced woman in black, Neale bought a jeton. I waited while he made the call. The woman stared at me, determined to be an enemy.

Neale came out. "He can't meet us till this evening."

He tipped the woman. She called, as we left: "Il fait beau aujourd'hui, monsieur."

Outside Neale asked me: "What did she mean? Did I tip too little? Or too much?"

"One can never tell what people mean in Paris."

"No. Well. Shall we go to the Louvre?"

"Yes, all right."

"Only we'll have to go by Métro," he said. "I can't work the buses."

As we walked along, Neale said: "Anyway, what is it about the shutters?"

"The slats," I said.

"Yes, it's clever. They give an impression you can see in, though in fact you can't. And isn't that the whole of romance?" In a moment Neale added: "So many streets in Paris look like a theatrical Seville."

"They look like canvas," I said, "because the stucco is so matt. The sunlight just lies on it."

"Or the lamplight," Neale said. "And then it's the shutters again. The figure who stands outside, below the window, believes he can almost see in."

"Don Giovanni, serenading Donna Elvira's maid."

"But Don Giovanni went to hell." Neale snatched my wrist and we plunged down the steps to the Métro.

We met François and he took us to a café in the Place Pigalle. We drank vermouth; he drank beer and smoked his pipe.

"Et qu'est ce que vous avez fait aujourd'hui?"

We told him we had been to the Louvre; and that we had seen, as we came out, a handbill advertising an exhibition of Manet's paintings at the Orangerie. We had gone there, but the exhibition was no longer there; we were directed to the Petit Palais. At the Petit Palais we were directed to the Eiffel Tower; but, disbelieving, we had not gone.

"Tant mieux," François said. "Cette exposition est finie—il y a—hoh—deux semaines."

"Dommage," Neale said. "Elle paraissait d'être très intéressante."

"Oui, oui, très intéressante."

"Une très grande collection des oeuvres."

"Collection definitive," said François.

"Vous l'avez vue?" we asked him.

"Moi? Non."

After a silence, François said: "Alors. Vous partez pour l'Italie?"

"Oui. Nous recontrons nos Américains à Nice."

"À Nice?"

"Oui."

"Oui."

"Moi j'adore les Américains," said François.

"Pourquoi?"

"Hoh—le jazz." He said nothing for a moment. Then: "Je n'aime point les Italiens."

"Pourquoi pas?"

"Ils ne sont pas très intellectuels."

We ordered more drinks. François asked us: "Vous partez ce soir?"

"Oui, vers dix heures."

"Gare d'Austerlitz?"

"Non. Gare de Lyons."

"O. Gare de Lyons." He added: "Quel dommage que vous partez toute de suite. Paris est très gai le soir." He waved towards the neon signs and the traffic. "Plus gai que Londres."

"Oui. C'est dommage."

Neale said to me: "What in hell shall we talk about now?"

"Tell him how we got the job."

"Ah, bon. Il faut que nous vous disons par quel moyen nous sommes employés par cet agence de tourisme. C'est une histoire très amusante." He began to tell it. François did not smile. Neale's French grew more blundering. "Vous comprenez—ce monsieur ne voulut pas accepter deux couriers—il croyait que l'un était assez."

François looked up from his beer. "Ainsi, ça suffira si l'un seul—ou si l'une seule—parte pour L'Italie? L'autre pourrait rester à Paris?"

Neale said: "Non. Il faut absolument que nous aillons ensembles."

François nodded. He knocked his pipe out and put it

in his pocket. Presently he wished us Bon Voyage, and left.

We arrived at the station long before our train came in. We waited on the platform; when it came we fought for seats and won two facing each other.

I took my Italian phrase-book out of my suit-case and switched on the light above my seat. I sat with the book open on my knee, dreading the over-night journey and doubting my own patience to bear it. The train started; we were clear of Paris almost at once, and looked out at darkened fields; I fell asleep.

We came out of the station at Nice and looked at the irregular square, elongated, haphazardly built on an incline. It was sunlit but not warm.

"We've got an hour," Neale said, "before we need go and meet them."

"What shall we do?"

"Let's each eat a fontainebleau."

"What are they?"

"Have you never had them?" We walked along the square and found a dairy on the corner. We went in— it was a tiny, triangular shop—and a thin woman of thirty-five, her hair dyed streaky blonde and done into sausage curls, sang to us: "Bonjour, madame. Bonjour, monsieur."

We responded. Neale asked for a fontainebleau apiece. As she took them out of the refrigerator, he said to me: "Doesn't this shop smell like your childhood? It does like mine. Perhaps everyone's childhood smells the same." He asked the woman: "On ne vend pas ici du sucre?"

She directed us next door.

"Merci, madame. Merci, monsieur.   Au revoir, monsieur. Au revoir, madame."

"Au revoir, madame."

In the shop next door an old man in a black apron was sweeping the sawdusted floor. We bought some sugar. As we came out, Neale said: "Isn't it silly to love people just for saying good morning and good-bye to you."

We each ate a fontainebleau awkwardly out of the paper bag, while we sat on a bench in the middle of the square, beneath a sub-tropical bush. We could not finish all the sugar; we packed it in Neale's case.

"We'd better go."

Carrying a suit-case each, we set off down a long lane of solid buildings, painted bright white, gleaming, squarely breasting the air like ocean liners. Many called themselves Guest House or Private Hotel. "It's just like Blackpool." "Or Eastbourne." "Or Scarborough." "No, Worthing."

Just before we reached the sea, Neale asked: "Do you feel terrible?"

"Yes."

"Let's have a drink."

We sat down at a circular iron table, warped and colourless, outside a café with dirty windows; it had once borne a name in white letters on the glass, but most of it had come off.

We waited. In front of us large, shiny cars awkwardly sailed down the narrow street. A fat man came out at last, wiped the table-top and said:

"What jew like? Amburger? Coke? Malted milk?"

"Two brandies please."

We drank them quickly and went on. We came in sight of the sea. It was glittering, a strong green-blue, the colour of a medicated swimming pool. We turned the corner and battled the wind along the Boulevard des Anglais. We came to the travel agency where we had our rendezvous. A pale green motor coach, empty, stood outside. We fixed our badges on our coats.

We went in. The shop door pinged behind us. A slight man in a beret came forward. "Thank God you are here at last." His accent was Franco–American.

"We're not late are we?"

The Frenchman looked at his watch. "No. Early. But my nerves are all to pieces. I am the one that has taken them through France."

We introduced ourselves.

"I can only repeat—thank God. I did not think I ever would see you."

"Didn't London let you know we were coming?"

"Sure. They cable they have made arrangements. I did not think the arrangements would stand. The other arrangements didn't."

"No. I gather the Italian courier backed out."

"As soon as he heard about them."

"Who let him know?" Neale asked.

"I felt it my duty. There is a fraternity in the profession. Besides, you cannot keep a thing like that dark."

"Well," Neale said presently, "where are they?"

"Les Américains? Not here yet. Don't worry—they will be here soon. Come, I shew you the coach while it is empty."

We filed out and walked round to the front of the bus, which was blunt and face-like. A man in a blue-striped smock, with a flat cap worn backwards, was leaning against the radiator. "Our driver. His name is Charles." To the driver, the courier said: "Permettez-moi de vous présenter . . ." The driver shrugged, moved round the far side of the bus and climbed into the driving seat.

"Anyway," the courier whispered, "you get a new driver at the frontier."

He led us back to the near side; unlocked the passenger door, which was near the front of the coach; and waved to us to mount the three grooved steel steps. He followed

114

us, pulling the door to. It did not connect properly. He wrestled to reopen it, and slammed it. "It is sometimes a bit difficult—the salt air."

He began to explain. "This front seat on the left is your seat. Good thing it is a double seat, since you are two. Here, just in front of you—you see you can pull it out towards you, so you don't have to stand up—is the microphone."

"The microphone?"

"You have to tell them which towns they are going through. If you don't know, ask the driver. Also, they like to know the age of the buildings you pass. You make it up."

He led us down the narrow aisle, between the pairs of seats, each with its tall, padded back, its antimacassar, its number. One seat had no antimacassar. The courier tapped it. "Mr. Wagner—don't pronounce it like the composer—refuse to have a lace thing. He thinks it leads to bugs. He thinks there are a lot of bugs in France. He is worried there will be more in Italy." We went on. The courier tapped the back of seat number thirteen friendlily. "Mrs. Luther has to travel in thirteen. She is sick if she sits anywhere else. She really is." We reached the back of the coach. There was a small compartment, with a door, like the one at the back of an aeroplane. Neale raised his eyebrows. "No, no," the courier said deprecatingly. "Unfortunately, no. There is just"—he opened the door—"a refrigerator." He pulled up the lid of the refrigerator; there were about a hundred bottles of Coca-Cola. "You take on fresh supplies," he said, "at wholesale rates, every day. Behind the refrigerator, there is—look." He stooped and opened a box. We stooped and peered round him. In the box lay a supply of paper mugs and five bottles of brandy. "Emergency ration," the courier said. "Declare it at the Customs—they'll understand—but don't let the passengers hear you. It is not to be used unless something happens very, very bad. In that case, you give it out with the compliments of the company."

Suddenly we knew from the noise that the passengers were upon us. The French courier poked the box away hurriedly. He turned his back on the refrigerator, placed his hands on its top and jumped into a sitting position on it. He drew Neale and me close in to him.

We felt the bus rock as the first foot was set on the first step.

The bus was filled with a noise like a parrot house.

I peered out, trying to distinguish Mr. Wagner and Mrs. Luther.

The noise grew a little less. The French courier said something we could not hear, but he pointed and we understood we were to troop down the aisle to the front. When we reached it, he took the microphone. "May I have your attention, please?" There was no drop in the noise. "I wish to introduce your new couriers, who are going to escort you through Italy." There was no response. "And now it is time for me to say adieu." He let the microphone go and it snapped back into its hole. He shook hands with Neale and me and climbed out of the coach. A man's voice from the back called, above the general noise: "So long, boy." Neale leaned forward and slammed the coach door.

Suddenly the coach listed towards the pavement side. I turned in my seat with difficulty. All the people sitting on our side were leaning as far out of the windows as they could; and the ones on the other side had left their places and come across, too, and were leaning their elbows on the others' backs. Thirty or forty cameras, still and moving, were pointed at the French courier.

Embarrassed, he stood on the pavement and raised his hand in a half-salute.

The driver started the engine.

I pulled down our window and leaned out, too.

The big gear-lever went noisily into first; we throbbed and began to move. My hair streaming in the wind, I blew the French courier a kiss. I looked back along the flank of the coach. The cameras, some held out at arm's length, were jogging up and down. Some followed round, planning to catch the last of the disappearing courier. My view was like a portion of a biology film, highly magnified, in which the bus was a monstrous micro-organism propelled jerkily by its stubby, waving cilia.

We pulled round a corner. The passengers went back to their places. For a minute or two there was a con-centrated silence, apart from the noise of film being wound on. Then the chatter, including an occasional hum of song, began again; intense, but throttled down enough to be bearable. The impression of travelling with performing animals was all the stronger because we periodically heard a peanut crack.

Neale took the microphone. "We are going to drive along the Riviera——" A woman's voice shouted: "Is this the famous Riviera?"

"Along the famous Riviera," Neale said. "The first important town we come to is Monte Carlo . . ."

A man's voice shouted: "Casino! Casino." The passengers laughed.

". . . Is the famous Monte Carlo, capital of the inde-pendent principality of Monaco, which is under French protection."

We drove on. A woman called. "Hey, miss."

I turned. A narrow-shouldered girl of about my own age was clicking her fingers at me. "I want a coke."

I fetched her one from the refrigerator. The aisle was full of peanut shells.

The man behind us tapped Neale's shoulder. "What do you call that plant on the walls?"

"Bougainvillia."

The man sat back and said to his wife: "It's like Southern California. Isn't it like Southern California?"

"No, it's not. I've seen something like it in New Mexico, but I never saw anything like it in Southern California."

"Why, you got the ocean here," the man said, "right alongside you, just like you got it in Southern California."

"It's more rugged than Southern California ever was. You got cliffs here. I guess it's just like New Mexico."

We drove into Monte Carlo, and Neale made an announcement into the microphone. "You will notice Monaco has its own police force, with their own uniforms."

"Which is the Casino?" someone yelled.

"That one, I think," Neale said, pointing at a dome.

"How old is it?"

"It looks as if it was built by Edward the Seventh," Neale said.

The woman behind tapped Neale. "Is that pretty old?"

"Yes."

The man behind said: "How do you mean, it looks like he built it? How can you tell?"

His wife answered him: "They put a kind of a stone in the front, with the fellow's name on it, and a kind of cross sometimes."

"All these countries are Catholic," the man said.

After a little we felt a jar at our backs. We looked up. A woman was standing in the aisle, swaying a little and leaning against our seat. Neale stood up.

"No, I can't sit there. I can't even stay here long standing, or I get sick to my stomach."

"Mrs. Luther?" Neale asked.

"That's right. I just want to say, on behalf of the party, we know you're going to give us a fine trip round Italy and we're going to do our darnedest to give you a fine trip too."

We thanked her.

She tottered back to number thirteen, then returned to us. "You English?"

"Yes."

"Married?"

"No."

"Going together?"

"No."

"Well. What do you know? That French boy——"

"The courier?"

"Yes, him. We gave him a pretty fine trip. I guess he wasn't used to having much of a time before he met up with us."

At last we came to a stop behind a queue of cars at the frontier. On our left was a patch of stony grass and a rock face that had been quarried; on our right the Customs building, apparently on the cliff edge.

The driver turned off the engine.

There was movement outside, occasional shouting, several uniformed men. No one came to us.

Mrs. Luther walked up the aisle, leaned across Neale and spoke to me. "On behalf of the women of the party, is there a john here?"

"I think so. I seem to remember——" I looked out. It was just to the left of the Customs building, with a steep staircase leading down to it. I pointed it out.

"Would you very kindly take us?" Mrs. Luther asked. "We don't speak the language."

"You hardly need to. The word Dames——"

"It's not only the language. The agency told us all

119

tips were included, and you always have to tip in these foreign johns."

I stood up. "Would anyone who——"

But the women were already flocking towards me. I led the way out of the bus. A Customs officer raised his hand across my path. "Interdit. Défense de descendre. Verboten."

"Neale," I called. "Come and explain."

The Customs officer listened seriously. Seriously he shepherded us out of the bus counting us; he counted us as we came back. I was delayed a little because the attendant had thought my five hundred francs too small a tip to cover so large a party.

As I sat down again in the bus, Neale whispered to me: "I declared the brandy. We're through the French part of the Customs."

The bus started. We drove a little way, jerking, and stopped.

An Italian official leapt up the steps of the bus and stood with his back to the driver's seat. "Qualchecosa da dichiarare?"

"Oui," Neale called." Sí."

"Che cosa?"

"I can only think in French," Neale said to me.

"He may understand English."

"But so do the passengers. Do you find this difficulty," Neale asked me, "in switching from French to Italian?"

"It's because they're both Romance languages."

"That must be why I love them."

The official reeled out: "Tabacco, sigarette, profumi, vini . . . ?"

I said: "Cinque bottiglie di cognac."

"Per i passeggieri?"

"Sí. In caso di necessità."

"Va bene. Altro?"

"Non so." I gestured to the passengers. "Ciascuno ha il suo bagaglio."

"Va bene," said the official. He leapt down, and waved us on.

"Are we all through with the Customs?" someone shouted.

"I think so," Neale said into the microphone.

We drove a little way, and halted again. Our driver climbed out, and a new one climbed in. Neale and I leaned forward and shook hands with him. He introduced himself as Carlo. He looked over the passengers, puffed one cheek out, smiled at us, turned to the front and, like a flamboyant pianist, threw the gear lever in.

After we had driven for a moment or two Carlo raised his hands completely from the wheel and called, basso: "Siamo nella bella Italia!"

I felt a spasm of tears pass behind my eyes.

From the back a voice I knew to be Mr. Wagner's said: "I guess Italy's going to be a pretty unhygienic country."

We drove through the suburbs of Genoa in the twilight. "Genoa," Neale announced. "Or, in Italian, Genova."

"Now I wonder why they call it that?" said the woman behind us.

Neale went on: "On our left you will see many new blocks of flats going up. Genoa is one of the biggest Italian cities."

The man behind asked: "What population?"

"Several thousand," Neale replied.

I whispered to him: "Try to keep off the size of things."

"On our right, the famous waterfront of Genoa. Notice the long promenade, the coloured lights, the masts of the ships."

"Do they get ocean-going liners here?"

"They do."

"Up to what tonnage?"

"Any tonnage you like to think of."

We drew up in front of a concrete hotel. We said good night to Carlo, and ran into the foyer. The manager was waiting.

Mrs. Luther was the first passenger to come through the swing door. "I hope it's fixed for me to have room thirteen," she said to Neale. "The agency promised me. I had it all through France."

I asked the manager: "É riservata la camera numero tredici per questa signora?"

"Tredici?"

"Sí."

"Tredici, no. Trentuno."

"Trentuno?"

"Sí, sí." The manager pulled open a drawer in his reception desk and brought out a cable form. He shewed it me. "IMPERATIVE RESERVE 31 FOR LUTHER."

"O Lord."

"Trentuno, sí sí."

"Sarebbe possibile—what is the Italian for a screw-driver? Può Lei riversare——"

The manager held his two fists up side by side and rapidly switched their positions. We nodded quickly. He indicated that we were to detain Mrs. Luther. He hurried away.

Neale drew Mrs. Luther aside. I heard him begin: "On behalf of my colleague and myself, I want to say how much we have enjoyed . . ."

I watched the luggage, carried in by the porters, piling up on the buff carpet. Finally it was all there; the passengers claimed their own; they were led away, with their cases, to the lift, going singly, two by two, some-times three by three.

122

Mrs. Luther broke away from Neale. "I can't wait any longer. I got to get to the john."

I took her arm. "Come along." I led her to one on the ground floor. When we came back, the manager was smiling in the vestibule. He bowed to Neale and me, and himself took Mrs. Luther up in the lift.

The last of our party was absorbed.

The reception clerk, the only one of the staff left, handed us our key. It was number 106. We waited for the lift and went up to the sixth floor.

We let ourselves into an attic room, furnished with a glaring yellow wardrobe with gilt handles, and a small brass double bed.

We washed, undressed and climbed in. Neale took my hand and pressed it, and we fell asleep.

★ IX ★

SUDDENLY I felt cold in bed. I opened my eyes and saw Neale bending over his suit-case in the corner of the room.

"What are you doing?"

"Some of that sugar has spilt."

"Badly?"

"Not very." He took out a pile of shirts, shook them and put them back. Carefully he lifted the sugar packet on to the floor. "I'm not going to take it any further. Can I leave it in the wastepaper basket, do you think?"

"Put it on the dressing-table. Perhaps the maid will be able to use it. And now come back to bed."

"It's time to get up. We're making an early start."

We breakfasted in a bar round the corner from the hotel, where we could be alone. "Thank goodness for some decent coffee." We ate large pieces of fruit cake, shaped like segments of a football, which came to the table wrapped in cellophane.

The bus, silver in the early sun and mist, was standing outside the hotel. Carlo was sweeping up the peanut shells from the aisle. He greeted us. "Ciao."

"Ciao."

We went into the hotel, saw the luggage carried out, thanked the manager and called into the dining-room: "Everyone ready?" There was no response. We went out again and sat in the bus. Carlo was in the driving seat, eating sandwiches. We wished him Buon Appetito. He held out the sandwiches to us. "Grazie, abbiamo già mangiato."

He finished eating, and told us we should have warmer weather.

A few members of the party came into the bus. They grunted when we said good morning to them. At last, in a rush, the rest came.

Neale slammed the door, and signalled to Carlo.

A maid ran out of the hotel, her arms piled with things, which she clutched awkwardly as she tapped at the glass of the coach. We lowered our window, and she passed the things through. "Mille grazie," Neale said.

As we drove off, Neale held up a packet of paper tissues and asked into the microphone: "Who left this in the hotel?"

No one answered; Neale was lowering his arm when a woman shouted: "Hey, that's mine."

We passed it back over our heads.

We found claimants for the other items the maid had brought: an electric razor, a pot of cold cream, a shoe, several coat hangers. The last item was our packet of sugar. We put it under the seat.

The woman behind us said to her husband: "I guess that about proves the Italians are honest."

"They just don't want to lose custom."

After a moment she said: "Well at least they're as honest as the French. At all the French hotels they brought things out in the mornings."

As we drove into it we seemed to disperse the mist. The sunlight first gleamed through, then matured into full brilliancy, pouring at us out of a deep blue sky, creating mirages of water on the road ahead, glittering on specks of quartz in the cliffs. We · wound along, flickered into tunnels cut in the rock, then out into the light again; the road rose and fell; constantly the cliffs would vanish and we would look sharply down on the blue, faceted sea.

On the other side a plain stretched a small distance inland, occasionally fields but more often whole areas packed with rose trees in bloom or with deep, almost black carnations. Beyond them the vineyards climbed up the hills.

"There's an awful lot of flowers," said the woman behind us.

The man said: "Not more than you'd see in Southern California."

Neale pulled out the microphone. "The Riviera dei fiori—the Riviera of flowers." He whispered to me: "Is this the Riviera dei fiori, or is that further up?"

"I don't know. It doesn't matter."

I took off my cardigan, Neale his coat, and we stowed them in the net above us. I was filled by early morning exhilaration; a feeling not quite of emptiness, but of having had just enough to eat, a feeling of readiness, of happy excitement. I found myself leaning forward, as if I was urging the bus on.

Carlo slipped off his cap and put on his sun-glasses. We went faster, swinging round the curves on the black, shining road.

We would pull out to overtake a cyclist or a small car, and Carlo would sound the horn too-too-tee-too. Often we passed a small dark, beautiful child wheeling a full-sized bicycle whose handlebars were hung with flowers; as we went by, the child would hold out a bunch of carnations towards the side of the bus.

The woman behind asked Neale: "What are carnations in Italian?" Neale looked at me.

"I can't remember."

"They don't know," the woman said to her husband.

I got up and went to the front of the bus, where I sat down on the steel hump beside Carlo. He looked, smiled at me, and turned to the road again. I waited till another boy tried to sell us carnations, then asked Carlo what they were called.

"Fiori," he said. "Fee-aw-ree."

"Sí sí," I said, "ma che specie di fiori?"

"Fiori," he repeated. "Fiori rossi—o fiori bianchi."

I went back to my seat. "You find out?" the woman said.

"I'm afraid not."

Presently I turned round and told her: "I've remembered. Garofani."

"O," she said.

I heard her husband ask: "What she say?"

"Some Italian word."

Neale announced: "Nervi."

Then, as we followed the coast: "Santa Margharita."

Later: "Rapallo."

"This looks like a good place for ocean bathing," said the woman behind us. "Say, is this a good place for ocean bathing?"

"Very," said Neale.

"I guess it might be quite a famous place for ocean bathing."

"It is." Neale took the microphone. "This is the famous resort Rapallo."

"It's pretty much like Miami," said the woman behind us.

I realized I had been, for some time, too hot. All the windows were open and a stream of air was bumping through the bus; but above each window there was a fixed panel of glass and the sun was grilling through it. I undid the short tweed curtain, and drew it across my window; but the breeze would not let it stay in place, and the clip which should have secured it was broken.

There was a stir throughout the bus. The general noise grew louder, and some of it seemed to be complaining. I felt as if I had found myself in an infant school at the precise moment when the children had concentrated long enough and were in need of a break. From all round the bus shouts went up for Coca-Cola.

I edged my way out. "I'll come and help," Neale said.

"No, there isn't room in the aisle."

I stood by our seat and stared down the bus, wondering what had become of its symmetrical arrangement. Coats flopped from the rack, where they had been ineffectually shoved; bow ties had been draped over the seats. The curtains were flying. Several people stood in the aisle trying to persuade others to change places with them. Two women were quarrelling. I set off. "Excuse me. Excuse me." The floor was deep under shells.

The back seats were occupied by four young men; two wearing pink crinkle nylon shirts, open to show the vest beneath; one wearing a sleeveless, neckless sweat shirt; the fourth wearing a string jumper. The fourth was lying across the aisle between seats, his head on one friend, his feet on another. He had stuck half of an empty peanut shell on his tongue and he pushed it in and out. His camera, in a leather case, rested on his stomach and moved up and down as he breathed. "Excuse me."

I took the tops off the bottles by twos and moved up and down the aisle distributing them. The straws I handed out were rejected; everyone drank from the bottle.

One of the four boys called at me. "Hey. Why don't you come and sit with us and look at the funnies?"

Mrs. Luther called to me for a Coca-Cola. I took it to her. "No straw?" she said. I got her one and went back to my own seat. It was occupied. Neale was in the middle of three or four women, all middle-aged except for the narrow-bodied girl I had noticed the day before. He seemed to be sitting at once on and amongst them, as if they had been a pile of plump, acid-coloured silk cushions. He tried to struggle up as I came, but they pulled him back. I heard exclamations that he was cute. I sat down beside Carlo. "Why, you're really English," one of the women said to Neale. "Do you wear a monocle?"

"No," Neale said. He indicated me. "My colleague does."

Briefly the women turned to me. "I guess a monocle looks kind of odd on a girl."

"I don't really wear one."

"Why did you say you did?" They turned back to Neale. The girl said to him: "Of course you have a lot of class distinctions in your country."

"Not many," Neale said. "Not now."

"That's because you've all gone socialist," one of the older women said. She dug at Neale with her fingers, and all the women laughed.

"No, seriously," the girl resumed. "All your *aris*tocrats have names you pronounce different from how you spell them."

"Do they?" said Neale.

"They certainly do. You can't fool me. You know what I mean."

"I suppose you mean things like Cholmondeley being pronounced Chumley."

The girl threw her arms up as she sat perched on the edge of the seat. "That's it! I knew you were just holding out on me." She pushed her face towards Neale's. "Say it again."

"Cholmondeley. Chumley."

"Isn't that cute?"

"I just can't believe it. I'm tickled to death."

"Tell us some more," the girl urged.

"Well," Neale said, "I suppose, oh—Featherstone-haugh is Fanshaw."

"No!"

"You don't say!"

"And Marjoribanks is Marchbanks."

"I can't believe it."

"It has a certain vers libre quality," Neale said. He chanted: "Featherstonehaugh is Fanshaw. Marjoribanks is Marchbanks. Mainwairing is Mannering." He paused. "Cirencester is Sissister."

"Go on!"

Neale looked at me. "Can you think of any more?"

"Beaulieu is Bewly," I said.

The bus halted. Neale looked out, struggled up from the women and took the microphone. "This is the famous Viareggio. We are going to lunch here. Your meal tickets will be accepted in that hotel on the left."

We saw the party out of the coach, straggling by twos and threes, and into the hotel, where they were expected. A waiter stood in the doorway and mutely directed each group to the lavatories.

We asked Carlo if he had a meal ticket. He showed it to us, but explained something quickly, making away from the hotel. "Non capisco," Neale said, and asked me: "Do you?"

"Something about a trattoria."

"Ask him if we can come too."

I did. Carlo seemed pleased. He led us off the main road, down a narrow street and in through a wooden

130

door. There was a long wooden table; round it a number of men looking like taxi drivers were eating. We found places, two side by side and one opposite; we stepped over the bench and sat down on it. A woman put a soup plate full of spaghetti in front of each of us, and a carafe of red wine between us. "It's worth it," Neale said, "even though it doesn't come out of expenses."

Presently Carlo leaned across and asked for our meal tickets. He took them to the end of the room and talked to the proprietress. He came back smiling and handed Neale and me five hundred lire each.

We finished, and followed Carlo out. Neale asked me: "What about the bill?" I said to Carlo: "Ma il conto?"

"Pagato. Già," said Carlo.

"How can it be paid?" Neale said.

I asked: "Come?"

Carlo made a long explanation. I told Neale: "I think it's this. He sold our meal tickets to the proprietress for our meals plus five hundred lire each. I think he says she's going to use them at the hotel with her family to celebrate her son-in-law's birthday. Anyway, we've made a profit."

"Bravo, Carlo," Neale said to him.

We waited in the bus, and presently the passengers came trickling out, talking about the meal they had had. "Did you see what that waiter put on the salad?" "I know they always——" "But did you see? Oil. Oil he mixed it up with. A thing like that could put on pounds. And you'd never know they done it to you."

Mrs. Luther stepped in, and stood in front of me. "Where did you get to?"

I hesitated, then asked: "Why?"

"I had to go to the john and leave my own tip. I gave her twenty. Was that too much?"

"No, too little."

"I don't mind about that. She should have spoken up. I only wanted to be sure I wasn't done."

"No, you weren't done."

"Well," said Mrs. Luther. "Aren't you going to reimburse me?"

I gave her two ten lire notes out of the profit Carlo had made for us.

We set off again, and the restiveness began at once. I moved up and down the bus handing out Coca-Cola; the empty bottles rolled noisily on the floor. I stooped to look out of the rear window, and saw that we had left the coast and were running along the wide, blanched bed of the Arno.

My place was occupied by the narrow girl. I stood leaning against the back off the seat.

"Can I call you Neale?" she asked.

"Yes, of course."

"You call me Joanie."

"All right."

"Go ahead—say it. Say Joanie."

"Joanie."

"I just love the way you say it. You say it a kind of English way."

Someone tapped my shoulder. Mr. Wagner was standing in the aisle. I looked at him carefully for the first time. He had cropped blond hair, squared off at the top; a fattish, whitish face, with pink lips. His white nylon shirt was so clean that I imagined that he must have changed it at lunch-time. He was about thirty. I shouted: "I'm sorry. I can't hear what you say."

He bawled back: "I say there's a seat vacant next to me. Come on back there, and we'll have a little talk."

I looked over Carlo's shoulders. "I'm sorry, but we're just coming in to Pisa."

"Okay." Wagner tipped me a salute. "I'll talk with you later."

We drove under the stone arch and drew up beside the dead, too green, lawn. We looked out at the dead white buildings.

"This," Neale announced, "is Pisa. If you look out you will see the famous leaning tower."

There was a scramble, and the bus was heavily weighted down. The cameras pointed out of the windows.

"Besides the tower, there is the cathedral, the baptistery and the Campo Santo or cemetery."

One of the boys at the back shouted: "Brrr!" The passengers all laughed.

"In the Campo Santo there is a famous fourteenth-century fresco of the Triumph of Death. We are going to halt here for half an hour, so that everyone can see what they want. We will reassemble here in half an hour's time."

Nobody moved. Neale and I got out of the bus. Joanie asked through the window: "You going in, Neale?"

"Yes. Do you want to come?"

"No. I got it in focus from here."

We walked up the path. There was no sound except the chatter from the bus behind us and the turning of ciné cameras. We went on into the Campo Santo, and there was total silence. We walked round the cloister, between the piles of broken-off columns and fragments of statuary. Even our footsteps ceased as we stood in front of the painted walls. "The silence of the grave," Neale said.

We came out, and Joanie hailed us from the bus. "You go up the tower?"

"No."

"I don't see why you got out if you weren't going up the tower."

We climbed into the bus. "You go up it," I told her. "There's still plenty of time."

"I would if I had my brogues on. These shoes aren't suitable." She tipped her leg up behind her, to shew Neale her high heels.

Neale said into the microphone: "If no one wants to see anything more, we'll get on."

Mrs. Luther appeared behind us. "Is there a john here?"

"Not exactly here," I said. "I daresay if we went to a café——"

"No, I don't need to go right now. I was just having forethought."

We woke Carlo, and he drove on for a few minutes. The engine stalled. He started it again; we moved forward; noisily we stopped. Carlo climbed out and opened the bonnet.

Presently Neale and I got out, walked round and joined him. He spoke to us excitedly. "Non capisco," said Neale. Carlo spread his hands and said what he believed to be his one word of English: "Kaput."

"No," Neale said. "We've got to get to Rome. Dobbiamo andare a Roma."

Carlo pointed across the road. The railway station was opposite.

Neale asked me: "Do you think he's faked it?"

"He couldn't have faked the noise it made."

"At least he's chosen a convenient place. Will you stay with them while I go and find out about the train? Or had you better go?" Grudgingly he added: "Your Italian's better."

I went into the station, found the capostazione and explained to him. He put through a call to our agency in Rome, and handed me the receiver.

A voice said: "Pronto."

"Pronto," I said.

"Pronto."

I repeated: "Pronto." The line went dead. I wondered if I ought to have said Pronta. There was a click; a voice said, "Roma. Pronto." "Pronto." The line closed up again. Finally I got through. "Pronto. Do you speak English?"

"Yes."

I explained.

"Do you have enough money to take the tickets? We will pay you back when you get here. You had better come in the first-class, because the train will be full. At what time will you arrive? We shall have a bus or taxis to meet you."

The stationmaster lent me ten porters, whom I led out. They moved the luggage from the bus to the station. We told the passengers to follow them. We shook hands with Carlo. "He says we've to get them to Rome by train, and then from Rome to Florence. He'll get the bus mended and meet us with it at Florence."

"Arivederci!" Carlo said.

"Fortunato, felice—Lei," said Neale.

Carlo grinned. "Arivederci. A Firenze." He held up two fingers pinched together and waved us good-bye.

As the train came in, Neale and I ran along the platform opening first-class doors and urging our party in. We climbed up ourselves, and the porters passed the luggage through the window. We piled it in the corridor. As we started, I ran up the train, pushing past quarrelling groups, until I found a seat marked number thirteen. I threw my cardigan down to reserve it, and ran to find Mrs. Luther. "Will you be all right here?" I asked as I settled her in.

"Sure. I reckon travelling by corridor train is a lot more convenient than travelling by road."

I found Neale in a compartment with Joanie and Mr. Wagner. I sat down. After a moment Joanie leaned into the corridor and pulled the hem of a pink crinkle nylon shirt. "Tad! You four come in here." The four boys came in and squeezed down. "That's right," Joanie said. "That way we won't get any outsiders filling the place up."

Mr. Wagner tapped my knee. "Come on in the corridor, get a breath of air."

I followed him out.

"You like American cigarettes?"

"Yes, quite."

He gave me one and asked: "Not too strong for you? After what you usually smoke?"

"No, thank you."

"Can you get American cigarettes in England?"

"Oh, yes, I think so."

"Well, that's something."

Presently he said: "You look kind of serious."

"Do I?"

"Yes. I guess maybe you're a serious kind of girl."

"Possibly."

"You know what I can't understand about Europeans?"

"No. What can't you understand?"

"Why do they hate each other so?"

"Do they?"

"Sure they do. Take that French boy we had along through France. He couldn't stand Spaniards. Could not stand them. Now what would a French boy like that have against the Spaniards?"

"Fascism, perhaps?"

"Well, I'm a supporter of the American way of life. But I haven't got anything against the Spaniards. I haven't got anything against anyone."

"No."

"Would you excuse me one moment?" He went off

down the corridor. Half an hour later he came back wearing what I took to be another clean shirt. "Travel by rail is not so hygienic as travel by road," he said. He propped himself against the corridor wall. "So. We're finally on our way to the eternal city. By gosh, that'll be a thrilling moment, when we arrive there."

He took a new stance. "Well, I certainly seen quite a bit of Europe this trip. The way I see it, Europeans are just hanging on to a lot of antiquated feuds and snobberies, and won't organize themselves to meet the changed conditions of modern life. Now, I don't want to say a word against our courier, especially if he's your friend, but I happened to overhear in the coach this morning he was boasting about the way the upper-class English pronounce their names differently from the spelling."

"You've got quite a few of those names yourself," I said. I noticed my accent had become tinged with American.

"Who have?"

"You Americans, Mr. Wagner."

"Call me Gottlieb. Now what is this about we have names like that?"

"What became of the c in Connecticut? What became of the c in Tucson?"

"Those are isolated examples. You can't prove anything by isolated examples. By and large I'd say the whole concept of pronouncing a word differently from its spelling—pronouncing it aphonetically—is absolutely incomprehensible to the mentality of anyone from the new world."

I nodded.

"And basically I'd say so is this whole idea of letting old-fashioned prejudices stand in the way of adjusting to present-day requirements."

"I think I'll go and sit down," I said, "if you don't mind."

"I don't mind at all. I'll be seeing you."

I went back into the compartment. Joanie was leaning her elbow on Neale's shoulder. "Here, write it down for me. Write it in the back of my diary." Neale took the diary. "Don't read it, will you?" she said. "No." He wrote, as the train jogged: "Beaulieu—pronounced Bewly."

"Why don't you give her your phone number, too?" Tad said.

We arrived in Rome in darkness, in a thunderstorm.

Neale and I were given a small room, high up at the side of the hotel. There were two narrow, white cover-leted beds. We lay down on them, too tired to undress.

Neale reached into his suit-case and took out the tour programme. He read: "Morning:—sightseeing in Rome with local guide."

"That lets us out," I said.

"Afternoon:—free in Rome."

"So does that. Let's sleep fairly late tomorrow." Presently I said: "Can you see a neon outside, through the shutters?"

"Yes." Neale switched off the light between the beds, and we watched the pinkness come and go on our wall.

We got up and opened our window. We looked on to a narrow road sloping down a hill. The façade opposite was sketchily baroque, its whorls marked more by grime than by actual recession. All the shutters were closed. The ground floor seemed to consist of lock-up garages.

The neon sign, on our own side of the street, perhaps marking the side entrance to our own hotel, was screened from us by a tree; it glowed rubily through the upper branches, turning the leaves an artificial, magical green.

We could see its ons and offs reflected in the damp pavement.

We leaned our elbows on the window-ledge. There came up to us a smell of tobacco, earth after rain, lilies, a freshness that was not too cold, and spiciness.

A Lambretta roared down the street. A voice shouted. One of the garage doors slammed.

A long way off we heard dance music. Almost equally distant, but coming from below us, perhaps from the hotel kitchen, we heard laughter and the sound of dishes being washed up.

✦ X ✦

Iᴛ was the full, hot, shabby Roman summer. Neale and I sat beneath a striped umbrella, drinking vermouth in the Piazza dell' Esedra, watching the children running round the gunwale of the shallow, basin-shaped fountains.

"Oh, why have we only two days here," Neale said. "I want to stay for ever."

I said: "It must be much worse for them."

"O, for them. Yes."

An unfamiliar bus, painted dark crimson outside, flatly and uncomfortably upholstered inside, had called for them at the hotel. We had piled them in, introducing them to their guide, a shrivelled, cynical Americanized Italian. As we closed the door on them, we had heard Joanie ask the guide what they were going to see. We caught a mélange of his reply: Colisseo, Catacombs, Christians, Caesars, Brutus, Borgias, Raphael, the holy father, the last judgment.

Thinking of it in the Piazza dell' Esedra, Neale said: "They're so bewildered, aren't they?"

Far off we saw a bus draw up at the Baths of Diocletian. Figures jumped out. Hubbub emerged, muted, from the warm distance. We could not see if it was our party or another like it. None the less we paid our bill and left.

We lunched early in the hotel dining-room, hiding ourselves away behind a gilt and white pillar near the door. As we finished our coffee, we heard the noise.

The party, roaring after its sightseeing, foamed into the room and encroached over the calm tables. Two of the middle-aged women spied us out, came across and confronted me. "We have the afternoon free. Could you tell us the best place to buy dress fabrics?"

I directed them to the Corso.

"I guess we went down there in the coach this morning. The stores looked to be kind of small."

"They're the best."

"I get you. You mean they're kind of exclusive. Right, I'll tell the girls."

We hurried out of the dining-room, out of the hotel. The stone streets were bleached by the furious light. We began to walk, following the shade as far as we could, watching our own feet because it was too bright, even through sun-glasses, to look up, treading the still pavements, making a metallic sound now and then as a grid, initialled S.P.Q.R., dipped under our weight. The trams ran less noisily, less often, for the siesta hour; the crowds packed into them were silent. We came upon labourers asleep under trees, or sitting on benches eating rolls and salami. We trudged along in the baking lee of ancient walls, guarded from any breeze; the air stagnated hotly. We passed posters advocating Christian Democracy, peeling, hanging down; posters denouncing Communism, defaced with scratches; inscriptions in chalk "W Coppi" as high as a man, which no one had tried to rub off.

We came into the damp water-darkened area of the Fontana di Trevi, crossed one of the narrow, traffic-jammed roads, and stood within the stale smell of spray, of unvital water artificially lashed into the air. Some small boys paddled excitedly in the shallows, bending down and scooping up the water towards the statues. Another coach drew up. Another party just like ours

141

debouched and grouped itself rapidly, just outside the water's arc. The guide bawled: "It is a tradition that anyone who throws in a coin will return to Rome." Their arms shot out straight. For a moment cameras turned. They were back in the coach. They had driven away.

"I wonder if they really want to come back to Rome," Neale said.

"Who knows what they really want."

We looked down at the coins lying on the floor of the fountain, the light making them wink beneath the churned surface of the water. Thirty or forty Italian coins, falsely bright; one or two French pieces, more solid, and discoloured silver-gold; one English sixpence.

"I suppose they got rid of their surplus currency."

"I hope the children manage to collect it afterwards."

We walked on. We turned into a tobacco shop where I bought a stamp and a gloomy postcard of the Coliseum. I addressed it to Annette and wrote: "I am having a holiday in Italy. I am being reminded every hour that Rome is the most beautiful city on earth."

We dined late, but even so we did not avoid all of our party. Joanie and Tad were still at a table at the far side of the dining-room. Joanie shouted across "Hey, Neale."

"Hullo."

"Did you know there was a place in that park arrangement where you can go horseback riding?"

"Yes."

"I went horseback riding this afternoon. I had all my clothes along—I just knew there'd be somewhere in Europe I could use them. I kept looking out to see if you were around. I certainly wish you'd seen me, Neale."

We walked in the dark to the Spanish steps. The flower seller at the bottom was folding his stall, like an easel, for the night. The long bunches of gladioli, luminously scarlet, lay on the ground. He picked them up, rested them on the saddle of his bicycle and wheeled them away.

Slowly we walked up, following the curving stone line of the banisters, stumbling over couples whispering in the alcoves. At the top, Santa Trinità del Monte faced us, gently floodlit, moon-coloured; and a patch of real moonlight, caught in reflection in a cloud, lay mistily behind a dark tree shaped like an up-ended paint-brush.

Balking at the last flight of steps, we rested against the stone balustrade, almost too high for us, and looked down into the cubic, private gardens, deep green and darkened. "It's like looking into one's childhood."

We walked across the steps to the other side, and sat on them. From the glowing, half-seen road above, the smell of lime trees came down to us.

Neale said: "The curious thing about the Spanish steps is that they really do look Spanish."

"Almost Moorish, by this light."

"It's Don Giovanni again."

A bunch of young Italians ran past us, laughing and panting from the climb. They vanished round the corner, and then two of them, a man and a girl, came back on to the flat platform before the final ascent. Giggling, they faced each other: the man flourished his arm and bent in a bow; the girl dropped a full curtsey. They ran off after their friends.

"In the history of one's love affairs with places," Neale said, "isn't the difficulty to choose one place? Isn't it like naming one's favourite film-star?—as soon as you speak, all the others seem to accuse you."

"I suppose so," I said. "Yet, about places——"

"Would you give up Paris? For Rome?"

"No. At least, I might."

"I have," Neale said, —"have you?—an instinct of

143

monogamy. I want there to be one place, one person, perhaps even one moment. I suppose like most of one's instincts it will have to go unsatisfied." Later he asked: "Could there ever be one moment so supreme that everything would be justified for evermore?"

"I believe so."

"All romantics believe so. But once the moment was over—supposing it ever came—once it was over, wouldn't you begin looking for new moments?"

"No. Not if it really had been the moment."

"You mean you couldn't tell till afterwards? You might cheat yourself like that for ever, going from one false moment to the next, getting tawdrier all the time. Promiscuity is an instinct as well as monogamy."

"Perhaps I'm wrong then. Perhaps there really is no mistaking the moment when it comes."

"But you thought it had come," Neale said. "You thought it had come with Cynthia, didn't you?"

"I was a child."

"Suppose Cynthia hadn't left you—do you imagine you'd love her still?"

"No. I was bound to grow up—to develop different instincts."

"Perhaps leaving you was the kindest thing she did to you. Perhaps it's the kindest thing anyone can do for a romantic. That, and whisking them away out of any city they fall in love with." Neale stood up. "If one lived in Rome don't you imagine one would grow—o—positively domestic with it?"

"One might. Yet it might be possible to keep oneself faithful, keep oneself alive to it."

"If one had a moment to look back on, it might." He leaned on the balustrade, burying his head. "O I'm so afraid that it's true about to travel hopefully being better than to arrive. It might be all in the quest, all in the search, all in the anticipation. When it came, there might be nothing there."

"That's what you're afraid of," I said.

"Yes, aren't you?"

"No, I believe there will be something there."

"I suppose I do, too, in a way," Neale said. "At least I'm willing to be convinced. Perhaps the moment will happen and convince me."

"Perhaps it will." I got up.

He looked down at me, as I stood on the step below him. "Will the moment just rise and overwhelm me?"

"Yes."

"I wonder where I shall be when it happens. I wonder where the place is."

"This place, perhaps."

"Yes, the place might well be Rome. Or some part of Italy, anyway. The only question is when."

We walked home. "I wonder," Neale said, "when the moment will be."

On the second day the party went on a day-trip to Naples. Another coach came for them very early in the morning, with another guide. Neale and I saw them off. We spent our own day between the picture galleries and the travel agency, where we were reimbursed, told that Carlo had wired to say the bus was mended and would meet us in Florence, and congratulated because only one letter of complaint had come in from the party. "It's from someone called Gottlieb Wagner. Do you know him?"

"O yes."

"He doesn't pronounce it like that," Neale said.

They shewed us the letter. "It seems particularly unfortunate that the party should be subjected to the conditions of railroad transportation when road travel had been promised throughout." It finished: "I trust you will pardon any inadequacies in this report, as I have only my portable typewriter with me."

"Well, I'm sorry," Neale said, "but it was hardly our fault."

"Don't be sorry. You're doing fine. During the French part of the tour, there was a complaint a day."

We lunched in peace and began dinner in peace; but Neale looked at his watch and said: "They'll be coming soon."

We heard them, and they came. "Adieu," Neale whispered, "vive clarté de nos étés trop courts."

Mrs. Luther stopped in front of us. "Pompeii was the most marvellous experience of my life. I had no idea those old fellows had progressed so far in practical engineering."

The tables filled up. Joanie was the last to arrive. She stood in the doorway, wearing a topless sun-dress, a cardigan slung over one shoulder. She looked round and spotted the four boys. "Hi, boys! Did you think I wasn't going to make it?"

One of them called: "Better late than never." The others whistled.

"I just had to get into something gay," Joanie shouted. "After all, this is our last night in Rome."

She came past our table, and we saw that her hair was wet, hanging in a sheet down her back. She paused and pushed a hank of it towards Neale. "Get a load of that, will you. I been swimming. I fell just head over ears in love with Capri."

"Did you?"

"We swam from a row-boat. I and some of the boys just happened to have our costumes along. I only hope mine didn't scandalize the natives. You ought to of been there, Neale."

We finished dinner. Joanie came back to our table. "Mind if I sit down? Why, that's sweet of you, Neale. You get a chair from some place, then we can all be seated."

He fetched one.

"I and some of the boys," Joanie said, "are going on a party. We thought we might go some place to dance. Would you come along?"

"It's very kind of you," Neale said.

"We were just going to make up a small party—just those of us that are okay."

"What does okay mean?" Neale asked. "Gay? I doubt if I'm okay."

"Well, gay, young—yes, I guess that comes into it, too. But I meant—well, you know how it is. Socially okay." She looked for a second towards the table where Mrs. Luther sat alone. "None of these hickory gals from the Middle West."

"Do tell me who's okay," Neale said. "I'd love to know."

"You would?" She settled her elbows on the table and moved her head closer to Neale's. She stared towards the table where the four boys sat. "Well, Jervis—that's the one in the T-shirt. Then Jimmy, next to him. Then Dean, the other side of the table. They were all at Saint Paul. And then Tad, of course. He was at Groton. Then we thought we might ask"—her eyes moved round looking for him—"Gottlieb Wagner."

"Is he okay?"

"Well, he doesn't come from any place, and he doesn't have any people—I mean, they're alive all right, but they aren't anybody. I don't think he even went to private school. But I guess he was a bright boy—he went through Harvard Law School—and I guess that makes him—well, just about so we could take him along."

Neale asked me: "Would you like to go?"

Joanie looked not at but briefly towards me. "O sure," she said. "Come along, too. I'll love to have a girl friend in the party to chaperon me."

We found an enclosure in the Pincio where there was a dance floor surrounded by trees, hung with fairy lights. As we went in, the band was playing 'Bella Ragazza Dalle Trecce Bionde'. We stood at the edge of the floor and Joanie shouted: "Can you play The Isle of Capri?" The music stopped.

"What you say, miss? What you want?" "Do you know The Isle of Capri?" "Yes, miss, sure we know it."

It began.

Joanie held up her arms towards Neale. He held his up towards me, and began to dance with me. "I can't tango. Is it all right if we foxtrot?" "Yes, of course." "We always seem to end up foxtrotting."

We danced round twice. Joanie, dancing with Tad, caught at us as we passed. "Neale! You're not going to do me out of saying I danced with an Englishman?"

"All in good time." We danced away. "One of my earliest memories," Neale told me, "is of my mother humming this tune."

"It's funny I don't know your parents."

"Yes. You'll have to, of course."

"Yes."

We danced past the other three boys, standing at the edge of the floor, drinking beer out of a bottle. Gottlieb Wagner was a little way apart from them, not drinking. As they saw us, they called, "Hey! The beer's kind of warm out here in the stag line."

The music stopped.

We heard Joanie's voice. "Play it again! I just adore that tune. It's going to be my signature tune from now on."

It started again. Neale and I danced again. After a moment, Tad tapped Neale's shoulder. "Orders. Joanie

148

says I got to cut in on you. She wants to dance with an Englishman."

Tad swooped his arms towards me, pressed his cheek against mine and pushed me sweetly into the dance. He sang into my ear:

> *She whispered softly 'tis best not to linger,*
> *And as I kissed her hand I could see*
> *She wore a plain golden ring on her finger—*
> *'Twas good-bye to the Isle of Capri.*

"Hey, gloomy," Tad said, and chucked me under the chin. "You don't talk much."

"No."

"I guess you're serious."

One of the boys beside the floor called: "Joanie! Come here a minute, will you?"

Her voice replied: "Let me alone, can't you, you wolves."

"No, Joanie, come on over here."

"Oh, all *right*."

"There are the boys," Tad said to me, "raising hell as usual. I guess we better go."

We found the whole group in the corner. Jervis was saying, "Joanie, there isn't much in this for us. Let's get the hell out of here."

"I was so *happy*."

"Come on out and let's walk."

"Okay," Joanie said. "Come on, Neale." She snatched his hand.

We followed them out. The three boys walked ahead; Tad, I and Gottlieb Wagner came next. From time to time we glimpsed Joanie and Neale uncertainly under the street lamps.

We walked over thick pine needles beneath tall pine trees.

149

The boys in front handed a flask to us. Tad drank some. "Rye." He gave it to me. I drank some, wiped the neck of the flask, and handed it on to Gottlieb Wagner.

"I'll pass it up this time," he said, and we gave the flask back.

Presently the boys in front stopped. Jervis said:

"To hell with this. Let's go on the town."

Jimmy and Dean agreed. Jervis cupped his hands and shouted "Jo—anie! We're going on the town!"

It echoed round the gardens.

Her answer came back, shrill and distant: "I don't want to go on the town. It's so romantic here."

"But we're going," Jervis shouted.

We said good-bye, and the three of them went off. Dean came running back. "You look after this for me?" he said, and slung his camera round Tad's neck.

I walked slowly on between Tad and Gottlieb Wagner.

At last, Tad said: "I'm going to find the other two." He set off, walking fast, down the main road.

"Shall we sit down?" Gottlieb said. We sat on an iron bench beneath a lamp. "You like to see a snapshot of my wife?" He took out his wallet. "She's making her vacation in North Carolina with her relatives. She wasn't keen on coming to Europe. She was afraid she might pick up some infection." He gave me the photograph; a small, plump, shabby woman in slacks.

"She looks very nice."

Gottlieb leaned towards me and kissed me. I felt my mouth engulfed, dampened, completely sucked in and absorbed by his fleshy lips.

He sat up straight again on the bench next to me, and put the photograph back in his wallet. He replaced the wallet in his breast pocket and took out a small glass phial. He tipped out a pill and put it into his mouth.

"Are you ill?" I said.

He swallowed. "Me? No. That's just a disinfectant tablet. Very few people know how many streptococci can be orally conveyed."

I said: "Good God!"

"Would you like one?" He pushed the phial towards me. "You're supposed to suck them, really, not swallow them like I did."

"I'm sorry if I shocked you into swallowing it."

"Honey, you couldn't shock me." He hurled himself at me, more violently this time, and bent me sideways under his full weight. He nuzzled into my neck, pulling at the skin with his lips. His hand was moving round my waist and I imagined he was feeling for my breast. He murmured: "Honey, you don't know what you do to me. You just can't leave me tonight. Stay with me, honey—you don't know what it does to a man."

I put my hand against his fat chest and pushed him off. I ran away. I scrambled up the road; and then, because I thought I heard him follow, ran off the road, over the stony grass between the trees. I made a circle, coming back past the place where I had left Gottlieb. He was not there. I stopped running, but I walked as fast as I could, making towards the artificial plateau overlooking the lights of Rome, meaning to take a tram back to the hotel.

Someone stepped towards me, from behind a tree.

"Hi, beautiful, what's your hurry?"

"O, Tad. Did you find the others?"

"Nope. But they're some place round here. I keep hearing Joanie laugh."

"Let's look for them."

"You look cute with your hair wind-blown. Come over here where I can see you in the light."

"No, let's find Neale."

151

"You are a serious girl. I guess you do a lot of reading. Don't you?"

"Yes."

"Have you read the Kinsey Report?"

"No."

He kissed me. As I broke away, he squeezed my arm.

"I guess you haven't much experience of the American male. Boy, have you got something coming to you!" He bent his head towards me again. I twisted away, and ran.

"Oh, for pete's sake. You're not starting that again."

"I must find Neale." As I turned my head back, I saw Tad make after me, stumbling over the roots of trees, the camera bumping on his chest. "I can't run with this thing round me." I fled him as if he was a satyr.

I ran towards the lighted skyline, with the dusky domes swelling into it. As I reached the gravel plateau I saw Neale just in front of me, standing alone beside a small fountain. He was dark in silhouette against the glow beyond, and his legs looked thin and long.

I ran up to him.

"Hullo." he said.

"Hullo. What have you done with Joanie?"

"O, she meant business. I got rid of her."

"How?"

"I told her I'd seen you kissing Tad."

"Did you really see?"

"No. It was all I could think of. I decided she wouldn't be so anxious to gain me if it meant losing him. She went to look for him. Did you kiss him?"

"He kissed me."

"How amusing."

As we walked home, Neale said: "Do you still want to sleep with me?"

I hesitated. "Neale, in the general sense, yes. You

know I do. But specifically, for tonight, I feel a bit sickened of the whole subject."

"Very well." He moved away from me on the pavement.

"Neale! I'm sorry! I mean yes."

"No, the moment's passed."

As we lay in our separate beds, side by side in the dark, watching the neon, I asked him: "Did you mean the moment had passed?"

"Who can say?" Later he added: "Perhaps it was only a moment."

We travelled to Florence in a compartment we shared only with Mrs. Luther. She told us about the cultural association of which she was a committee member. "Last semester we had a most interesting programme. We had a lecture on the political face of Asia; two which covered the whole history of painting; and we finished up with an open debate on relativity."

When she left us to go down the corridor, Neale said to me: "Which is she more, awful or pathetic?"

★ XI ★

THE day in Florence was to be spent sightseeing with a local guide, again no concern of ours. We saw the party off and went back into the hotel to finish breakfast. Neale said: "There's Carlo."

"I suppose he's got the day off, too."

He came over. "Ciao."

"Ciao." We found him a chair and poured him some coffee.

Neale said: "Tell him I'm sorry we didn't have time to say more than hullo when he met the train yesterday, and that he looks like a man who's had a nice long holiday."

"I can't. It's much too hard. Speak your own Italian."

"O, I've given up trying," Neale said. "You do it so well."

Carlo asked Neale if he wanted to sell any meal tickets.

"Non capisco," Neale said. He pointed to me.

Carlo began to explain to me.

I told Neale: "He says do we want to sell the ones for today, for lunch and dinner at this hotel."

"Well, we do, don't we? We could find somewhere quiet to eat."

We gave Carlo the tickets.

An hour later we met him by appointment in the Piazza della Repubblica. He took us to a café, treated us to orange spremute, and gave us two thousand lire each.

We left him and walked down to the Lung'arno, then along it to the Uffizi. As we went through the gallery, we forgot the slight quarrel we had felt with each other all morning. We stood for some time in the tiny Botticelli room; and standing in front of the Venus, Neale said: "He is the artist, isn't he? For ever and ever?"

I said nothing. Neale said: "Isn't he?"

"Don't press me."

"Why not?"

"I always do think he is—always have thought he is —except today."

"O. I see."

"He's gone dead on me."

"Then there's no point in lingering," Neale said.

While we stood in the next room, we heard a chatter approach; a beating of feet, the high voice of a guide. "Observe the painting of the flesh tones, and of the muscular development of the arms and legs. The next picture . . ."

Neale whispered: "It might be any party." But even as he said it, we heard Gottlieb Wagner's voice. "What arrangements are made for regularly cleaning the pictures?"

We ran out of the room into the marble corridor. A surge of women we knew was coming along it towards us. We dodged back into the room we had come from, and the voices closed in on us. We ran into the next room, then the next, the voices pursuing. We tried to escape: there was a crimson cord across our path. We ran on again, through another arch, through another room, and found a way clear into the corridor. It lay empty of tourists. We ran down it, past tapestries, past busts of Caesars; we saw an attendant gasp at us, and debate with himself whether to stop us; we bumped into an elderly French couple and brushed past them, as the man commented: "Américains." "Well, I suppose," Neale said, gasping, "Americans have a reputation for taking their culture at speed, but not, I should have thought, at this speed."

We reached the lift shaft just as the lift came to rest, and through the opening doors heard another voice we knew. "I don't care if I do get left behind the others. I must find it."

Neale pushed me on, to the stairs, and we fled down them; we came out laughing into the sun-dappled square and found a bench under the colonnade where we sat to cool ourselves.

We heard a noise from the vestibule of the Uffizi.

We hurried down to the Lung'arno, dived into the traffic and ran towards the Ponte Vecchio.

As we crossed it, we heard an international voice upraised behind us. "This is the Ponte Vecchio or old bridge, a very famous medieval old bridge with many jewellers' shops on it."

We hurried across and plunged into the quarter on the wrong side of the river, dusty, continually in building, thronged with workmen wearing whited-over khaki caps made of paper. "Not that way," Neale said. "They might go that way to the Pitti." He drew me over to the right. We walked down the Via de' Serragli, terrified each time a tram clanked past us, encroaching on the pavement.

We crossed the road and went up a dark side-street; we came into a vast, sunny, dusty square, crossed it, and entered a smaller one where there was a market. Neale lingered by a stall of fountain pens; went on to a basket of scarves, then to ties, then to postcards. "Aren't they cheap here?" He bought one shewing the cathedral. "Who shall we send it to?"

"Tanya?"

"All right."

We walked on, past blood-red slices of
said: "I've got an idea. With all this mone
for us, we could not only eat out—we could

"How do you mean?"

"We needn't spend the night at the hotel.
find a pensione."

"Do you think we could leave them all alone?'

"We could give our address to some responsible person
—Gottlieb Wagner—in case anything did happen. I once
stayed at a pensione near here. I daresay I could find it
again."

We found it, but it was full.

We came back to the square, and found a gelateria,
half hidden by the temporary stalls in front of it. We
pushed through the bead curtain and asked for two ice-
creams. The fat man beside the refrigerator asked Neale,
"Che colore preferisce?"

"Tutti i colori."

He made us up two tubs, from dabs of twenty kinds.

We sat down at a marble table and Neale wrote the
postcard to Tanya. "This is to confirm that Florence is
the best city in the world." He passed it to me. "You
sign it, too."

When we paid, we asked the fat man to recommend
us a pensione. He gave us an address. We asked how to
find it. He sent his son with us. He took us five minutes'
walk and left us outside a courtyard. We went in and
up a staircase. We found the pensione, but that one, too,
was full. We asked the proprietress if she knew of any
other. She gave us an address in the next street.

We followed her directions, found a doorway, went
in and up. Our ring was answered by a maid in full
uniform. We asked if there was any hope of spending

night there. "Credo di sí," the girl whispered. Shyly she asked us in; in the hall she left us.

We looked round. "I wouldn't have believed it possible," Neale said. "Not since Ouida." The floor was tiled, not unexpectedly; but these were enormous squares, with an *art nouveau* design. In the centre was a marbled plinth; on it a leather flower-pot; in it an aspidistra. There was a long table, covered with green baize, and several occasional tables, of marquetry or mother-of-pearl inlay. An epergne stood on one of them. The walls were hung with drawings reconstructing ancient Roman buildings. The windows were stained glass. On the green baize lay an amber cigarette-holder.

Neale wandered towards one of the tables, and beckoned to me.

"What is it?"

"The visitors' book."

I looked over his shoulder. We read the most recent entries.

"Ecstatic thanks to Stephanie, for unforgettable Florentine days—and nights. Muriel Senege, Ohio, U.S.A."

"I shall never forget. Vivienne Bletchforth, New York, N.Y., U.S.A."

"A most enjoyable experience. Rosemary Blaynes, Northwood, Mddx."

I moved away to the other side of the hall, to look at one of the drawings. A door opened beside me, and a woman came out. She was wearing a black dress; above it, a flowered smock; above that, two or three fringed shawls. She was black-haired, white-faced, beautiful in an ovoid way; about forty. She was smoking, and I noticed her red nail-polish was chipped.

"I'm Stephanie. Do you want to spend the night here?"

"Are you English?" I said.

"I'm everything, my dear, as the occasion requires."

"Could we have two rooms?"

"O, are there two of you? It's dark in here, isn't it?"

I indicated Neale. She peered at him, then looked back at me. "Do you know, I simply haven't got room for two."

"O, I see."

"It's sad," Stephanie said, "isn't it?" She opened the front door for us. Neale asked her: "Could you recommend us anywhere else?" "O, if you want somewhere, yes. Number twenty in this road."

I laughed as we went down the stairs.

"Shut up," Neale said.

"It pays you out for François. And even, to some extent, for Joanie."

We were taken in at last by a tiny old lady, who stood very upright, had silver hair and a wrinkled, brown, peasant face. I asked on the doorstep if she could possibly find us two rooms; she held the door open, making way for us, clacking in Tuscan. "Due camere? Sí sí, sí, sí."

She took us to our rooms, which were clean, bare and whitewashed like monastic cells. Behind Neale's back she secretly showed me the bathroom. She asked if we would like to lunch immediately. "Sulla terrazza?"

We followed her out. Neale whispered to me: "Is she like your grandmother? She's like mine. Is everyone's grandmother like her?"

The terrace lay folded in sun, shaded in one corner by a tree growing up from the garden below. A table stood in the shade. The signora whisked a white tablecloth from under her arm and spread it. She signed to me to sit down. "Si accomodi."

There was a sound of bees. The walls of the house, three of them enclosing the terrace, drooped with honeysuckle. We looked over the balustrade into a tangled garden. The signora brought out a tray and gave us each a plate of soup. Two white pigeons appeared at once, the bigger edging the smaller along the balustrade towards us.

After lunch, the signora asked us what we were going to do. I explained we had to collect our things. "Ma dopo," she said—"Fiesole."

We shook our heads.

She led us into the hall. There was an old municipal map of Florence stuck to the wall with sticky paper. She jabbed the middle of it. "Da Piazza San Marco. San Mar—co. Filobus effe."

"Tell her we've been to Fiesole before."

"L'abbiamo già visto."

"Filobus effe," she repeated. "Ef—fe." She held up six fingers. She gave us the key of the front door.

Neale went to the hotel while I went back to the Uffizi. We met again under the copy of the David statue. "I've taken our night things to the pensione," he said, "and I left a message for Gottlieb."

"And Botticelli came back to me."

"Ah. But I wasn't there," said Neale.

We wandered about Florence until it was time to go home to dinner. We let ourselves in, and the signora came hurrying into the hall to meet us. "Sono stati a Fiesole?"

I began to make an excuse for not having gone, but Neale said: "Sí sí."

"Va bene," she said. "È bello, non è vero? Una bella veduta?"

"Molto bella," said Neale.

"Bellissima," she said.

We dined alone on the terrace, and as it grew dark the signora brought out a candle stuck into the mouth of a wine bottle. We could see glow-worms in the garden below. I asked her what they were called.

"Luciole," she said, giving it a soft Florentine sh-sound.

✭ XII ✭

WE drove out of Florence along the riverside, making towards the fat smoke-blue hills. We left the part that we knew, and yet the city seemed to linger on: a wide, modern road; blocks of flats under construction; children playing in municipally provided shade. Only the river remained recognizable: the same pebbly expanse between deep, dried walls. Wherever, for a brief patch between mud deltas, the yellow water ran deep, bathers were standing in it, up to their knees or sometimes their waists, splashing one another, occasionally launching into a clumsy crawl.

We began to climb. "I suppose it's not so bad to be leaving," Neale said, "since it's Venice we're going to."

We went up the fertile hills, glimpsing sunlit villas and churches between the trees. Neale asked me: "Do you think it's any good telling them they've seen this sort of landscape at the back of Florentine primitives?"

"No."

We began on the real mountains. The narrow black road led up and down, riding along crests, spiralling round ascents. We looked out on rocky humps covered with thin pale green grass, more like moss or slime; and then on dark grey cavernous formations, overhung, gothic as icicles, with no vegetation at all. "They must recognize this," Neale said. "It's pure Leonardo."

"I should stick to facts."

He took the microphone. "We are going to drive right over the Apennines."

"Are they pretty high?" said the woman behind. "How high are they?"

"Very," Neale said. "We shall lunch in Padua, and then go on to Venice."

The day ripened; the sun gleamed down on us; we were gripped by the exhilaration of the drive. The passengers had not become restive yet; the continual hum behind us was almost pleasant, business-like, early-morning. Gottlieb Wagner came up the aisle, tapped me and said: "Good to be in a motor-coach again." I nodded. He went back to his seat. I whispered to Neale: "They're not so terrible, in their way. And in any case, we shall have finished with it all by tonight."

Carlo looked briefly round and kissed his fingers to us.

Neale said: "Tell him it'll all be over by tonight."

"I don't know if I can." I leaned forward and said to Carlo: "Sarà tutta finita stasera, la gita."

Watching the road, Carlo smiled and nodded. "Sí. Va bene."

"Not that he did much," Neale said. "He got out of most of it. Tell him he's a lazy hound."

"No."

"Why not?"

"Because I don't know how insulting it is in Italian."

"Go on."

"They may have some quite different animal for laziness."

"Just tell him he's lazy, then."

"O, all right. But I'll tell him you said so, not me." I moved forward and sat beside Carlo. I looked through the windscreen; the road was a succession of blind curves. I waited for a moment when I should dare to divert his attention. We pulled to the top of a hill; for a little way the descent was clear before us, with nothing coming. Gesturing strongly backwards to where Neale sat, I told Carlo: "Lui dice che Lei è pigro."

Carlo made a wide grin and glanced at me for a second. He tapped his chest with his left hand, then put his hand quickly back to the wheel to keep us to the intricately winding verge. "Io?" he said. "Pigro?"

"Lui lo dice, non io," I repeated. I got up and went back to Neale. Carlo must have touched the accelerator. The bus tipped suddenly down the hill. I was shot into my seat. I heard Mrs. Luther give a hiccough.

Neale shouted: "Bravo, Carlo! Avanti Coppi!"

"Avanti Coppi!" Carlo responded, and raised his hands above his head.

"Look out," Neale said.

Carlo gripped the wheel again and pulled us sharply across the road; another bus, coming the other way, crept past us, almost grazing us. Mrs. Luther called: "Can't you tell him to look where he's going?"

Neale leaned forward to speak to Carlo. "Piano, piano."

"Pigro? Io?" Carlo said. He glanced at Neale, and they grinned at one another. Neale sat back.

We were going uphill, round a spiral. Carlo took it at a run, straining the engine, pulling us all over the road, driving on the left as often as the right. Only as we came near the summit did he shudder the bus into third and then, as soon as he could, slipped back into top. We could see the road ahead intermittently, as the twists permitted; it was narrow; and it lay along a series of crests, all high, with the rocky ground falling sheer down on both sides of it.

We began to career along. The bus shook, and rocked down its backbone; from moment to moment it would swerve, turning suddenly as we seemed to head straight over the edge, and then turning back again equally suddenly, with Carlo pulling the steering wheel round with all his force. There was less noise from the passengers, more noise from the engine, creaks and crackings from the metal coachwork all round us; deep beneath all the mechanical sounds we heard Carlo's voice humming: Zoom, zoom.

"O Lord," Neale said, "he's pretending it's an aeroplane. He's having a sexual-aggressive fantasy."

A man's voice yelled: "Can't you make him watch what he's doing?"

Neale tried to struggle out of his seat. He was jerked back. "Piano," he shouted. Then: "Lei non è pigro."

Carlo made no answer, but we heard him go on humming.

Neale and I collided with one another's shoulders. It was a moment before we could recover balance. Then I gripped the edge of the seat with both my hands. Neale stretched his feet out and braced them against the stanchion opposite.

The passengers were no longer silent. At each sickening hump-back, at each swivel, a woman shrieked. Mrs. Luther called out: "Can't you stop him? Can't you stop him?"

"So long as it's only the women," Neale whispered. Almost at once we heard a man groan.

I watched Neale's feet extended before us. The right foot was plunging at the floor as if feeling for a foot brake. I asked, "Could you drive this bus?"

"Better than he can."

I tried to edge forward to come near to Carlo, but I could not force myself against the bias of the bus. I shouted to Carlo: "Lasci fare a Neale."

"Lasci fare a me!" he replied.

Neale said: "It would be fatal to try and get the wheel from him."

The road was bordered on each side by a fragile white fence, only two or three feet high, consisting of widely spaced wooden slats, set right up against the precipice edge. At almost every other bend the fence had been broken away, some of it folded forward on to its face, some simply missing. The vista immediately beyond the fence was of sheer, sunny space; and then, in the middle distance, other mountains, some of which we had come along already in our tortuous course. By looking at the other mountains we could see what had happened to the missing parts of the fence. They trailed down the precipice side, like flowers over a wall, hanging, barely connected, in the empty air.

We heard a bang and managed to twist ourselves up and round in our seats for long enough to see what was happening. Mrs. Luther had contrived to stand up in the aisle. She stood stiff, thrown from side to side, looking as though she was dancing Petrouchka. She said: "I'm going to stop him."

"We'll have to grab her," Neale said, "if she tries to grab Carlo."

However, she was unable to urge herself along the aisle, and presently she was tossed back into seat number thirteen.

Sometimes, where the fence was broken, two of the smashed slats had been pinned together and propped up to make a cross. The woman behind us asked her husband: "What are all these crosses we keep passing?"

"What you say?"

"What are these crosses?"

"All these countries are Catholic."

She was not satisfied. She shouted to Neale and me: "Hey, what are these crosses?"

"I'm afraid," Neale called over his shoulder, "that they mark the site of accidents."

"Oh, how awful!" We could tell from the sound that she had put her hand up in front of her mouth.

With difficulty Neale leaned out into the aisle and peered down the bus. Turning back, he said to me: "Messieurs les voyageurs are in a bad way. Do you think this is the moment for the emergency ration?"

"Yes! I'd forgotten it."

"Can I get at it, though?" Neale said.

"You stay here, in case you get a chance to take over. I can't drive."

"Do you think you can get down the aisle?"

"It ought to be easier in that direction. It's certainly impossible in the other." I hauled myself up and set off.

At first it was no easier. I was pitched from one side of the bus to the other, jarring my pelvis on the seats. I made a little progress. I was thrown on to Gottlieb Wagner. I pushed free by levering myself against his flesh as carelessly as if it had been inanimate.

The bus tilted uphill. I slid down the aisle. The strip of fibrous stair-carpet which covered the back portion of it rucked up under my feet. I came to a stop by putting my hands out as buffers against the refrigerator, where a drift of peanut shells had gathered, ground into small pieces, like clippings of canvas.

I opened a bottle of brandy and jerkily poured some into a paper cup. I set out with the cup; but the brandy in the bottom leapt up in stalactites and slopped over the side. It sank into the carpet. Brandy fumes began to rise. Tad, in the back seat, turned round. "What's cooking?"

I pulled out all the paper cups, gave them to him, and told him to pass them forward, one to each passenger.

"What's up?" he said.

"With the compliments of the management."

I took the brandy bottles and began to fight my way

up the aisle, slithering, going the last few feet almost on hands and knees. Beginning at the front of the bus, I visited each passenger, slopping a little brandy into each cup, saying: "Compliments of the management. Drink it up before it spills." Sometimes a cup would be drained and held out for a refill before I had passed.

As I reached Mrs. Luther, I guessed she would object. I said: "Medicinal", and clumsily poured it out.

Gottlieb Wagner asked me: "Have these cups been handled much?"

I had a bottle almost empty, and I gave it to him. "Drink it out of the bottle." He took it, and tossed his paper cup out of the window. I watched it shoot towards the fence, totter between the slats and disappear.

When I reached the back seats, the four boys were holding out their cups and shouting: "We want brandy."

Joanie had somehow moved to them. She was lying across Tad and Jervis, and with their free hands Tad was caressing her arms, Jervis her legs.

"We got her over here so as we could protect her," Jervis said.

"We were brought up to be chivalrous," said Tad.

Joanie pushed her cup towards me. I gave them a three-quarters full bottle between them, and set off up the aisle again with a half full bottle for Neale and myself. As I went, I noticed a relaxation. There were no more screams; chatter was beginning to fill the bus.

I was flung down beside Neale. "There were no cups for us."

Neale took the bottle and tilted it. A little brandy trickled out of one corner of his mouth and he caught it back. "This is on a fairly empty stomach," he said. He gave me the bottle, and I drank some. "None for Carlo," Neale said.

We careered on.

Gottlieb Wagner began to sing:

> 'Twas on the isle of Capri that I found her,
>> In the shade of an old walnut tree,
> She was sweet as the flowers blooming round her,
>> When we met on the isle of Capri.

Tad's voice called: "You ought to get up to that microphone, Gottlieb!" Gottlieb stood up, staggered, and sat down again. "I can't make it."

"I guess that show laid an egg," Tad said.

The boys laughed.

Mrs. Luther took up Gottlieb's tune, humming it gently. The woman behind us took it up from her.

From the back row, the four boys began in unison: "Two, four, six, eight—who do we appre—ciate? Brandy! Hurrah!"

They repeated it, and cheered again. Then it changed to:

"Phi Chi Psi—Oregon! Ra Ra Ra." They broke into laughter and whistles. They began again: "Phi Chi Psi. . ."

At the third or fourth repetition, Joanie's voice joined in, getting the words not quite right. "Phi Psi Phi—Oregon! Ra Ra."

"Ohio!" shouted Gottlieb Wagner.

"Ra Ra Ra," they all shouted. They laughed and laughed.

I whispered to Neale: "What do the English sing in a crisis?"

"Hymn tunes," he said. "Sad ones."

"I suppose that's why they so often find themselves singing the German national anthem as the ship goes down."

Neale bent quickly forward and pulled the microphone towards him. While the bus continued to roll, he sang

169

into the microphone, in a slow, baritone voice, with the words carefully articulated:

> *Life presents a dismal pi-icture.*
> *All around is sin and gloom.*
> *Father's had another stri-icture,*
> *Mother's got a fallen womb.*

I put my head near the microphone and joined him, as contralto as I could:

> *Uncle He-enry's been depo-orted*
> *For a most unnatural crime.*
> *Aunty Mabel's been abo-orted*
> *For the fo-orty-y secon-ond time.*

Neale let the microphone snap down.

There was no sound whatever except from the engine and the road. We kept our backs stiff against the seat backs, rocking from moment to moment, not daring to look behind us, realizing we had at last silenced our passengers.

Finally Mrs. Luther said, "O *no!*"

After a moment Joanie's voice sounded at the back, reedily. "I consider that in *very* bad taste."

Carlo leaned sideways and backwards towards us, his left hand pursed up into the shape of a crocus.

"Watch the road," Neale shouted to him.

"Guardi la strada," I said.

He gave a brief tug to the wheel, and then turned to us again. "Bel canto," he said.

"Grazie."

"Bel canto," he repeated. "Bis. Ancora una volta."

"No."

The bus rocketed forward.

"All right," Neale said. "Bene." He took out the microphone. We sang it through again.

"Bellissimo," Carlo said. He withdrew his foot from the accelerator. We shook, and slowed down. Carlo drew us in to the edge of the road and pulled on the handbrake.

We were beside a low-built country inn. A small boy stood in the doorway waiting for us.

The passengers crammed the aisle before we could get the door open for them. They poured out past us, not looking at us; the boy directed them. We gave them time to get clear, then followed them. After a moment Carlo followed us.

We came downstairs again and went into the main room of the inn. Our passengers were assembled there. They fell silent as we entered. Neale announced: "As we are a good bit ahead of schedule we shall stay here half an hour, so that everyone can have the refreshment they want." There was no response. Neale and I went up to the bar. Sausages in silver paper were hanging from the ceiling. We asked what we could have to drink. "Aranciata. Birra." We had the orangeade; it was flat, with a taste of ginger.

Carlo came in and walked up to me.

"What does he say?"

"He wants to know if he can have his share of the brandy now."

Neale told him: "No. Finito."

"Che peccato," Carlo said.

"Neale, he's trembling all over."

"O Lord." Neale found the proprietor, and said to me: "Ask him if he's got any brandy for someone who's sick."

"Ha Lei dell' aquavite per un ammalato?"

The proprietor looked at Carlo. He went away, and came back with a small glassful, which Carlo drank.

Neale, Carlo and I went out and sat in the bus. Eventually the passengers came, stepping in without speaking to us. We slammed the door. Carlo started the engine and gently slipped into gear. The bus began to trickle down the hill, the engine driving softly; Carlo's foot eased down on the brake, keeping our speed low, and he steered carefully along, keeping to the right.

In the afternoon Carlo chugged along without hurry. We had time to read each of the advertisement placards propped up along the verge of the road like the sandwich boards carried by card kings. We turned off and crawled along the dusty road beside the sun-dappled Brenta; in the late afternoon we reached the sea, saw the gasworks and shipyards lying under smoke to our right, and at last found ourselves on the long bridge to Venice. Undeviating, the road stretched ahead like an airstrip. Militaristically straight, the railway went side by side with it. We cut our way over flat, razor-blade blue sea, that seemed to be nearly on a level with the road. The sun behind us lit up the rear window of the coach. Occasionally, on the surface of the water, it touched off a light on one of the faces of a ripple.

Mrs. Luther said, "Are we near Venice? We're behind schedule."

"Very nearly there."

"We got to get there soon."

At last we came to land. We drove past the notice pointing, in English, to the ferry. Carlo carried us on, into the Piazzale Roma. The yellowish tiered garage rose on our right. Carlo drove carefully between the local buses and their concrete islands, and drew up at the far end where patches of oil glistened on the road, under the shade of trees hanging over from the small public garden.

We got out; I gave Mrs. Luther directions; we engaged porters.

Carlo climbed down from the driving seat. "Allora."
"Allora."

We shook hands with him.

"Arivederci."

"Arivederci."

The porters went ahead, the luggage slung 'round them. We led the party down the short path through the garden. One side was shaded; peasant women in black were sitting on the low, artificially rural wall. The other side was in the sun, and ants swarmed.

We emerged on to the bright, broad quay. The church opposite, its stone shimmering in the sun, seemed to rock gently on the far side of the canal.

"Gondola, signori, gondola, gondola."

We calculated, and engaged ten. We grouped the party at the steps. The gondolas queued, nuzzling each other. We tried to make up parties to offend no one's friendships, no one's snobberies. We filled one boat, Neale and the old man with the boat-hook handing the passengers in; we piled the suit-cases, up-ended, at front and back; the boat pushed off, the next one moved up. Each woman, as she stood with one foot on land and lowered the other over the edge until it touched the bottom of the boat and felt it softly give way, made a tiny shriek.

The men said: "You're riding too low in the water." "What payload do you carry?" "Does a gondola ever sink?" Tad tried on a gondolier's hat.

We saw them off.

A gondolier approached us. We shook our heads. "We can beat them to it if we go by vaporetto," said Neale. "If we get a direct one." We queued at the kiosk, bought tickets for ourselves and our luggage, and passed on to the rocking landing-stage. The boat came: the platform jarred mildly. The official rattled open the brass rail, jumped on to the stage, secured the rope; he unchained our exit and we stepped on to the boat. We piled our luggage on the steps beside the helmsman's cabin, and moved forward, deep into the crowd, deep into the prow. "It's fantastically efficient, isn't it?" said Neale.

The sides of the boat curved high round us. When we cut another boat's wake we got wet.

We sailed up, between deep orange and rose-pink; between Venetian gothic and Venetian baroque. The sun divided the surface of the water first into strips and patches, then into transparent tesseræ.

We stared, not minding that the brightness wounded our eyes.

"Is it a little more decayed," Neale said, "a little more peeling, than when one saw it last?"

We drew level with the gondolas, stretched in a line like a water-dragon, each segment marked by its gondolier standing up, its irregular slab of luggage protruding; the undulating body was fatter towards the middle, where two gondoliers rowed side by side, keeping pace dab for dab. As we overtook them we looked back; as our wake caught them slappingly, the gondolas ducked up and down, as though they acknowledged us, and we heard, carried over the water, the sound of Joanie's laugh.

Our boat ran bravely ahead. We came in sight of the open basin. The Salute drifted roundly towards us; San Giorgio, low in the water, squarely heaved. The boat slewed across to the left. We landed, our knees trembling with the shivering of the platform. We carried our luggage on to the Molo, and paused while we pinned on our badges.

We walked along, past the Customs office, glass-fronted, partly open, looking like a conservatory, with a young sailor or marine standing inside, holding a rifle, wearing gaiters too big for him; past the white, biscuit-shaped benches, where workmen sat playing dice; past the corner of a café, and we came to the Piazzetta.

On the steps at the base of St. Theodore's column sat a number of hotel porters. Standing up amongst them was a slight young man wearing a beret and khaki shorts. On the beret he had a badge like ours.

He saw us and came towards us. He was brown-skinned, his face sharply aquiline, like a Red Indian. "Was Sprache?"

"English."

"I am Alexis. Have you lost the party?"

"I'm afraid not. They're coming by gondola."

"Let us go down here to meet them. I have got the porters to carry their luggage."

"What hotel are they going to?"

"A rather nasty one behind San Marco."

We stood watching the water lap the stone. Gondoliers moved towards us, flocking, cooing and nodding like the pigeons. "Gondola, signori, gondola, gondola."

"No, grazie."

"Gondola. Un giro. Mille lire."

"No, aspettiamo degli amici."

Alexis said: "Tell me, are they as bad as one has heard?"

"No," Neale said. "They have great charm."

The gondolas came in, nosing like swans at the quay. The boathook grappled them. The party climbed out. We moved among them, paying off the gondoliers, tipping the man with the boathook, counting the luggage. The hotel porters unstrapped their belts and began hanging the luggage on their shoulders. Joanie went up to Alexis. "Are you our Greek guide? Are you a Greek? A real, live, modern Greek?"

From the Piazza a bustle of vendors approached our party. A man offered to take their photograph; another took it, as a speculation, and tried to hand out the slip saying where prints could be collected. Conical paper bags were thrust at them, containing big orange seeds to give the pigeons. Drawers were pulled out and displayed, from the middle of wooden cabinets carried under one arm: trays of mosaic brooches, glass beads like old-fashioned marbles, beads of cloudy glass, beads of pastel-coloured glass flecked with gilt. Accordion strings of photographs of Venice were dangled, were squeezed in and out. Guide books were offered in three languages.

"Hey, will you look at this?" Tad called. I went over. A fat, unshaven man in a khaki overall was pressing a thumb-marked book on him.

"How much is he asking?" Tad said. "What's that in dollars?"

I looked at the book. It was the photographs of Finnish nudes. I took it from the man and turned to the back page. There, in pencil, was Finkelheim's code mark.

"English," the vendor said. "Come from England—all the way."

"He wants too much," Tad said. "You can get that sort of thing back home at half the price."

The porters set off across the Piazza, lost to us in the crowd and the dazzle of the light. We caught them for a moment as they moved under the shadow of the arcades; then they plunged into the dark Merceria.

The party followed, heaving their camera straps over their shoulders, stripping off cardigans, folding coats and mackintoshes over their arms.

Alexis ran after them.

"Good-bye," we called to him.

He raised an arm. "Good-bye! Auf wiedersehen! Au revoir! Ciao!"

"Ciao!"

176

"Let's sit down," Neale said.

"The cafés here are expensive. We're poor now."

"Just for once."

We sat down facing the side of the Doges' Palace.

"Are you exhausted?"

"Yes. Aren't you?"

"Totally."

A waiter came slowly out to us. The cafés were still almost empty. One or two tables were occupied at the far end, near the waterfront: and at one a yard or two from us, with an empty table between us and them, sat two people. The man, who wore a blazer, had his back to us: the back of his hair was neatly cut in a shelf. We could see the woman only when he moved his head. She seemed to be tall, and not young; she was wearing a navy blue linen dress and sun-glasses with royal blue lenses.

Neale leaned forward and asked me softly: "What do you make of that accent?"

"Those two? Are they talking English?"

"Yes."

I listened. One or two words reached me, but without any connection of sense. "You're nearer than I am," I said to Neale. "The man's English, I think."

"Yes, he's English. What about her?"

So far as I could tell she was speaking plain, Quaker-like English. Yet at one moment I thought I heard her call Italy I—aly, the 't' merely indicated, brushed at, the 'l' sounded very faint and not rolled. "Is it slightly Scotch?" I said; then at once: "No, it's not that."

"No, it's not Scotch." Presently he leaned towards me again.

"Got it. We've heard so much lately I can't be wrong. It's American."

I could hear nothing for the noise in the Piazzetta. From what I had heard before, I said: "You may be right. But it's very, very faint."

"Isn't it? And isn't it charming? Surely Henry James spoke like that."

"Quite possibly."

Thick crowds of people were coming into the Piazzetta, across the Ponte della Paglia.

"Presumably they've come off the boat from the Lido," Neale said.

"But just as many are going from here towards the boat stop."

"Perhaps at this time of the evening everyone in Venice goes over to the Lido, and everyone on the Lido comes over here. I wonder what they do when they get here."

"They walk round," I said.

We watched: young, well-dressed parents, with well-dressed children; groups of girls, groups of youths; lovers; elderly women arm in arm with their middle-aged daughters; sailors in white uniform. We would notice a group pass our table several times. Then they would go round the corner into the Piazza itself, which took longer to traverse. At last they would come back to the Piazzetta and pass us again, then again. Down the middle of the Piazzetta a boy was riding his scooter, up to one end, then back, then up again. He wore tiny white shorts, a pale blue silk blouse, smocked, ruched and embroidered, and a white knitted skull-cap, appliquéd with coloured flowers and pointed at the top with a red tassel. His hands on the handlebars were wearing white cotton gloves.

"I suppose that scooter is as near to a bicycle as a Venetian child can come."

The cafés began to fill. A party of German tourists

entered the café area, hesitated noisily, and sat down behind us.

The furiously dying light almost blotted out San Giorgio, and turned the brickwork of the Doges' Palace deep, peachy orange. The benches beneath the arcades opposite us were full up with old men, and occasionally an old woman, sitting side by side, wearily, ignoring one another.

We heard the spurt of a note of music. We turned. On the rostrum outside our café, a small band was arranging itself.

The Englishman and the American woman stood up to leave. For a moment, while the man paid, the woman took off her sun-glasses.

"Isn't that Helena Buchan?" Neale said.

I tried to remember the picture of her singing Vissi D'arte.

"I'm bad at recognizing people from their photographs."

She put her glasses on again.

As she launched herself into the crowd, she was pulling a black stole up round her shoulders. The man in the blazer hurried after her, and adjusted it.

"I'm sure it was," Neale said.

"It may have been. She's much older than when she made that film. And much more beautiful."

"Beautiful?" Neale said. "O, no."

"O, surely. That face . . ."

"Like a lump of granite that's been exposed to the weather."

The child on the scooter was called by a woman's voice somewhere in the crowd. He disobeyed, and began to scoot faster. He ran into a young man, who smiled and patted the child's head. The child pulled the scooter petulantly up, pivoting it on the back wheel, and set off towards the Piazza. After a moment he fell off, and began to cry. The mother ran to him, and several of the crowd stopped.

Behind us the band began a Viennese waltz.

"Well," Neale said, "we'd better start to look for somewhere to stay."

"Yes."

He said something else.

I shouted against the music: "What?"

"And for Cynthia."

"O, yes."

We did not move. My eye passed above the crowd to the façade of the Doges' Palace. At first it merely traced the pink pattern in the bricks, along, down, along, down, following the diamond lozenges. Then it slipped into the tracery, ran round the quatrefoils, outlined the fishtailed arches, played over the delicate balustrade as if over the fringe of a marine creature; it descended to the next tier; at last it came bumping round the capitals and slid down the short, stumpy, girth of the pillars to the ground.

The waiter brought our bill.

"Come along," Neale said.

✸ XIII ✸

WE found a pensione in an alley behind the Merceria.
It was run by a Swiss woman with a bun. She
offered us a choice of seven languages. We chose English,
and she said: "I have not two rooms. I have one room
with two beds. I give you a screen you can have between
them."

We asked to see the room. As we followed her upstairs, Neale whispered to me: "It doesn't seem very
nice. Shall we try elsewhere?"

"No. Venice is always full. I'm tired of lumping the
bags round."

The room was dingy and small; the lights were arranged
so that both could not be lit at the same time, and each
was weak.

Neale whispered: "It's not positively dirty. There is
a wash-basin."

We took the room.

"I get the screen," the woman said. We asked if we
might have dinner. "We don't have meals. You have to
go out."

We dined in a trattoria where a man played the violin
from table to table and then brought his hat round.
Someone outside in the street was playing a piano
accordion. We finished and wandered out. "Shall we go
to bed?" "We might take a last look at the Piazza."

We wandered along the narrow paths, and lost our

way. "I'm sorry, I thought this led on to the Piazza."
"The next one's bound to." We stopped at a newspaper
stall, lit by flares. Under the eaves hung a copy of *Oggi*,
with a cover photograph of a man called Bradbury
Washington. The caption said he had come to Italy to
act in a film.

"Do you think it's anything to do with this thing
Cynthia's come for?"

"I doubt it. I shouldn't think Cynthia's much involved
with actual films, would you?"

"I suppose someone's sent her to Venice. But I doubt
if she does more than pose in her bathing suit."

We stared at the sullen, fleshy face of the film star.

"I wonder if he's queer," Neale said.

We walked on, and suddenly came out on the Piazza.

"How odd. I thought it was a long way yet."

We crossed it, and stood looking out over the gently
lighted water.

"Don't the Italians manage floodlighting well? Look
at San Giorgio. Look at the Doges' Palace."

A big steamer, storied and turreted like a castle,
moved slowly across the sea, carrying a string of white
lights between the masts.

We wandered on, and crossed the Ponte della Paglia.
At the silver kiosk on the Riva we bought an evening
paper, just before it shuttered up for the night. I read
the paper while we walked past the decaying façades, with
black arches between the buildings leading to unlit alleys.
The lights became fewer, the waterside cafés less kempt.

I paused. "I wonder if this is it. International Congress
of Film."

"Almost certainly. What does it say about it?"

"Nothing much. It starts tomorrow. Somebody called
George Girdler has come over from London to organize
it."

"Listen," Neale said. The water was gently slapping against the quay.

Neale asked me: "Where would a man like that stay?"

We looked up the Riva, in the direction we had come from.

"Up there, I suppose."

"Shall we go and see him? Or are you too tired?"

"Yes, but let's go all the same."

The ground-floor windows of the hotel showed orange light. They were divided into round faces like the rim of a cheap tumbler. We went in. Neale asked the reception clerk for Mr. Girdler.

"He expects you, sir?"

"No. Would you ring through to him?"

"What name, sir?"

"We're from the Tottenham Court Road Express, London."

Into the phone the clerk said: "Here are a gentleman and a lady from the Express, London, sir."

He turned to us. "Mr. Girdler says will you go up."

A pageboy conducted us.

As we went in, Mr. Girdler half rose from behind an eighteenth-century desk that was both too small and too ladylike for the typewritten papers heaped about it. He was an abnormally tall, blunt-limbed man of forty, with a plain, earnest face and tired eyes.

"How do you do, how do you do. Let me get you a drink. I put it in one of these pigeon-holes—there's one that's big enough for a bottle. Not its original purpose, I imagine. Do sit down. Have you been in Venice long?"

"We arrived this evening."

"Pleasant journey?"

"Very smooth," Neale said.

"Wonderful nowadays, isn't it? Now, if you will forgive

183

me, I'm going to treat you good people very badly indeed. The fact is, I'm up to my eyes. I've kept my poor secretary working to this unholy hour, and what I propose to do is this. If you will excuse my apparent inattention, I'm just going to go through these letters and sign them, while you sit there and ask me anything you want to know."

He half turned his back on us. We lay in our arm-chairs, beneath the chandelier of frosted tulips. For a while we were too tired to speak. Neale stirred.

"About the congress. Could you give me an idea of its purpose?"

"Its purpose. Simply an exchange of views, on an international level, between practitioners of film."

"And your programme?"

"Some of our meetings will be formal, and some"— Girdler signed a letter and blotted it—"informal. Gala opening tomorrow morning in the Doges' Palace."

"Are you expecting any big names to attend?"

"Some of the biggest names in documentary. Blenkinsop. Bracegirdle."

Neale and I looked at one another. I shrugged.

"Any film stars?" Neale asked. "Will Bradbury Washington be there?"

"He may be. He well may be."

"Did you know Helena Buchan was in Venice?"

"Is she? No, I hadn't heard that. Funny thing—she made one or two films, years ago. They were just photographed operas, of course. Film, as we shall be discussing it, is essentially something to be looked at. A succession of visual images. That's basically the theme of the congress."

"We were wondering about Cynthia Beaulieu," Neale said.

"Cynthia Beaulieu."

184

"The young actress."

"Is she promising?" Girdler asked.

"Very. We wondered if she was coming to the congress. Will she be at the gala opening?"

Girdler turned round.

"I'll tell you what. Come along tomorrow yourselves. To be perfectly frank, I can't for the moment recall anything about Cynthia Beaulieu. But I've no doubt she'll be there. I've got an invitation card left. I'll make it out for you. What is your name?"

"Mr. and Mrs. Gottlieb Wagner." Neale spelled it. Girdler copied it on to the front of an invitation card four pages thick, tied up with red cord like a Christmas card. He delivered the invitation into Neale's hand.

"Don't lose it. You might have to show it at the door. We're being given the works, rather. Carabinieri, and so forth. One or two big politicians coming, with their wives. The President's sending a deputy."

We thanked him.

"I hope to see you tomorrow if I'm not snowed under with people. Sit near the front so you can hear properly. Will you forgive me if I don't take you downstairs?"

We went back over the bridge and crossed the Piazza.

"Neale, I've got nothing to wear. For tomorrow."

"That dress we bought."

"It's just a cotton frock."

"I suppose it is."

"I haven't even got a hat."

"You'll just have to endure it," he said. "It's one of the ordeals for Cynthia."

Beneath the arcades a crowd stood watching television. The set was in a lighted shop-window, surrounded by gramophone records and electric irons. As we passed, we saw the shop was still open.

"What's the Italian word for a record?"

"Disco."

Neale drew me back, into the shop, and asked the salesman: "Ha Lei un disco di Helena Buchan?"

"Sí. Che cosa vuole?"

Neale turned to me. "What's she recorded?"

"She sings the Countess in the recording I've got of Figaro."

"O, I know. Can you think of anything else? She's a wonderful Countess."

"Tanya has one of her doing something from The Magic Flute. I'm not sure what."

Neale asked the salesman: "Qualchecosa di Mozart?"

"Sí." After a moment he came back and handed us a record. "Don Giovanni."

"Ask if we can hear it."

"Possiamo udirlo?"

The assistant put it on a turntable. For a moment it revolved tickingly; then the shop filled with Donna Elvira's voice.

The crowd outside shouted; one or two people hissed for silence.

The assistant came over and switched off the gramophone. He pointed to the television, lifted the record on to another machine and handed Neale and me a small round earphone each. I blocked my free ear, holding the earphone to the other. We stood listening to the high, tragic, betrayed voice. The record finished, and we put the earphones down. The assistant asked if we wanted to buy.

"Tell him we're too poor."

"Siamo troppo poveri."

He smiled at us.

We asked the Swiss landlady if we could have Neale's suit pressed for the morning. She followed us up to our room. The screen was there. Neale undressed behind it, and I passed his suit out to her.

"What time you want it tomorrow?"

"Half-past ten. We have to be at the Palazzo Ducale by eleven."

"You are going to the conversazione?"

"Yes."

"That is very big," she said. "Very important. That will be grand fashion."

She left us. I unpacked my new cotton dress and hung it on a hanger with a long wooden prop. It was rather creased from the suit-case. Neale said: "Venice is the only part of Italy that could be called grubby."

"Poor Gottlieb."

"He's only here one night."

"Poor Gottlieb all the more."

"It's funny to think of them, isn't it?" Neale said. "They're somewhere in Venice tonight."

We stood beside the mantelpiece, looking at a small wooden model of a châlet.

"Well, let's go to bed."

I went behind the screen and began to wash my hair in the basin; it was cracked, and there were one or two black hairs there already.

I heard Neale get into bed.

"What are you doing?"

"Washing my hair for tomorrow."

"O Lord: Are you going to be damp all night?"

"How can I help it?"

"It's just as well there are two beds."

We went out for breakfast in our old clothes, and then came back and waited in our room for the landlady to bring Neale's suit.

"What time ought we to get there?"

"About five to?"

"Ten to. I don't want to make a conspicuous entrance, Neale."

"No. You may as well start getting dressed. You'll take longer than I will."

I was in my petticoat when the landlady knocked. Neale went outside to get the suit from her. I heard him thank her. She said it was a cold morning.

He came in and changed into the suit. He looked at me. "Have you got any ear-rings?"

"Only these." I put them on.

"Your hair rather hides them."

"It's bushy from being washed." I began to brush it.

He opened the window and looked out.

"The calle's so narrow you can't see the sky. But I think it's going to rain."

"We haven't got anything."

He took out his plastic mackintosh.

"We can't go in that."

"It's a question of going under it, anyway. We can't both get in it."

"We'd arrive soaked."

"If we get really soaked," he said, "we'll just have not to go. We'll give Cynthia up."

He folded the mackintosh into his pocket, spoiling the hang of his suit.

"I wonder how the other guests will get there. I hadn't thought of it before, but you can't take a taxi in Venice."

"They'll have flunkeys with big umbrellas to escort them across the square. Are you ready?"

As we left the room, I looked at the chalet on the mantelpiece. Its front door had half opened.

"Look."

"O Lord," Neale said. "I didn't realize it was one of those. That means it will rain."

Outside there was a stagnant, dangerous heat; but occasionally a cold wind, an inch or two above the ground, carried grit and sheets of paper towards our ankles.

We hurried, and I became hot.

"Is my nose shining?"

"Not much."

"Wait a minute. . . ."

"No. We want to get there before it rains."

Outside the Palace a crowd waited to watch the guests arrive. There were policemen in control, keeping a trough open; the way was clear to the Porta della Carta.

"Have we got to run the gauntlet?"

"No. Let's pretend to be part of the crowd and then slip through."

We stood behind the back row. People were standing on their toes and craning forward. Several children had been lifted up to see.

"We'll never get through," Neale said.

I said: "Permesso. Permesso."

People made way for us, without stopping peering.

Two carabinieri stood in the doorway. We passed through.

"Perhaps we have to shew the card further in."

Carabinieri splendidly lined the Giants' Staircase. We went up it between them, along the balcony to where two more stood, into the Palace. The route inside was marked all the way by silent pairs of magnificent uniforms. We made our way through them as if through a series of triumphal arches.

We came out at the back of the grand hall. It was filled with rows of seats, about a third of them occupied. Ten rows at the front were more comfortable than the rest; they seemed to be upholstered in plush. Just where the quality of the seats changed, a footman stood in each aisle, wearing blue livery and white gloves, holding a mace, keeping guard.

"Shall we go as far up as we can," Neale whispered, "without encroaching on the posh part?"

We walked quietly up a side aisle, and found two seats only just short of where the footman stood. None of the best seats seemed to be occupied. Neale pushed his mackintosh on to the floor and whispered: "Well. Can you see Cynthia?"

I looked round the audience. It seemed to be mostly Italian. I saw two men wearing dark suits, and three or four women wearing hats, but not fashionable ones. Behind us the hall was filling up. Most people were in raincoats. Some left their umbrellas at the door, propping them against the wall. Others took them to their places and hooked them over the seats in front or laid them along the floor. Two rows behind us sat a mother and three children, who swung their legs backwards and forwards ; the white ankle socks flashed rhythmically.

"I don't think she's here. Do you think we've come to the right place?"

"I'm beginning to doubt it."

Next to me was a man in a bright blue suit. He pulled his brief-case out from under his chair, and unzipped it. His elbow touched mine. "Scusi." "Prego."

"What's the time?" Neale said.

"Five past eleven."

Suddenly a tumult passed over the hall. We heard chairs scraped back; and our own staggered as neighbouring ones moved. People began to push, then to flock, then to run forward. There was a crash as a whole row of seats at the back fell over.

We looked up the aisle. The footmen had retreated.

They were now reserving only the front two rows. The people fought to fill the free places.

Gradually the audience settled down. There was a dispute in our aisle. The footman was called in, but he refused to adjudicate. The three children who had been behind us were well up towards the front.

I noticed an apple lying on the floor beside me. The man in blue had gone. I looked round the hall; he was two rows ahead. I picked up the apple, leaned across and gave it him. "Grazie." "Prego." He offered me an apple. "Grazie, no."

Some of the crowd began to clap faintly. Others said "Sssss" to them. The clapping stopped. There was a quiet chatter over the room.

Neale started to laugh. "O Lord. It all goes to shew the absurdity of ever being afraid. Do you realize you're the best-dressed woman in the room?"

Presently some formally dressed men, one of them in morning dress, filed through a small door on to the platform. The chatter from the audience grew neither more nor less.

The men sat down. One of them poured himself a glass of water. After a little, the man in morning dress moved to a rostrum and began to speak, reading in a flat voice from a piece of paper. The words came to us through a microphone. I heard Venezia, Italia, bellezza, arte.

"What's he saying?" Neale whispered.

"Welcome to Venice."

The speech stopped. On or two people clapped.

Another man went to the rostrum, and began to speak in French: Venise, international, l'art.

I asked Neale: "What does he say?"

"How glad he is to be in Venice."

One or two people clapped again.

The next speaker was George Girdler. "Film is essentially and basically international. To receive images through the eye, conveyed from the eye to the brain, is the property of all men, of whatever country. It is therefore fitting . . ." The microphone clicked, and the voice became fuzzy. The microphone was switched off. We heard Girdler's natural voice, disconcertingly distant, the words scarcely distinguishable. "Great results have been achieved—not least by Italian films—with amateur actors. The professional actor is basically only a subordinate part of film making. In some cases actors can be dispensed with altogether. It may well be that the future of film lies with the animated cartoon. The appeal of personality had its uses in popularizing the medium in the early days of Kinema, but film in its maturity must be independent of the star system."

Someone was standing in the aisle pressing against Neale's legs which were stretched out to the chair in front. I looked up from black slacks to black jersey; I recognized the mutinous face of Bradbury Washington. He said: "Let me through."

Neale looked up at him, and did not move.

"I got to get to the front. I'm late."

Neale did nothing. I saw Washington's hand turn in on itself like an ape's; the nails picked at each other. "Hey!" Neale did not respond. Washington bent down and said: "You stand up and I'll hit you."

"Don't be silly," Neale said. "Go round the front way."

After a moment he did, and we saw him climb up on to the platform. The audience clapped loudly. Washington sat down. A flashlight photograph was taken. Girdler resumed his speech. "Film proper is a succession of visual images. It is no more and no less than shadows cast on a screen. The real star of any film is the director.

The director is the man the public does not see, the man"
—his voice sank—"who manipulates"—the loudspeaker
came through again with a roar—"the shadows."

Girdler sat down; there was a little applause.

A fourth man came to the rostrum, and began to speak
in a flowing tenor voice, wheedling the microphone,
phrasing and moulding the words beautifully, as if he
was singing an aria. La più bella città del mondo; questa
conferenza non solo nazionale ma internazionale; film;
una poesia misteriosa; lucidezza; artisti, attori, attrici;
l'anima umana . . .

"What's he saying?"

"Mysterious poetry," I whispered, "of film. Great
actors portraying with lucidity the human soul. The
exhibition is in the next room. He declares it open."

The audience gave itself no time for applause. For the
second time it rushed forward, overturning chairs again,
shouting or fighting silently. The two small doorways,
one at each side of the platform, were jammed. A balloon
of people stuck out of each, struggling towards it; soon
they became stationary. Neale and I alone were left
sitting. The men on the platform had all disappeared,
presumably through one of the doors before the crowd
got there. "It must have been quite a chase," Neale said.

We joined one of the queues. People pushed us.
Against our will, we became part of the crowd and for
a moment were jammed immobile. We eased ourselves
a little, falling back as far as we could. "I wonder what's
holding it up." I said to someone next to me: "Perchè
non si muove?"

"La polizia."

Through the top of the open door we felt a draught.
Some of the men in the crowd struggled to free their
elbows and put on their hats.

The crowd moved forward a little, then stopped again.

"Is it worth it?" Neale said. We looked back. The doors at the top of the hall, where we had come in, were closed. "There seems to be no other way."

We moved forward again. Peering through the spaces in the crowd, we could now see that policemen stood in the open doorway with their hands linked across it.

Slowly we reached the front. The people behind pressed us up against the policemen's hands.

At last they parted. Neale and I, with three or four people from just behind us, were allowed to pass; then the hands closed again.

We were in a small exhibition room, with fawn coloured fibre screens standing about it; crowds pressed round the screens.

We pushed up to the nearest. I could just glimpse a glossy photograph, about twelve inches by six, pinned in the centre of the vast screen. It seemed to shew a café table, with no one sitting at it; it was photographed upwards, from somewhere near the floor, and lit in such a way that one half was bright and the other darkly shadowed. A man at the front of the crowd was sketching in the air before the photograph, referring to it delicately with the back of his hand. "Che composizione! Che poesia!" One of the women responded: "Bellissima!" All at once the little group turned and ran at one of the other screens.

"Do you think Cynthia's here?"

"We'll never find her, even if she is."

"Shall we go?"

We went down. The crowd was still outside. It paid us no attention. One or two other guests straggled out after us. We looked to our left. The sky was grey. The sea, without colour, swelled formlessly, high against the quay. Wind blew across it suddenly in a strip, turning down the points of the waves before it.

We walked away into the Piazza. The pigeons were flying in long elipses, at shoulder height.

Heavy and sudden, the rain began.

We ran into the porch of San Marco. Standing on the uneven, smooth marble, we peered out and saw the Piazza empty as if in a dumb-show conjuring trick. Some tables and chairs vanished indoors; some were tilted; we found ourselves looking at a dark grey expanse of paving stones, running with water, with nobody there.

The crowd that had been waiting outside the Palace came pressing towards us to share our shelter. We held on to a pillar and kept our places at the front. They came in clucking, in groups, pushing the children by a hand in the small of their backs; the few who had mackintoshes waved their arms as they tried to put them on.

We stood looking out. Cold blew round our knees. Water splashed up at our ankles from outside. Behind us there was the unnatural warmth of bodies and mackintoshes, pierced occasionally by a draught or a shiver.

"Should we run for it?"

"Yes."

Neale took out his plastic mackintosh and we pulled it over our heads.

"Now."

We slipped as we ran round the corner, clutched at one another, and set off up the alley-way. We could hear jointed shutters in front of shops being run down, shutters of upstairs windows being slammed to. We saw a boy run across the path ahead of us and dash, screaming, into a shop. We ran on. The water coursed down the basins at the side of the path. We saw pieces of hail land and bounce. There were voices above us, as people gathered at windows and peeped out.

The whole street was flowing under shallow eddies.

"Come on." We ran.

"I thought it was here," Neale said.

"So did I."

"Perhaps it's the next. The one parallel with this."

We tried it. Our pensione was not there.

"I'm sorry. It all looks so different without anybody in the street."

"Is it over there?"

We stumbled up a bridge. I paused on the flat top and looked along a grey, deserted side-canal sprigged with raindrops. "Come on." We ran down the other side and under a small arch. We found ourselves in a passage running along beside another canal. We were partly protected.

"I'm lost. Are you?"

A man overtook us, pushing past, manipulating his umbrella under the low roof. He left the passage and, leaning forward, the umbrella in front of him, scrambled over another humpbacked bridge. He disappeared.

"These little bridges—one solitary little figure with an umbrella," Neale said. "It's like Willow Pattern."

The wind changed, and the rain began driving in on us.

"Let's get on."

We hurried over the bridge the man had taken. "I recognize this," Neale said. "I think it's going to bring us out."

But it brought us into a campo we did not know, derelict under the rain. A locked church jutted out into the middle. The grass stood soaked between the paving stones. Some geraniums, growing on top of a wall, had been battered sideways by the rain.

We ran across the campo and came to a dark, drenched alley. "Down here." We went. "Let's get into the first doorway we find." We ran past shabby front doors all built flush to the street.

We came at last to what seemed to be the side entrance of an hotel. There was a broad shallow step. We mounted it and drew ourselves in. There was just room for the two of us. Below, above and on two sides, we were encased in yellow marble. Behind us were glass doors, with a gilt bar across their waist. Looking in, into the dark, we could dimly see some sort of foyer. In front of us the rain fell in heavy straight lines like a curtain of beads.

"O, isn't Venice beautiful," Neale said.

He slipped the mackintosh off our heads. I put my hand up and tried to comb out my hair.

"Are you wet?"

"Just at the top here. And at the sides." I wiped raindrops off my forehead. "I imagine it's an even chance whether I look bloody or quite amusing."

He looked at me. "Actually, it's all right." We faced one another, staring. Neale sighed. "I feel touched by the exotic."

I looked away, down at the uninteresting modern marble floor, up at the uninteresting sheet of marble beside me, secured by screws which had rusted and stained a little. "So long as nobody comes through this door," I said, "and jabs us in the back."

"Nobody would come out in this weather. Only us."

"Yes, only us." I looked at him.

"Could it be," he said, "that the moment might overtake one when one was out of breath and not at all dressed to receive it?"

I brushed at my hair again.

"Are you afraid?" Neale said.

I felt how straight my knees were, how I was pressing with all my weight into the floor.

He said: "Are you afraid to rise?"

"I know I've got to rise to your occasion when it comes, because you'd never rise to mine."

"But are you reluctant? Have you reservations?"

I found that I answered quite loudly and without calculation. "No. No, I've no reservations."

"We shall have to die, one day," Neale said.

I turned aside and laid my forehead against the marble wall.

Neale said: "Suppose one had the courage to throw all one's vitality into a single occasion. Suppose one dared to pin on it all one's appreciation, all one's sense of beauty, instead of keeping some of it for the next moment, the next place, some other person . . ."

"Suppose one did."

He whispered: "Wouldn't that moment, and ourselves at that moment, be immortal?"

I said nothing.

"Shouldn't we have made the beauty safe? Shouldn't we have broken through?"

Out of the corner of my eye, I saw a cotton dress move in the hotel foyer. I turned. So did Neale. We stood against the glass doors, our hands on the bar, the doors slipping slightly under our weight.

Inside the hotel, Cynthia was facing us, but not looking out: we were the direction, not the object, of her gaze. We could hear nothing, but she was talking to the hotel clerk, who, behind his desk, was just within our vision to the right.

Neale whispered to me: "Don't do anything. Let her go."

"Yes," I said. "I'll let her go."

Cynthia turned her back to us and began to walk up a staircase that would carry her out of our sight.

We both pushed the bar and burst in.

"Cynthia!" I called. "Cynthia Bewly!"

She turned, peered, stooping, into the dim foyer, and then came down the stairs again, holding her hand out to me. "Susan! How extraordinary to see you here!"

I shook hands with her.

I introduced Neale. As she held out her hand to him, I realized I had no memory at all of the moment immediately before, when my own hand had held hers.

Neale grinned at her. "Ah. The photograph made flesh."

Cynthia giggled incuriously.

"You should be chained to a rock," Neale said, "and in danger of being eaten by a dragon. Actually, we've dealt with the dragon."

"What dragon?"

"Oh, the lances we've broken for you," he said. "At one moment it looked as if the dragon was going to eat us. But we tamed it—we forced it to let us ride it over the Apennines."

Cynthia turned to me, smiling. "I see you've found someone who talks as much nonsense as you do."

"No, seriously," he said. "We've been looking for you."

"For me? Why?"

"It's a long story."

"Well, you must tell it me, but not now. I'm sorry to be rude but I'm in a frightful hurry—I'm going out to lunch and I must change first. It's gone so cold." She looked at us, and added: "You *are* wet."

"I'm sorry to keep you," I said.

"I'm sorry to dash away. Look, when shall I see you? Are you here for a few days?"

"We could be," Neale said.

"Oh, good. I'm vaguely trying to get a film part, you

know, but nothing much is happening. Are you free tomorrow?"

I said we were.

"Well, look, let's meet—do you like swimming?"

"Not much."

"O no. I remember. You never did. I was thinking we could have all gone to the Lido. But if you don't . . . Do you know Totobar?"

"That cave off the Piazza?"

"That's the one. There? At eleven, tomorrow?"

"Yes, all right."

"I must fly. Do forgive me." She set off up the stairs. The clerk came running round to her and gave her her key. "O thank you. I almost forgot." She looked down at the number. "O, good. I've got my own room again."

The clerk said: "All your things have been moved back, madam. We are very sorry you had to change."

"O, that's all right." She explained to Neale and me, while she walked slowly, backwards, up the stairs: "I had to have a different room last night. A dreadful party of trippers came, and a terrible woman insisted on having number thirteen."

"Mrs. Luther," Neale said.

"Was that her name? How do you know, anyway? You are mysterious. You must tell me everything tomorrow." She laughed and disappeared up the stairs.

Neale walked over to the clerk. "Could you tell me how to get back to the Piazza?"

"The Piazza, sir?"

"Yes. San Marco."

"But how did you come, sir? The Piazza is just round the corner—first on the left. I think the rain has stopped now, sir."

We went out, and followed the clerk's directions. "What a damn muddling place it is," Neale said.

We lunched in our trattoria. The man with the violin came round again, and so did a man selling postcards. I bought one.

"Who's it for?"

"Miss Falconbridge."

I wrote it at the table, turning my pen over and writing with the back of the nib so as to get all the words in.

I hope you didn't think I came to see you only so that I could ask you next day to stand referee for me. The idea of applying for the courier job hadn't occurred to me when I saw you. It cropped up suddenly, and I got it, with the result that I am here in Venice. There's no point in saying anything about it. It's still Venice. Oddly enough, I ran into Cynthia Bewly a few minutes ago by accident. She is here, looking for a job. She is vaguely on the fringes of films, and now spells herself Beaulieu. I had only a minute with her, but we are meeting again tomorrow. Affectionately, Susan.

Over our coffee, I asked Neale: "What did you think of Cynthia?"

"She seemed quite nice."

We finished, and paid.

"Well, what shall we do now?"

"Wait for tomorrow, I suppose."

PART THREE

✶ XIV ✶

CYNTHIA came into Totobar with Helena Buchan.
We had been watching the doorway. Cynthia
stepped in, clean-looking and angularly graceful, in a
yellow dress with bars of flowers across it; as she came
out of the sunlight, I felt myself clench, and I was bound
to my chair by a paralysis of fear.

She was followed by a much bigger woman, whom
I recognized at once. I did not realize they were together
until Cynthia turned back for her and led her towards
our table.

I felt irritation and boredom. My thought was that
a mature and successful world, and the obligation to meet
a stranger, would impose itself formally over whatever
intimacy I had hoped to re-establish from our giggling
past. I looked at Neale, but he was standing up. I
followed his example. Cynthia joined us, introduced us,
and said: "This is Mrs. Buchan." She was taller than
any of us.

Neale moved out, and we indicated that Helena Buchan
was to take the innermost place. She passed behind the
table with a constrained stateliness. She was big-boned
but thin; powerful; perhaps athletic. Large and fine-
shaped, her jaw jutted over the table. There were lines
on her neck. She was younger than I had thought, as
little as thirty-seven, or as much as forty-five.

We all sat down. In the inner chair, against the stone

wall, Helena Buchan was almost in darkness, and she took off her sun-glasses.

I was next to Cynthia. "Isn't it wonderful weather," Cynthia said. "After what we had yesterday." She stooped sideways and deposited on the floor her handbag and another longer bag, made of green plastic, which might have contained knitting. She saw me look, and said: "Bathing things."

The waiter came. Cynthia stooped to push her bags further under the table; then she smiled up at him.

We ordered four coffees.

"I do think the waiters are nice in Italy," Cynthia said. "By the way, where are you two staying?"

Neale told her.

She began to chatter about hotels and pensioni. "If I don't get a part soon, I shall have to move into your little place." I watched her. A band of sunlight penetrated from the Piazza and touched the top of her hair to auburn. Without colour, completely beautiful, her face smiled and pleasantly grimaced, never still for an instant; the long lips moved in the way I remembered, and I remembered that I had used to wonder if Cynthia had grown out of a speech defect; the words came, a little slow but carelessly numerous, in a voice high, carrying, pretty and just perceptibly tainted with cockney.

I might have triumphantly ground to death something that had saddened me. For a moment, even the piercingly mortal beauty of Venice was destroyed, negatived by Cynthia. As the waiter brought the tray, the image in my mind was of a Woolworth's, a Scotch Wool Shop and meeting for coffee in the High Street.

I felt inert after strain. I almost dozed. Cynthia was chattering. Nobody spoke to Helena Buchan. I felt that Cynthia was probably unaware of the discourtesy and Neale careless of it; but I could draw no words out of myself, and my admiration of her singing made me stiff. I could not make myself look at her direct; she sat silent and, it seemed, completely still.

Cynthia took a teaspoon out of the frosted glass of water and stirred her coffee. Feeling me watch her, she turned to me. We smiled broadly at one another. I realized without disappointment that we should never be friends, and that the affection I had, as a duty, brought to her would never be required.

"Now do tell me," Cynthia said, "why you were looking for me."

My cheeks became steamily hot, and I wondered if I was blushing. "Well. We saw you in *The Lady Revealed*."

"You didn't! Not in that old thing! I must say, you look at some funny things."

"You appear in some."

"I never know whether to do those things or not," Cynthia said. "Some people say they get your face known, if not your name. Other people say they just get you associated with those kind of things, and you never get any further."

I was silent.

Out of the shadows, Helena Buchan said: "Will one of you enlighten my innocence?" Her speaking voice was low, difficult to catch because she seemed to be looking down; at the centre of the sentence, her voice grated, like a boat passing over shallows. I heard Neale draw breath. Before he could answer, Helena Buchan pursued more loudly: "Was this thing Cynthia appeared in a show? Or a newspaper? Or just a machine in a pin-table saloon?"

I turned to apologize to her. Neale, leaning towards her from the other side, interrupted. "Ha, you're so right. It's a portable version of what the butler saw." He described *The Lady Revealed* to her. I looked at the open neck of her rough linen stone-coloured dress. Shadowed, the flesh was grey-green like flesh in an early painting. The bones lay big and exposed, with declivities beneath them. Where the deep lapels met, her bosom rose thin and slight.

Neale began to recount our quest for Cynthia. Without changing the inclination of her head towards him, Helena Buchan felt in her handbag, or in a pocket, beneath the table. Without deviating from Neale, she passed a packet of American cigarettes to Cynthia and me. She offered them to Neale. Impatiently he refused. Without deflecting her attention, she lit her own. The face, bent over the table, was for an instant illuminated from below, but the lighter's flame threw no colour; the face was like a statue, suffering, restrained and over-large.

Cynthia touched my arm. She was holding out a match to me. We smiled at one another, and she whispered, as Neale went on talking: "What an intriguing story."

Breathing out the smoke, I turned back, more at my ease, even amused, and began to join in Neale's narrative. Our two voices performed like strings and woodwind, in canon or taking the burden from each other. We could feel rather than see that Helena Buchan turned cumbrously to each of us as we spoke, following the line we developed, acknowledging each of our dénouements.

Neale described our telephone call to the wrong Cynthia Bewly. Cynthia herself interposed, her voice lying above Neale's like a line of piccolo melody. "How ghastly! Fancy someone with the same name as me being such an old battleaxe!"

Neale swirled on, into the depths of the story, into the depths of winter.

"O, I know what it's like," Helena Buchan said, "though I've taken care not to spend a winter in London for—o, longer than I'd like to remember."

He brought us out into the spring. "We traipsed south of the river to some desolate art school——"

"You didn't!" Cynthia cried. "Did you see old Bingley?"

"Yes. We found the place at last——"

"He was a great pal of mine. But I can't think how you——"

Neale brushed Cynthia away. He talked with his head bent sideways, watching Helena Buchan. In the darkness, her gaze apparently fixed on the table top while she listened, she was like the audience to a play we were giving in a small lighted circle. She was outside the arc. We could only project our words towards her, sensing her attentiveness from her silence and immobility; from the dimness there came to us now and then a rustle, occasionally the sound of a spoon against a cup, often a laugh—unexpected by us, because we could not see its preliminaries on her face.

Neale went on excitedly, working himself up, as if it was a justification which he was flinging into the dark. The shape of the big woman against the wall was vague, as the shape of an audience might be in the theatre, and for a moment, while Neale talked alone, I had a fantasy that the audience had slipped away and that he was throwing his words to the bare wall.

He took us to Nice, and to the tour. As he launched us into Italy, I bent forward and tried to take the narrative from him. For a moment, I had it; but he contended with me, wrested it back and at length brought us on our furious journey across the Apennines. He landed us at Venice. "There was nothing for it," he said, "but to go and see George Girdler. So we went to his hotel——"

"O do you know *him*?" Cynthia interrupted.

"No. We went in——"

"How *did* you get in? He's ever so difficult to see."

Neale stopped. After a moment, he held up his hand for the waiter. He asked us: "Shall we have some more coffee?"

There was a pause of hesitation: Neale poised himself to renew the atmosphere he had created.

Helena Buchan said: "Do you have some. I'm afraid I must go."

"*Must* you?" said Cynthia.

"I'm meeting Philip at the Campanile."

We all stood up.

"Don't you any of you move," Helena Buchan said. She thanked Cynthia. I saw Neale awkward and appalled, as if he had caught himself back on the edge of a precipice. The atmosphere had engulfed him; and now that it was at disrupting point he was disconcerted to find himself deeper sunk in it than anyone, and unable to pull himself lightly out. Helena Buchan said to him: "It's a fascinating story. I hope I hear the end of it sometime."

He said nothing.

She looked from Neale to me, and then at Cynthia once more.

"You must have a very beautiful body, to make them both come so far."

"O no," Cynthia said. "Not really."

Helena Buchan walked out into the sunlight.

We sat down again, in the fragments of her departed presence. No one moved round into her place. Cynthia began gathering the empty coffee cups.

The waiter came and took them. Cynthia ordered three more coffees. "This is on me," she said to Neale.

The waiter brought the fresh coffee and added another slip of paper to the one on the table. Cynthia picked them both up and put them in her handbag.

"Well?" she asked Neale. "How did you get in to see Girdler?"

He told her, not spiritedly. "Fortunately," he finished, "the clerk couldn't manage such a mouthful of English words as Tottenham Court Road Express."

"There's no such paper, is there?" Cynthia said. "I live near there."

"Near Tottenham Court Road?"

"Yes." She named the street parallel to ours.

Neale began to laugh.

"But you're not on the phone," I said.

"Yes I am. I have to be, in case a casting director wanted me suddenly."

"It's not possible," Neale said.

"All the time you were talking, I kept wondering why you didn't find me."

I said: "Did you spell your name Beaulieu in the phone book?"

"Yes, of course. That's the name I'm known by." She giggled. "If I'm known at all."

We drank our coffee.

"Well, what did Girdler say to you?" Cynthia asked.

"Invited us to the Doges' Palace."

"O, were you there?"

"Yes. Were you?"

"No. I was dying for an invitation, though. Was it frightfully smart? I would have gone to watch outside—to see the fashions—only it was such miserable weather."

"There wasn't much fashion," Neale said.

"O, I'm sure there was. Men never notice. Were any celebrities there?"

"Bradbury Washington," I said.

"How lovely. Did you get close to him? He's terribly good-looking, isn't he?"

Neale said: "Queer, I imagine."

"They say that about everyone," Cynthia said, "in films. It's only gossip."

At last she rose, took the two bills out of her handbag and went across to the counter to pay them. Neale whispered to me: "My God, you were right. She's fantastically beautiful."

"Cynthia?"

"O yes, Cynthia is, I suppose. But no, I meant Helena Buchan."

"Why couldn't you keep quiet," I said, "about the tour?"

"Why should I? She was amused."

"Had you forgotten that she's an American?"

Cynthia came back to us. We thanked her, and we all walked out into the Piazza. She took my arm for a moment. "Shall we just look round the shops?"

"Let's go this way," Neale said.

He led us straight across, under the noonday sun, to the Campanile.

"Well, she's not here. I suppose she must have met Mr. Buchan all right."

"Do you mean Philip?" Cynthia said.

"Isn't he Mr. Buchan?"

"No, he's a Mr. Caswell."

Neale demanded: "Is he her lover?"

"I don't think so." Cynthia giggled. "They have separate rooms at the hotel."

"How well do you know her?"

"Well, you know, just like anyone you meet at the hotel. I was a bit at sea when I first got here. Venice is muddling, isn't it? Helena was ever so nice to me."

We began to walk along the arcades, Cynthia pausing to look in the shop windows. Neale said: "Do you call her Helena to her face?"

"Oh, yes. She's not a bit sticky like that."

We walked on.

"I call Philip Philip, too," Cynthia said.

Outside the television shop, Neale paused, and told Cynthia how we had gone in and heard Helena sing Mi Tradí.

"O, did you?" She led us on to the next shop. "Funny, I'd gone round with them quite a lot before I found out she was a singer. Philip told me. Is she good?"

"She's immortal," Neale said.

Cynthia asked me: "Do you think so, too?"

"Yes."

We finished the circuit, and Cynthia began to take leave of us. I said: "Thank you awfully, Cynthia. You must let us take you somewhere next time."

"You could take me to the Lido this afternoon—o, no, you don't like swimming, do you? Well, I'll get in touch with you, now I know your address."

Neale said: "I've got an apology to make to Helena. I must see her again."

"Well, I should think you quite easily could. She seemed to like you."

"Will you fix something?" he said.

"I don't know how long she's staying in Venice. Sometimes she has things to do. But I'll try."

After luncheon we lay in our room for the siesta, but it was too hot to sleep. The Swiss landlady knocked on our door and called me to the telephone. "A Miss Büly to speak with you."

I put on my dressing-gown and went. I lifted the receiver and said: "Hullo. How brave of you to make an Italian phone call. They scare me silly."

"O, I got the man at the hotel to do it for me." Her giggles came metallically through the machine.

"Haven't you gone to the Lido?"

"I'm just going. With Philip. Helena's too busy, or tired, or something. But look—are you free tomorrow?"

"Yes."

"Helena wondered if we couldn't all go somewhere together. To look at some churches or something."

"I should think we could."

"Could you be at the Campanile by eleven?"

"Surely. Incidentally, who are we all?"

"How do you mean?"

"Who's coming?"

"O, I see. Well, just the same as today, but with Philip as well."

I asked: "Is Philip a man who sometimes wears a blazer?"

"He does sometimes. Is this another mystery?"

"Not in the least. We once saw him with Helena, that's all."

"O, well, I'm sure you'll like him. He's awfully kind."

"I expect I shall."

I went back to our room and told Neale.

He said: "Good."

I lay down again and fell into thick, hot unconsciousness.

Neale said: "Tomorrow, if you get a chance to be alone with this Philip, you might try to find out about him."

"What about him?"

"O—what's Helena to him, and he to Helena."

"I'm not going to ask him if he's her lover."

"No, I suppose not. But you could try to sound him."

"Why should I?"

Neale rolled over and faced me.

"For me," he said.

✶ XV ✶

THEY stood in a group at the foot of the Campanile. As we joined them they opened into a line, receiving us, and Helena said, smiling: "Well, it's banging day in Venice."

We had heard hammering since early morning. As we crossed the Piazza we had seen metal oblongs, rather like bedsteads, lying on the paving stones, while workmen moved round them. In front of San Marco the flags were up on the flagposts, but they hung downwards, like a single strip of ribbon, in the fierce morning stillness.

"Some festa, I suppose," Philip said. He was tall and substantial, younger than Helena by five or even ten years. He gave no impression of unusual height; yet he was several inches taller than she and so well built that she looked frail beside him.

"I almost forgot," she said. "You haven't met. This is Philip Caswell——"

Vibrantly near at hand, a bell began to toll fast and painfully. Cynthia shrieked and covered her ears. Helena continued to introduce us, speaking louder.

Philip smiled at us. He shouted gently: "I can't really hear, but I can guess which of you is which. How long is this thing going on?"

"Till they're tired, I think," Helena shouted.

"Shall we take the vaporetto to the other side?" Philip

asked. He had made no shock about meeting us. We had drifted already into his friendship, and without exerting himself he contrived to direct us in a group towards the Molo. I noticed he was carrying Helena's black stole bundled beneath his arm.

"Anywhere out of the sound of these bells," Helena cried.

She seemed to me more animated than she had been the day before. She was still stately, but her vitality was less intense; and as she abruptly skipped away from the noise I felt the monstrousness dissolve from the picture of her I had held in my imagination.

Neale ran round the little group of us and urged himself at Helena's side.

"I have an apology to make to you. But no one except you must hear it, or I shall blush."

"I can't hear," she shouted.

He hurried her forward, ahead of the rest of us, worrying at her elbow without daring to touch it.

Philip followed, walking between Cynthia and me.

As we passed the garden, the bell suddenly stopped. It rolled twice more, clumsily, under its own weight. A brazen aftermath was left in our ears: the buzz of Venice came to us at second hand as if we had been turned deaf; then it came through again, a comparative peace.

Cynthia said: "How beautifully Helena walks. Anyone can see she's been trained."

"I wish you could convince her of it," Philip said.

I asked: "Does she need convincing? What of, exactly?"

"O, of everything," he said.

Outside the vaporetto stop, Helena waited for us, turned back to receive us. Neale talked to her urgently. As we approached, I heard Helena answer: "No, I'm not unpatriotic, I hope, but I'm not obsessional about it

—if that's the right word." She faced us all. "Neale thought I might be having a fit of Yankee pique. I've assured him I'm not."

Philip smiled and passed us, to join the queue at the ticket kiosk.

"No," Helena said while we waited for him, "I don't seem to set much store by all those distinctions any longer. You know, all those ones we were brought up to think so important—class, colour, nationality, sex— even age. The only distinction I recognize now is between the quick and the dead." She laughed. "That used to be a line about pedestrians in the traffic—they were all either quick or dead. Or was that before your time?"

"I seem to remember it," Cynthia said, "from school." She asked me: "Do you?"

I nodded.

"How you children date me," Helena said.

We got out of the vaporetto at the Ca Rezzonico stop, and wandered into an alley. For a moment we progressed in an awkward bunch, each giving way politely to the others, so that we seemed to roll along, head over heels. Then Neale manœuvred again to Helena's side; and again he drew her out ahead of us. We kept them in sight, their figures fluffy in the sunshine as they stepped between the umber sunlit walls. We, walking three abreast, came more slowly, meeting obstacles. A crowd, running to- wards the vaporetto stop we had come from, over- whelmed us, and we stood aside, buffeted. Afterwards we had lost Neale and Helena.

They appeared again, far off, the sun on Neale's hair, and we saw them go into a church. We walked towards it. Cynthia stopped to adjust her sandals. We gave way to two nuns. We reached the church, and went in. It was empty. We stood for a moment in the stone coolness. Hearing footsteps, we turned round. A small boy ran into the church, reached above his head to the holy-water stoop, crossed himself, genuflected totteringly, and skipped across the nave to a side altar where candles were burning in front of a painted wax madonna which stood, crowned, behind glass.

"Shall we go?" Philip whispered, and we filed silently out.

We walked along the hot, hard paving stones, into churches; out again; making flickering transitions from sunlight into dimness, from unendurable heat into enclosed chill. Sometimes, when we came out, we would glimpse the two figures ahead, concealed from us now by a dazzle, now by the sudden shade of a wall, now by the mistiness of the heat.

At every church door, Philip would stand aside, Cynthia would hesitate, and I would push through the crimson tongue of silk hanging in an oval swathe across the doorway and silently enter the dark. Sometimes there was a rounded, sculptural magnificence; occasionally the interior was overgrown with pious, brown nineteenth-century mahogany. Not lofty, unspiritual, but varied, richly ornamental, civic, baroque, moyen sensuel, the churches of Venice received us in.

Once we found an empty nave with an aisle traced up it by two lines of tall lilies; they stood in clumps, in big oval Chinese vases; the sweet, soprano scent wove above the smell of incense. A priest came in and hurried up the church, his shoes squeaking, a brief-case under one arm, his hat held in the other hand. He genuflected hastily, and went towards the vestry.

"Let's go," Philip said. "There may be going to be a service, or a wedding or something."

We had come almost right across the spit of land, and I recognized where we were. I led them into another church.

"Who did this?" Philip asked me.

"Veronese. He decorated the whole church."

We spoke to the sacristan, and he led us upstairs along corridors that seemed to belong to a private house; then we stepped through a door and found ourselves in the wooden gallery, unsafe beneath our feet, looking down at the decorated body of the church, and up at the giant-size, partly defaced frescoes clamped close beside us on the walls.

We came right through on to the Zattere. I looked along the grassy waterfront, but the others were not there.

"Come along."

They followed, Philip patient, Cynthia tired. I took them in and out of the churches.

"Who painted that?"

"Tiepolo."

"Who painted that?"

"I don't know."

We came back to the waterfront. As we emerged, I saw Helena, sitting on a bench, looking out over the stretch of sea so wide that it seemed un-Venetian and almost sunless. Neale stood thinly beside her.

She turned. "We lost you."

I was afraid of shewing my despair. Helena, as if seeking it out, looked directly at me, taking off her sunglasses. I met her deep-set eyes for the first time, and for the first time noticed their colour: a deep blue, but artificial-looking, like a paint mixed with white, the colour of bluebells or dark hyacinths.

Cynthia sat down on the bench next to Helena, and loosened her sandal. I sat next to Cynthia.

"Did you see the Veroneses?" Helena asked.

"Did we?" Cynthia turned to me.

"Yes."

219

Standing behind Helena, Philip said quietly: "I'll get a gondola." He moved away down the quay.

Neale asked: "Are you going to celebrate the festa tonight?"

"We might have a coffee on the Piazza," Helena said.

"Why don't we take a gondola for the evening——"

"Why don't you take account of my age?" Helena replied.

"Because you haven't any," he said abruptly. "You're no age."

"They say it's not what you are but what you feel. I feel a thousand."

"J'ai plus de souvenirs que si j'avais mille ans."

"O, so you like Baudelaire," she said.

He raised one foot from the ground and nearly over-balanced. He blushed.

"Well don't be so surprised that I understood," Helena said. "A singer has to learn languages, more or less. I can make love quite eloquently in four. And die in four."

"Well, do you like him?" Neale said aggressively. "Do you like Baudelaire?"

"O, I don't pretend to judge. I don't know about these things."

Philip came back to us along the quay; and a gondola pointed its prow towards us.

"I should think it will take us all," Philip said. He handed Helena in, then Cynthia; they sat together leaning against the music-stand back of the seat.

"No, thank you," Neale said.

Philip looked at me.

"I'll stay with Neale."

Philip got in and they pushed off. Neale walked to the edge of the quay. "After dinner tonight," he called. "In the Piazza."

"Probably," Helena's voice replied. "If I find you haven't worn me out."

Neale stood with the front of his feet projecting over the quay. Worriedly, I said: "Come and sit down. Come away from there, anyway."

"Very well."

He sat next to me and we stared across at the line of brick warehouses with their dutch gables.

"Isn't it ugly," he said.

We slept all afternoon. Neale woke up excited; he hurried me out to the trattoria to dine. It was fuller than usual, and the service took longer. While we waited, Neale said:

"I told Helena we went into that shop and heard Mi Tradì."

"Did you? What did she say?"

Neale laughed. "Isn't she wonderful? She said: 'Yes, it's terribly good, isn't it?'"

"She may have meant the music."

"She meant both. Because she said afterwards: 'I was young then and Mozart was mature. We made a fine combination.'"

The waiter brought our spaghetti. Presently, the violinist came up to our table and, swooping down over us, rocked while he played a sweetly Spanish tune in our ears.

"I wish he wouldn't watch me eat spaghetti," Neale said.

The tune drifted away. We finished eating, and asked for coffee. "I wonder what her sex life is," Neale said.

"Helena? I couldn't guess."

Neale made an embracing, splendid gesture. "O I imagine her as gloriously bi-sexual," he said. "I see her with three concubines and four lovers."

221

"Is Philip one of them?" I asked.

"I shouldn't think so. Would you?"

"No, I don't think he is. He's a dear," I said.

"Yes, he's a dear. But he isn't up to her."

We went out and into the Piazza. The bandstand had been put up in the middle, and it faced us, darkly drum-shaped in the twilight. No players had arrived yet, but a thin crowd stood round it waiting.

We began to walk round the edges of the cafés, peering in at the rows of tables.

"They won't be here yet."

"We'll just make sure," Neale said.

We walked round twice, fast the first time, slowly the next. The centre of the square was becoming crowded; the cafés were about a third full; and it grew dark. Shaded lights appeared on top of the bandstand: lights in shop windows, in the inner part of the cafés, glowed but did not fall beyond the arcades. On our second revolution, the floodlighting had been switched on, gently touching the front of the buildings. The centre depths of the square seemed all the darker, more impenetrable, more velvet; all the passages of light merely lay soft on its surface like bloom.

We found them, sitting at a table near the edge.

"Come and sit down," Cynthia called. Philip brought an extra chair. Neale said to Helena: "So you weren't exhausted?" "No," she said, "not quite." Philip said: "She nearly was."

The others were drinking coffee. Neale and I ordered Cinzanini.

The band began. Ragged and second-rate, they jogged into the overture to The Marriage of Figaro.

"Tonight is highbrow night," Neale said.

"I was going to say," Helena replied. "They usually play Puccini."

"This is very special. We saw the programme on the front of the bandstand. They're going to do a movement from the Seventh."

"That will be too much for the poor things," Helena said. "They should have stuck to Puccini."

Neale said: "You weren't always above Puccini yourself. You made a film of Tosca."

"How do you know that? O, I suppose there's no reason why you shouldn't know it. I can't have it cut out of the books."

"Are you ashamed of it?"

"It was quite a good performance," she said. "At least, I thought so at the time. I don't know how it's worn. I made it in the days before I got this feeling that time was short and I'd better concentrate on the best." She shook her head, and smiled at us. "Here, I don't know why I'm running down Puccini. After all, it's wonderful in its way."   .

Philip said quietly: "It's the kind of music that makes you cry and then makes you ashamed."

Cynthia asked him: "Are you interested in music, too?"

"Yes," he said. "Yes, I am."

"Are you a singer?"

"O no, not anything. Just a camp follower. I've carried the bouquets on, in my time — haven't I, Helena?"

"O, your time doesn't go back very far," she said. "You're just a boy."

The overture came to an end. Some of the crowd in the Piazza clapped a little. We heard chairs scraping on the bandstand.

In the silence, Helena said deliberately, looking round at us slowly:

"I've sung Tosca, in whole or in part, in the Metropolitan Opera House, in the Casino at Deauville—I can't for the moment recall why it was there, some charity performance I daresay—and also in the Concert Hall on Worthing Pier."

"She has also," Philip said, "at the end of a performance of Tosca, kicked her bouquet into the orchestra pit."

"Yes, I did that," Helena said seriously.

"Why?" Neale said.

"I don't like bad orchestras. In those days, I couldn't stand them."

"Did the bouquet hit anyone?" Cynthia asked.

The conductor on the bandstand rapped his baton.

"I didn't see," Helena whispered to Cynthia.

The band stumbled into the second movement of the Seventh Symphony. We stared into the dark Piazza, listening. Softly Helena said: "It's a mournful choice. Also," she added, "a mistaken one."

Lamely the rhythm plugged on. There was a weedy sound. Some of the strings trailed behind the rest, out of tune.

"O dear," Helena said.

The music grew so faint, so disorganized, that I thought it was going to give out. Some deep part of the orchestra, perhaps the cellos and double basses, began marking the rhythm. The other instruments took it from them, and seemed to rally.

Helena whispered: "They should have stuck to Puccini."

After a moment, Neale leaned towards her, his voice excited. "Helena, why don't you——"

Somebody at the next table called Sssss, loudly and self-righteously.

Neale finished in a whisper.

Helena looked at him. I saw her neck stiffen, as if with fear. Slightly but quickly she shook her head.

"Yes," Neale whispered. "Yes, yes."

"In a way I'd like it," Helena whispered back, "but——"

"Sssss."

"We can't talk about it now," she whispered.

The music went on. Cynthia tapped her foot to its beat on the floor. Neale tapped with his fingers on the table, but continually he was ahead of the orchestra, leading them on to their conclusion.

At last it came. The clapping was of medium volume, but serious, almost pious, and dense. Neale jumped up and ran towards the bandstand.

"O no," Helena said. "He's not gone to ask."

We saw him push into the crowd. There was a pause. The conductor stepped off his eminence and disappeared, presumably to talk to Neale. Helena stared, straining, towards the bandstand.

Neale reappeared, standing at the outer edge of the crowd, beckoning to us.

Helena looked suddenly at Philip.

"Come on," Neale called. "He seems to be thrilled."

Helena and Philip stood up. Together they began to walk to the bandstand. The crowd parted for them. I saw Helena touch Philip's arm for a moment.

"Come on," Cynthia said. She and I ran after them, darting in before the crowd closed up.

Neale was saying, excited, squeaking: "He can't do Mozart, but——"

"I'm not in practice for anything else," Helena said.

"Vissi D'arte," Neale said, taking her arm, "Vissi D'arte."

A few people in the crowd caught his words and repeated them; one or two clapped.

Helena stood at the foot of the bandstand, quite still. Then she turned her back on Philip and slipped her stole off into his arms. Gently he handed her up. She appeared

225

on the bandstand. She was wearing a white cotton dress, with a wide pleated skirt; her thin arms were bare. She seemed half luminous.

The conductor spoke to her, and she nodded. A player sounded a note; she nodded again. She turned and faced outward, over the heads of the crowd, drawn away towards the conductor's desk with a certain awkwardness, as if one of her limbs was broken; like a long-legged animal frightened by efforts to make friends with it.

Standing next to me in the crowded dark, Cynthia whispered: "O, I'm scared for her."

The music began. Helena's voice began.

I felt Cynthia move convulsively and her hand seized mine. Hand in hand we stood and watched the stage. In long, lapsing syllables Helena's voice tumbled into the square. I looked round. The crowd was silent, all solemnly facing the bandstand. I saw Neale a little way from us, looking up. Philip, next to him, stood looking down.

When she finished, the clapping was loud. It went on. It grew; the noise of stamping joined it, and a few cheers.

Helena stood awkwardly inclining her head. She held her hand out to the bandmaster. He touched it. She moved to come down from the bandstand. The crowd shouted. She stood a moment longer; I could not tell in the dark but I thought her eyes were searching for one of us. She bowed again.

I saw Philip move forward.

Suddenly, on the bandstand, Helena dropped slowly and with perfect command into a full, tiered curtsey.

She came down, leaning on Philip's hand that was reached up to her. We ran forward. "Let's go back to the hotel," Philip said.

"No!" Neale cried.

Philip unwrapped the stole from his arm and put it about Helena's shoulders.

"I must go back," she said. "Are you coming, Cynthia?"

"You were *wonderful*," Cynthia said.

Helena smiled. "Come along."

Philip pushed into the crowd; Helena and Cynthia followed him. Some of the crowd, suddenly recognizing Helena in the dark, touched the back of her shoulders, as if superstitiously, or in congratulation, as she passed.

Neale called: "Tomorrow, under the Campanile, same time!"

"Probably!" Philip called.

Suddenly Helena stopped. She turned, stepped back towards Neale and me, and we heard her grin. "I used to sing that lying on the floor," she said.

I had been asleep. In his bed Neale turned suddenly, and the straw mattress shifted. I heard him thrust his head into his pillow, and sigh. I became asleep again. He sighed again. I said:

"Are you awake?"

"I can't sleep."

"Why?"

"Helena." He let a pause fall. I knew I was asleep again. Neale said: "Well. What do you think?"

"What can I think?"

"Do you mind? Do you think I'm silly?"

"No," I said.

"O God," Neale said. He sat up. I vaguely saw him prop himself against the wall at the top of his bed. "Isn't she just like her voice?"

"How do you mean?"

"O, the two, her voice and her personality, seem to

227

me so integrated. It's the very *quality*—the *quality* of their quality, if you see what I mean."

I said: "She's a very fine singer, as well as having the voice. It's something to do with the way she separates the notes from one another. She gets a sort of purity."

"O, but all the art," Neale said, "only enhances the voice. And the voice only enhances her."

I reached to the table between the beds, and took a cigarette.

"O God, what shall I do," Neale said.

I lay smoking in the dark.

He said: "It's an appeal she makes, isn't it?"

"An appeal? What against?"

"Pain? Mortality? Sadness? When she was singing tonight, I kept feeling she was looking round that crowd for there to be just one person there who would understand, who would come through to her . . ."

I said: "I think she appeals for someone to protect her from the beauty of the music."

"From all beauty," he said.

"From life, then."

"O, but she wants life, doesn't she? And she's got it, hasn't she? My God, how she's got it."

"She's afraid," I said, "that someone might answer her appeal."

"And afraid that somebody won't. God, she's independent. God, she's courageous. But I can't leave her to be lonely," he said. "I can't endure that."

After a moment he asked: "Would you come over here? To my bed?"

I got out and stretched myself beside him, lying on top of the sheet, propped up, as he was, against the wall. He put his arms round my waist and began rocking me from side to side. "Comfort me."

"Try and go to sleep."

"O, I can't." He pulled himself up suddenly and bent over me. Then he laid his head on my breast and began rocking again.

"If it's as bad as that, you'd better ask her to marry you. She seems to be unattached."

He wrested himself away from me. "One doesn't *marry* an object of romance."

"I'd hoped one did."

"One has an *affaire* with them," Neale said. "For as long as one can stand their beauty."

I sighed. "You'd better ask Helena to have an *affaire* with you."

"I wonder. What do you think she'd say?"

"How do I know. I expect she'd say she was old enough to be your mother."

"Ha, I know the answer to that," he said bitterly. "I'd tell her that if she knew anything about it, she'd realize that only increases the attraction."

I leaned over and stubbed out my cigarette. "Will you try to go to sleep now? You can ask Helena in the morning."

His arms brought me back. "No, stay here. Hold me."

★ XVI ★

WE waited beside the Campanile. I could feel tiredness round my eyes; the light hurt them. Neale was white-faced, but he chattered with excitement. Helena and Cynthia came to us out of the brightness.

"It's my fault we're late," Helena said. "I slept late. Philip isn't coming. He has to write some letters."

Cynthia said to Neale: "So you've got three girls to look after, all on your own."

"That doesn't frighten me one bit. I adore girls. What shall we do?"

"I'm not going far today," Helena said. "I really was tired after last night."

"Then let's just sit down at a café."

I said: "No, Neale. They're too expensive just here."

Helena said: "Please let me pay."

I looked at her, perhaps hostilely. "No. I don't see why you——"

"But I'm the one who won't walk any further. I should be made to pay for my age." She led us to a table.

We ordered coffee. Helena held out her cigarettes to Cynthia, then to me. As I took one, she said: "Cynthia's heard some good news."

We looked to her. Giggling a little, Cynthia said: "I've had a note from George Girdler. He wants to see me."

"Ha, that's because we recommended you," Neale said.

"Did you really?"

"Yes. We said you were promising."

"Well, thank you very much." She coughed a little, over her cigarette smoke.

Helena said: "She's going to Mestre tomorrow, for a screen test."

"He's sending a motor-boat for me. I shall be all alone in solitary state."

"Would you like Philip to go with you?" Helena asked.

"Do you think he would?"

"I'm sure he would. If you're scared?"

"I am a bit," Cynthia said.

"It'll be all right," Helena said, "if you just relax. Not that I'm the person to give that advice to anybody."

Neale leaned towards her and said harshly: "Why. Do *you* find it hard to relax?"

She stared at him.

He added: "I've never seen you on the stage."

"At least," she said, "I could stand still on the stage." She broke her gaze, and said to us all, generally: "I was no actress. No singer is. But I could stand still. Unfortunately, the people who produce opera—well, I suppose they can't find anyone with the musical talent and the dramatic talent at the same time. But they were always trying to get singers to act, and that seemed to mean hopping around or working your face like a rubber monkey all the time you were on the stage. I don't know anything about it, but I always thought you shouldn't *try* to act opera. Not in the ordinary way of acting. I just thought a singer ought to stand still." She added: "And it isn't easy to stand still on the stage."

"A lot of real actresses can't do it, even," Cynthia said.

Neale said to Helena: "You were obviously perfectly

231

right. If they'd known anything about it, they should have let you have your own way."

"O, but *I* don't know anything about it," she said. "I expect they were right after all."

We watched the people on the Piazzetta. A pale, fat-faced little boy in rompers came toddling along the edge of the cafés, trailing a wooden engine on a string, looking along the spaces between the tables and making as if to go in, and then looking back towards the square. His mother was a pretty fair-haired girl; she was walking with her mother, a woman no more than middle-aged, but bundled up in black, black stockings, a black shawl over her head. They were parading up and down, talking to one another, keeping well clear of the café area; whenever the child brushed against it and looked back soliciting their disapproval, they would call him or dart forward and pluck at his clothes.

"I once sang Zerlina," Helena said. "In the days when I was just starting. My voice was lighter then—more in the head, less in the chest. It was a good part for me to get."

"You must have been terrific," Neale said.

"My voice was all right. What was wrong was me. They wanted me to be coy. I was supposed to trip around being the arch little peasant. I can remember how I used to blush under the wig they stuffed me into. I always hoped nobody I cared about would come to see the performance."

"Yes. How awful for you," Cynthia said.

The fat child stood beside our table, looking up at us; he began to come further into the café.

It was the grandmother who swooped after him, this time; and as she came she slipped and fell flat, face down, on the paving stones.

We all moved, as if towards her. The fair-haired girl

shrieked: "Gesù Maria! La mamma!" The waiter ran out, holding a table napkin. Some of the crowd joined the fair-haired girl in picking up her mother; several others stopped and made noises of scandal.

She was standing up again, unharmed; the daughter brushed at the knees of the long black skirt. The child had run to them. He howled.

The crowd moved on; they moved off.

"I've heard of fallen women," Neale said. "That's the first fallen mamma I've seen."

Helena said: "Don't be unkind. She might have been hurt."

Presently Neale asked: "Shall we go?"

"Where?" Cynthia asked.

"Not far," Helena said.

"Just for a stroll. Down the Molo."

"I suppose we might go and look at it, just once again," Helena said. She paid the bill.

As we rose, Neale was at her side. "Seriously, haven't you noticed? If there's one thing Italians prefer even to a bambino, it's a mamma."

"What's wrong with that?" Helena asked.

"O, you Americans," he said, and skipped. "It's why you all come to Italy, of course."

"Why?"

"Straight out of one mother-cult and into a worse one. In America you have only one mothers' day a year. In Italy it's mothers' day every day of the year."

Helena paused, waiting for Cynthia and me, and we walked four abreast.

"Which direction is Mestre?" Cynthia asked.

Helena pointed. "Well, vaguely that way." She smiled at Cynthia. "Philip will be with you."

"And I daresay the man who runs the boat will know the way," Neale said.

We reached the giardinetto. "No further," Helena said. "Would you like to go and sit in there?"

"No, I'd rather look at the water." They strolled across and leaned on the balustrade. Cynthia and I followed. Cynthia stood between me and Neale.

Below our feet the water licked at the sea wall. The line of small boats tied up there nodded continually, the water clicking on their planks. When the vaporetto passed, they rocked deeply, and their enormous masts, on a level with our eyes, swayed from side to side, disproportionately solid. A man stepped quietly from boat to boat carrying a rope.

Helena said, almost too far from me to catch the words: "It doesn't look like a city built on water. It looks like a city built on air."

Neale propped his elbows on the broad roughened top of the balustrade. We looked out over the glittering water at the glittering buildings. "O, it's too beautiful to bear," Neale said. He hid his head in his hands.

Cynthia turned round and leaned her back against the balustrade. "Look at those ice-creams," she said. "I've never seen ones like that before."

I peered round. Coming along the path behind me were two girls, sucking melon-pink ices; a thick cylinder of water ice, shaped like a long thumb, held by a stick.

I heard Neale say: "Ha." He, too, turned round and leaned backwards.

"What's so funny?" Cynthia said.

"Nothing." Suddenly he said: "Do you know why all of us from the North have this urge towards Italy?"

"Because of the sunshine," Cynthia said, lazily. "We don't get much at home."

"Ah, but why do we want the sunshine?"

"It's natural. It's nicer."

"I'll tell you why," Neale said. "It's because in Italy

the summer just seems to go on and on. And that's what it seemed to do in one's childhood. So one comes to get one's childhood back."

After a moment, Cynthia giggled. "I don't want my childhood back."

"O you unique person," Neale said. "You'll end up as the prop and stay of some poor nostalgic man." He added: "George Girdler perhaps."

"Don't be silly," Cynthia said. "Actually, I don't remember much from being very small. But I wouldn't like to be at school again."

Neale asked: "What about you, Helena?"

Distantly her voice said: "I opt for the present. I just want it to go on like this."

"Ah, but it doesn't," he said. "One comes to Italy to get the illusion that it does."

"There may be something in your idea," said Helena.

Cynthia felt the balustrade behind her. "Isn't it a nuisance. It's too high to sit on."

"No it's not." Neale laid his hands flat on it and jumped himself up. He sat swinging his legs, his back to the sea.

I reached along behind Cynthia and put my hand just behind Neale, where he could not feel it.

"Well, it's too high for me," Cynthia said.

"And for me," said Helena's voice.

I looked over at the Salute, roundly urging itself towards the water, roundly rising up into the sky, like a perfectly shaped breast.

Neale said: "I'll tell you something else." His legs kicked up, projecting into the path beyond Cynthia. "Do you know why all Italian journeys must end in Venice?"

"They don't all," Cynthia said. "Some people——"

"Figurativement," said Neale. "It's because Venice is

235

built on water. Salt unsavoury water. It's warm and it's wet. And at its most most beautiful, it's dark."

Cynthia said: "It certainly is a very unusual place."

"Unusual? No, it's usual. It's so usual that it's the earliest thing any of us would remember, if we could allow ourselves to. It seems so exotic because we're not allowed to go there. But we do, of course, in fantasy." His voice became grave. "The only problem is, what to do when one's got here. Have you—I don't mean this personally—has anyone, ever, had a sexual experience that was as good as fantasy?"

After a silence, Cynthia said: "I think that's morbid."

"Ah, do you? You mainstay, you," he said. He squinted down at her. "And what does a canal remind *you* of?" Suddenly he hauled himself up. He was squatting on the balustrade. Then he stood up on it. Laughing, he began to run along the top, jumping over Helena's hands which were still resting there, clasped. "O, don't," she said. He laughed. Cynthia called: "You'll fall off. Get down at once."

He jumped neatly down.

He turned and stood facing us, some way from us up the path. He held his hands together, interlaced, just beneath his chin, like the strings of a bonnet. "Come on," he called. "Let's go and find those ice-creams."

"We don't want any," Helena said.

"I'll get up on the balustrade again."

"O, I'll come with you," Cynthia said. "Even though I don't want one. They don't look nice."

"That's just the word."

"You're not safe to be alone," she said as she went to him.

I watched them go, into the straggling crowd.

I felt Helena move up to join me. "Are you going to marry him?"

"I never know," I said, "from one moment to the next." I realized I was alone with her for the first time. I felt small beside her. I strained over the balustrade, my clenched hands making a lump against my chest. I looked down, deep into the shell of a boat. I asked: "Should I?"

"He's a nice boy. He will be, when he gets over the urge to épater."

"I don't think you count as the bourgeois."

"Cynthia does, perhaps."

"It wasn't aimed at her."

"She seems to have received it, though."

"At the moment," I said, "he's in love with you."

"O" she said quietly. "That's why he was going on about mother, so."

Presently I said: "I realize, now, I was jealous of you even that first time we met in Totobar."

"Uh-huh."

I asked: "Why did you come that day? Why did you let Cynthia bring you?"

"O—I had two reasons," Helena said. "One was that Cynthia had got all hot and bothered to pay me back for hospitality I'd given her. I thought I'd better let her buy me a coffee. But when I came, you all made me feel old."

"I'm sorry. What was the other reason?"

"O, Cynthia had told me you were clever."

"Really?" I said. "I didn't think she'd noticed."

"She went on about how clever you used to be at school. I must say, when I pressed her, she was a bit vague about exactly how. She said you were good at French."

"I was good at practically everything else."

I felt my forehead heavy from leaning over, and from the sun hitting the back of my neck. I stood up straight, and shook my head. Helena gave me a cigarette. She lit it, shielding her lighter, smiling at me. "You wouldn't

237

think there was so much wind. We are on the sea, after all." She lit her own, hollowing her cheeks, and pointed the cigarette for a moment into the air as she drew in the smoke. "I had a hunch, that day I came to Totobar, that you might be a person who could tell me something. Or teach me. Or transmit it in some way, if that's the word."

"I wonder what about."

"O, something on the lines of what Neale was saying. What's the secret of pure enjoyment. Is there any such thing. Can one ever, for a moment, live wholly in the present."

"Don't you get it from your music?" I said. "I get it when I listen to you. Or nearer to it then than at any other time."

"No," she said. "Music means the most to me, of course, in one way, because, so far as I know anything about anything, I know about music. But just because of that, if you see what I mean——" She looked out at the Salute. "In a way, I get it from looking at buildings. I seem to—o, forget myself, I suppose. You know, when one's eye seems to travel over the shape."

"Yes," I said, and we stood silent.

Behind us came Neale's voice. "I didn't get you any because you were so firm about it." We turned. He stood holding the ice in front of him. Deliberately he put his tongue out and licked the pink cylinder. He swallowed. "Perhaps after all it's more suitable for me than for you."

"Where's Cynthia?"

"O, she said would you excuse her, but it's nearly lunch-time anyway and she's gone back to the hotel to look out some clothes for tomorrow."

For a moment Helena looked afraid.

"I'll walk you back to your hotel," Neale said. "If you want to go now."

"Very well," Helena said. "Thank you."

We set off. I tried to drop back; Neale tried to let me; but Helena put her arm into mine and leaned her weight on me.

"All right," Neale said. "I'll ask you in public."

"What?"

"Will you come away with me? Helena?"

"It's an idea," she said. "Where to?"

"Anywhere in the world. Where would you like to go?"

She was silent for a moment. "It's an odd thing, but I have the feeling I'd like to see Provence again before I die." She turned to me. "Do you know Provence?"

"No."

"Well, why don't we——"

"I don't think Neale meant a trio," I said.

She looked at him. "O, you meant come away like that. I'm sorry I was slow on it. The answer's no, I'm afraid."

"I see," he said. "That's all there is to it."

"No," she said gently. "Friendship is an experience you shouldn't underestimate. It's not unpoetical, though there's not much poetry written about it."

"I'm not interested in it," Neale said.

We crossed the Piazza.

"I don't see why you shouldn't both come to Provence with me," Helena said. "If for any unaccountable reason you wanted Cynthia to come along, my car takes four. I'd like to shew you Aix."

We turned up the alley. "What's Aix like?" I said.

"Oh, it's a watering place, old, a bit decayed. Not unlike your Cheltenham. I seem to remember a big square, and plane trees, and sunlight, of course, and having breakfast in the square for some reason."

We stopped outside her hotel.

239

"It's a trick of the old and weary," she said, "to want to shew the world to someone else. Maybe that's why it's nice to have children. I wouldn't know. Maybe I really got acquainted with Cynthia so as to have someone to shew Venice to. You sort of renew your own impressions that way. Maybe when you're really jaded you can only enjoy someone else's enjoyment." She smiled at us. "Also, of course, it's always a pleasure to shew Europeans some corner of their own continent they don't know." She looked at each of us. "Are you coming to Provence?"

"No," Neale said.

"No, Helena," I said, "I can't. I haven't the money."

"Oh, now, look——" she began.

"You're too generous. I'm sorry to be bourgeois and Cynthia-like, but I couldn't let you."

"All right," she said. "Very well. Perhaps we'll go somewhere on a day trip."

Neale said suddenly: "God, it's got a glamour."

"What has?"

"O, that you should be rich. And American. It's so outlandish."

"I'm not all that rich. And not all that outlandish."

"O, but by my standards——"

"O, your standards. By your standards I'm just a cornucopia. That's rich and outlandish enough. But you won't believe I'm drying up." She moved into the hotel.

"Are you coming out this afternoon?" Neale called. "Or tonight? On the Piazza?"

"No. I don't think so."

He ran forward to her. "Helena. You're not——"

"No, I'm not. Don't worry," she said. She smiled at us both. "I know where you're staying. I'll contact you."

She came the next morning. We were dressed and just

going out to breakfast, locking our bedroom door. The landlady called us. We ran down the narrow, dingy stairs. Helena stood in the little cubicle of a hall, surrounded by the stained flowery wallpaper. I held my hands out as I went down to her, and for a moment she took them. "I have to go and get my photograph taken in Padua. Will you come?"

"Surely," I said.

"Can you drive?"

"I'm afraid not."

"I'll have to do it all myself," she said.

"I drive," Neale said.

She turned to him, smiling. "I'm afraid you're not invited. This is a ladies only trip, like going to the hairdresser."

"It doesn't become you to be arch," he said.

"No, I know it." She turned away. She asked me if I had breakfasted. "We'll buy something to eat in the car."

As I followed her out of the hotel, I turned back to Neale. "I won't go if you'd rather I didn't."

"Why should I?"

"Will you be——"

"I shall be *perfectly* all right," he said.

✴ XVII ✴

THE car was brought out to us in the Piazzale Roma. We stood beside it. Helena asked me: "Is it all right?"

It was medium-large, a metallic silver-green. Either it had no roof, or the roof was rolled down at the back where there was a fold of canvas. It was very new: but its shape belonged to the thirties; it was a roadster.

."It's wonderful," I said. "The only word is ritzy."

Helena smiled. She got into the driving seat and opened the other door for me. She stowed her handbag, a scarf and a pair of big leather gloves in the pocket beneath the dashboard. Starting the engine, she said: "I have a passion for fast cars—and nice, homely men."

We set off along the black, industrial road across the sea. Helena hoisted herself up in her seat and loosened the folds of her skirt. She began to drive with one hand, her elbow resting on the frame of the car. I looked at her. Her hair was flying. "O, it's going to be a lovely day," she said.

"Would you like something to eat?"

"Not yet. Do you."

I took out a roll.

"It's good to get out of Venice for a bit," Helena said. "Although this is certainly a miserable road. But when we get to the mainland it'll be fresher."

"It's fresher already."

"Does Venice make you homesick?" she asked.

"Not particularly. Why?"

"O, Philip was talking—last night—you'd almost think he'd heard what Neale was saying down by the Molo."

"I shouldn't have thought Philip had ideas like that."

"O, it wasn't *like* that. It was just that Venice apparently makes him think of home. I thought to myself Neale would have an explanation for that." She reached up and twisted the driving-mirror slightly. "No, Philip was saying it got him down after a bit, always hearing Italian round him, and only half understanding it, and having to think before he asked for a box of matches. And all the newspapers, he said, written in Italian. He went on about how he'd like to buy an evening paper on a warm evening in London. And how the newspaper sellers chalked their own placards to mislead you—The Queen: a surprise. And when you buy the paper you find she's gone on her vacation, or something, just as usual. Or Race-horse Owner in Dock. And you find a tiny paragraph on the back page, saying that someone who once bought a carthorse has been fined for parking it in the wrong place."

"There are little nests of offenders," I said. "All round Marble Arch they put up terribly scaring posters."

"There you are," she said. "You've got it, too. You're homesick."

I laughed. "No, I'm just susceptible to atmosphere. You and Philip between you built one up. Actually, I've no reason to think well of Marble Arch. I always remember walking round there and down Park Lane to a sort of employment place, where I had to go to get a job."

"Didn't you like that?"

"No. I was scared silly."

Helena nodded.

We came to the mainland.

"Well, we're out of Venice. Do you mind if we don't take the autostrada? I thought we might go on the country road. Would that be all right?"

"Yes, indeed," I said.

I settled down, and the winding white road half hypnotized me. We turned in and out beside the deep river. Eventually I asked Helena: "Does Venice make *you* homesick?"

It was a moment before she said: "O, it would. If I had a home."

"Where, actually, *do* you live?"

"O, everywhere. I have a place, you know, in England."

"Have you? Where?"

"Cumberland. I bought it because the country was so beautiful. I bet you've never even been there."

"No, I haven't. When are you coming to England again?"

"Sometime," she said. "Never. It's too cold. Part of the house is rented. I just have a bit of it, in case I wanted to go there. I have a sort of secretary-housekeeper who lives in it and takes care of things for me. And then I have a place—well, it's not mine, but it's a place I can go—in Paris. And—my ex-husband lives in Kentucky."

We drove on.

"Let's have a cigarette," she said. "They're in there." She tapped the bevelling of the dashboard. "Would you light me one?"

I put it into her mouth.

"It's funny," she said. "Although it all ended so messily—and so soon—we divorced after two years— I still feel a sort of romance if I think of it. I look back on myself, you know—as a bride."

"Yes. Of course."

"Oh, I wasn't really the girl, you know, for tripping up the aisle looking cute in white. I was even a little taller than the groom."

"Was he a nice homely man?" I asked.

"No. No, he wasn't. Perhaps it was the scare I got from him that put me on to nice homely men. Anyway, although I wasn't the type, I got through it all right. I gave a performance. I didn't fall over my dress or anything." She looked out of the side of the car. "This is Strà. Have you been to the palace here?"

"The Villa Pisani? Yes."

"We won't stop then. I like it, though."

"So do I." We drove past the long stone blocks of the entrance lodge, with their twisted giant caryatids; and then along beside the stone wall, with the occasional iron gates giving us a glimpse of the deep park beyond. "Were you married in white, after all?"

"O yes. I was married in London—didn't I tell you? I happened to be singing there, at the time. So we had all the trimmings. A June wedding." She added: "It rained like hell."

"Of course it did."

"As you say, of course it did. We came out of the church and just stood there on top of the steps, looking at it. Then we made a dash for the car. I was scared all the time the hem of my dress would get muddy on the pavement. I don't know why I was so worried, since I wasn't ever going to use it again."

"What flowers did you have?"

"O, roses."

"Yes, of course," I said.

"I told them yellow, because I didn't think I was the girl for pink. But they got pink. I was mad." She threw her cigarette out of the car. "Now tell me about yourself."

"About myself? What?"

245

"Oh, anything that comes to mind, as the psycho-analysts or psychiatrists or whatever they are say. Or no, don't do that. I'd probably get your dreams or your earliest memories, or something. I always feel sorry for the psychoanalysts. I can't think of anything more boring than people who tell you their dreams and their earliest memories."

"Nor can I."

"Go ahead and tell me something else, then."

"I could tell you about Neale. And Cynthia."

"That sounds fine, for a start."

"I've never really wanted to tell anyone before," I said. "At least, I have. There was a woman who used to teach me at school. I wanted to tell her."

"And didn't you?"

"She wouldn't—or couldn't—let me. I would have liked to be friends with her. But something held her back."

"Some people are inhibited," Helena said.

"Yes. She had some inhibition."

"Well, go ahead and talk to me," Helena said. "I have no inhibitions."

"O yes you have."

"Yes I have. Go ahead and tell me all the same."

We drove into Padua, and Helena parked the car in a square outside a restaurant. "Isn't it a funny little town? I never know whether I really like it or not. Anyway, there are far too many bicycles."

I pointed into the pocket under the dashboard, where there was still a paper bag full of rolls. "We can hardly take them into the restaurant."

"Leave them there, and let's hope somebody steals them. You didn't have much appetite."

"I can't eat many rolls." I didn't move from the car.

"Why do you have to come to Padua to have your photograph taken?"

"O, they want it in a hurry, to go in a catalogue or a publicity hand-out for a recording."

"Have you made a new recording?"

"No, they're just putting some of the old ones on to long-play." She stepped stiffly out.

"But why Padua?" I said.

"You mean why not Venice? Well, I've been to this man in Padua before—a long time ago. I don't know any of the people in Venice."

"Do you hate having your photograph taken?"

"Yes. Let's draw our lunch out as long as we can. That'll give him time for his siesta and me time to compose myself."

I got out of the car. "Why do you hate it?"

"O, I don't know. Makes me self-conscious, I suppose." She walked ahead of me, a little stridingly, into the restaurant.

We stepped along small, crowded pavements, in the sun; under arcades out of the sun but hardly cooler. Helena had to lead the way, but I was taking her, and whenever the crowds did not knock us apart she leaned on my arm. "Incidentally," she said, "where do *you* live?"

"Nowhere. That's my answer to your living everywhere."

She halted. "Haven't you an address." Someone pushed into us.

"It is amusing, the way you say *add*ress. Well, there's a girl called Tanya. We left our things at her flat, so I suppose that's our address."

"Would you give it me." Helena asked. She opened her handbag and tore a thin leaf of lined paper out of a diary or a note-book. She gave me the bag to hold, while she pressed the paper against the wall and wrote down Tanya's address. The pencil lines appeared: thick, and intermittent, like a flagged path, where the cast of the stone pushed through.

"Do you really want it, or are you just using up time?"

"I never do that," she said quickly, "even when I am scared. No, I thought I might want to write to you some time."

"Good," I said.

She folded the paper and took her handbag from me. We walked on.

"I shall have to go home soon," I said.

"Have you got tickets?"

"Not for any particular date. But the money's running out."

"Are you flying?"

"O no. Rail and sea. That's all the agency would give us."

"Will you get another job, back in England?"

"I shall have to."

"Mm." she said. "I shall be leaving Venice soon, too."

"Why?"

"O, I get the urge, you know." She led me into the photographer's. It was low built and cramped, with a wooden lintel. Helena had to stoop as she went through. I caught sight of the small shop window as we passed it: draped in shiny, striped taffeta, with framed photographs standing about on it, portraits of young men in army uniform, and full-length pictures of first communicants, little girls in long white dresses, little boys in white suits with rosettes, standing sometimes in pairs and looking like sugar figures on the top of a wedding cake.

Inside, there was a carpeted box: a reception room. A small ornamental chair, with gilt stick-like legs, stood against the wall. The latch of the front door rang a bell as we closed it. A girl came. Helena introduced herself. The girl went to the back of the shop, and descended some stairs. Helena took out her comb and began to pull at her hair.

Stooping, the photographer himself made his way up the stairs: a short, young, rather pretty-faced man. "Ah, I am so glad," he said. He indicated Helena's comb. "You have plenty time for that, downstairs."

"O yes," she said. She stood holding it. The photographer smiled, and stood back for her.

I took the comb from her.

"This is a friend," she said, "that I brought along to hold my hand."

"Yes," the photographer said. "Pleased to meet you. You come down to the studio now?"

There were three stone steps down. He reached his hand out in advance of us. "Excuse me. I light the light." He pulled the switch down.

We were in a cellar: so I judged by the stone floor. The walls were hung with white sheets, roughly draped. At one side, a curtain on a rail stood pulled back, and I could see a dressing-table inside, with sticks of make-up lying on it.

In the middle of the floor stood a throne. The photographer indicated that Helena should sit there.

"And the friend," he said. "She sit down"—he pulled up a wooden kitchen chair for me—"behind the machine. Behind my back. So. Then she say something to make you smile."

Helena and I sat down, opposite one another, separated by four or five yards.

The camera was a brown wooden box, long, old-looking, with a front that pulled out like a gas-mask. The photographer pushed it towards Helena, tipping the tripod along from one foot to another. He halted it, and pulled the black cloth over his head like a beekeeper's veil.

Helena stooped to put her handbag down beside the throne; then she picked it up again and set it on her lap. "I don't know what to do with my bag."

"Is all right," the photographer said, under the black cotton. "It doesn't matter. Just try to relax." He came out. "We get some background," he said. He went round behind Helena and disappeared into the sheet hanging in front of the wall.

Helena sat stiff on the throne.

He came out again, pushing the sheet with him. He hooked it loose, and began to edge out a tall, folded screen. It was green, covered in a miniature, rather Persian-looking, pattern of leaves, branches and blossoms, with occasional blue peacocks and parrot-like birds with long tails, perching, each about three inches high.

Manœuvring it as if it was in some way human, he got the screen into place behind Helena's throne, and opened out its wings into a semicircle.

He ran back to the camera, and under cloth again. "Is better. Now we have some light."

He pushed a lamp to Helena's side, adjusted its angle and turned a wheel. The stem lengthened. The tilted shade towered above the throne, the naked bulb pointing at Helena.

He switched it on.

I saw Helena's eyes water. She looked down.

The photographer came back, into the camera cloth again. "Don't look so sad," he said. "We want a happy picture. Look at your friend and laugh."

Helena tried to look up. "It's this damn light," she said. "It's like being grilled by the Communists."

Immediately the light fizzled and went out.

The ordinary lighting of the cellar was dim by comparison.

Neatly, the photographer held his finger up to Helena. "Uh. You said Communist to it. That is a naughty word. I get another light."

He hurried across to the dressing-table and began pulling out the drawers. I saw electric-light bulbs rolling about in the spilt powder. He brought one out, dusted it, lowered the lamp, fitted it: he switched on: no light came. "O-o-oh," he said, and shrugged. "I have to go out and get another. You excuse me? I try not to be long."

"That's all right," Helena said.

For a moment after his departure, she sat still on the throne. Then "How long do you think he's gone for?" she said. "Long enough for a cigarette?"

"Don't you think this place is full of inflammable stuff? I mean, film and photographic chemicals and so on."

She opened her handbag. "Let's break the rules."

She lit our cigarettes.

"It's rather a nice screen, isn't it?"

"I wonder what's behind it," she said. "Behind the curtain, I mean, where he got it from." She got up, turned back the screen and parted the curtains. I peered round her shoulders. "You can't see much," I said.

She lit her cigarette lighter and held it out, between the curtains. There was a small recess, which seemed to be piled with silk and screens.

"I'm sure all this is inflammable, anyway."

"O well," she said, "if we burn his shop down, we'll just have to pay for it."

"Neale's right. You are glamorously wealthy."

"To be as wealthy as a photographer in Padua? O, I don't think that's aiming too high." She pointed down at a corner of the recess. "What's that?"

I went on to my hands and knees and crawled beneath the curtain. "It seems to be a pillar. Or a bit of one." Holding my cigarette in one hand, I tried to roll the pillar out. Helena held the curtain up, to give me light. "Lift it," she said. "It won't be heavy."

I tried. It was made of cardboard. I carried it out into the light and set it down near the throne. It was made to represent part of a classical column, broken off. It stood on a square base, and the fluting was painted in with grey paint. Some ivy leaves had been painted on the irregular top, trailing down one side. It was naturalistically and clumsily done; but from a distance, or beneath a strong light that cast deep shadows, it would have made its classical effect.

Helena looked at it. "Heavens."

She went behind the curtain again.

I touched the pillar, tilted it, tapped it. "It's got something," I said towards the curtains, "simply because it is cardboard. I mean, it's not so much a thing as a motif."

"How do you mean?" her voice said from the dark.

"O, it's a trapping. Pierrot in love with the moon."

"Here are some real trappings for you." Her hand came through the curtains, jangling a wreath of roses, some paper, some silk, with dark green leaves of canvas, all tangled up together. She shook them; one silk one fell on to the floor.

She tossed the others back, and picked up the fallen one.

I said: "Why don't you have your photograph taken with it?"

"O, I'm no good for wearing flowers. I'm not feminine enough." She held it out to me. "You wear it."

I took it. "Where? Behind my ear? Between my teeth?"

"Now don't be silly," she said.

"How repressive you can be."

"No I'm not. But I meant you to wear it seriously."
She pushed it through the lapel of my dress. "It suits
you. Leave it there."

She sat down again on the throne, but now she leaned
back, her knees apart. I rested my wrists on the column.
"You know what you said to Neale about underestimating
friendship?"

"Yes?"

"I was just thinking I've never experienced it."

"Now you're being silly again," she said. "I'm sure
you have. I'm sure you're a very warm-hearted person."

"No. I've been in love, or acquainted with people
because I wanted to use them in some way, or I've hated
them. I hated you at first." After a pause I said: "How
odd. It was only a day or two ago that Neale was asking
me to sound Philip to find out if he was your lover."

"Did he ask you to do that?"

"Yes."

"He's not, you know. I mean Philip isn't."

"No, I know."

"I reckon you were impatient with people," Helena
said. "That's why you weren't friends with them. You
wanted them to give you something, always."

"I suppose that's it."

"Whereas, in fact, if you don't look for it, you often
get given things. Still, it's natural to be impatient when
you're young."

"I once told Neale I could stand anything but a status
quo."

"And now," Helena said, "one would give anything
for a status quo. If only it would last. What were you and
Neale really looking for?"

"A moment," I said, "that should be immortal. A
moment to set up against those moments when you wake
in the night and realize—o, that Venice will crumble

into the sea one day, and that even before that you'll be dead yourself."

Helena nodded. "O, those moments in the night," she said. "When they come on me now, I just say to myself: Well, you know now. You're going to die. That's all there is to it."

I looked at her, smiling, over my pillar. "O Helena, I do like you."

"That's a good thing." She gathered herself robustly in her chair. "Because I like you."

"I wonder why?"

"Why?" she said. "O, sympathy of some sort. Tu sei molto simpatica."

"Everyone is in Italy," I said. "It's worse than mamma. Perhaps you've seen the flaw in my personality, and your imagination has made its way in."

"Have you seen the flaw in mine?" she asked.

"Some of it. A little crack. It's why one likes you."

After a moment, we heard the photographer's footsteps. "Stub out your cigarette," Helena whispered.

He came in, carrying a paper parcel. "I am so sorry—Ah, you have found my column. You have found my roses."

"May we keep one of them?" Helena asked.

"But of course. Would you like us to make the picture of you with the column? You hold a rose?"

"No," Helena said. "Certainly not. It'll do right here."

He fitted the new bulb and put on the light. Helena winced. "And now—one last thing." He approached her, and knelt at the foot of the throne. He reached up and began rouging her cheeks, filling in the hollows at the side. She moved slightly, like a dummy, under his pressure. He added some brown grease-paint to the eyebrow pencil she already wore, and she blinked as he did it.

Awkward, she sat in the throne, scowling a little against the light, while he took the pictures.

"That is all," he said. "I have finished."

She got up. "Thank God. Look, if I give you the address, could you send the proofs to me in Vienna?"

"Certainly I could."

We walked back to the car. When we got in, Helena took her powder compact out of her handbag. "I want to get this stuff off my cheeks. You look somewhere else. I don't like to look at my face when there's anyone else there."

I looked out of the side of the car. "Why do you want the proofs to go to Vienna?"

"Because I'm going there. I thought I'd go and see some old friends, and then I might go on to Salzburg. I'd like to hear some Mozart well done before I die. It'll be odd to be in the audience."

"Write and tell me about it," I said.

"O, I will. You won't· come with me? You and Neale?"

"No, I can't."

"No, right. I'll send you a report on the music. A pretty pernicketty one, I daresay. I'm hard to satisfy nowadays. I've got something else for you than that, though."

"What?"

"A sort of present. Something I'd like you to have Now I know your address, I can wire my housekeeper-cum-secretary and get her to send it you in London."

"You won't say what it is?"

She started the car. "You may have a use for it," she said. "Or you may not. It doesn't matter if not. Don't feel I'd mind."

"When are you leaving for Austria?"

"Soon." She smiled at me. "I've driven quite far on

my own today, haven't I? I reckon if I take it in easy stages, stopping, you know, at little places in the mountains, I can make it."

"You're not going to take Philip, then?"

"No, that's part of the idea. I'm going to give Philip a rest."

On the drive home, we stopped at Strà. We went into an inn, and had dinner in the courtyard in the evening coolness. Helena said: "Why don't we stay the night?"

"Don't you want to drive any further?"

"Not much. Would you mind?"

"No. I could ring Neale, I suppose."

"You do that. And I'll send this wire. I'll ask the proprietor if he has rooms."

After we had engaged them, we went out to the car. Children were scrambling over it. Helena got in, and drove it into the courtyard of the inn. I walked after her. I got the paper bag of rolls out. "That's all our luggage," Helena said. "Will you be all right?" I nodded. "Let's find the phone," she said.

There was a box in the hall of the hotel. Helena went in and sent her telegram. She came out and held open the door for me. I asked: "You wouldn't get through for me, would you?"

"Surely."

She came out again, holding the receiver towards me. I went in, and she shut the door behind me.

"Neale? Are you all right?"

"Yes, of course."

"We're going to stay at Strà. Helena doesn't want to drive any more."

"Yes. I don't mind."

"We'll be back early tomorrow."

"Well, you'll probably find me here."

"Yes. I'll come straight to the pensione."

"O, take your time."

I said: "What have you been doing all day?"

"O, wandering round. I ran into Philip and Cynthia."

"How was her screen test?"

"No good."

"Can they tell? So soon?"

He laughed. "They didn't bother to look, even. Girdler just apologized and said she wasn't the sort of actress he'd thought she was."

"O Lord. It's probably our fault."

"I'm not taking any blame," he said.

"I hope you were nice to her."

"I wasn't nasty."

"What will you do this evening?"

"Wander round, I daresay. I expect Cynthia will want to go to bed and mourn. I might have a bachelor night out with Philip."

"Don't sound so bitter, Neale."

"I'm not," he said.

I told Helena about Cynthia's screen test. She shook her head.

My room was a whitewashed attic. The ceiling sloped down to a square window, with a narrow, wooden window-seat.

I lay in bed naked beneath a sheet. I could see the basin and ewer on the table. The maid had told me that all the water came from the well in the courtyard. She had brought it up, and I had washed; it was cold and pale brown.

I could see through the window the trees of the courtyard with stars behind them.

Helena came into my room. "I'm not going to say I couldn't sleep. It just seemed too good to waste." She sat down on the window seat. "I had to put my dress on to come. I guess they wouldn't like me to run round the corridors with nothing on."

She threw me a cigarette. I saw her light her own. Then she threw her lighter on to the bottom of my bed.

She leaned out of the window. "I can smell horse dung and lime trees."

She smoked, then stubbed her cigarette out on the window-ledge and threw it into the courtyard.

"All this about finding the moment," she said.

"Yes?"

"There's nothing in the world but people, is there?"

"No, nothing. How do you mean?"

"Well, like what you said about imagination and sympathy. People find their way into one another's personalities. You give to one person, take from another —give and take vitality, I mean. But nobody has all the vitality. Nobody is a reservoir. It's just an exchange. It goes round in an endless cycle."

"I suppose so," I said.

"Just as one gets one's vitality, in the first place, from one's mother's body. Just as I should have liked to pass it on to a child of my own."

"Yes."

She sat for some time perfectly still. She got up, said Good night, and went.

✶ XVIII ✶

WE took the vaporetto back from the Piazzale Roma to San Marco. I saw Helena to her hotel; then I walked round to the pensione. I went up to our bedroom. The maid was just coming out, carrying a long brush; she wished me Buon giorno.

Neale was not there. I lay down on my bed and smoked.

He came in at about half-past eleven. He looked tired. In his lapel he was wearing the shabby silk rose which Cynthia had given me underneath the stage at school. He looked at me and said: "Ho, you've got one too."

"Yes. How are you?"

"Fine. Did you have fun at Strà?"

"We stayed at rather a nice place."

"Good."

I said: "You look a bit worn. Did you go on the town with Philip?"

"No," he said. Then: "I slept with Cynthia."

"O. I see."

"Well?"

"Well what?" I asked: "Are you glad about it?"

"Quite. Why shouldn't I be?"

"No reason at all. Is she glad?"

"I imagine so. I didn't ask her."

I said: "Where?"

"Where? O, at her hotel. It was funny, there were no

difficulties at all. I just went up to her room. And came down again next day."

"There's no point in asking why?"

"Why? O, well she was fed-up, I suppose, at not getting a job with Girdler."

"Yes, but why did you?"

"Me? She told me to, I suppose."

I nodded. I lit another cigarette. "It's funny how it seems to seal two people up together, so that one's imagination can't approach them."

"I suppose it does."

"If you're glad about it," I said, "you've no reason to be ashamed with me."

"I'm not ashamed."

"You seem on edge. I thought you might think you'd treated me badly."

"You? O no. I've treated you better than I've ever treated anyone."

"Have you?"

"Yes, of course. I kept you travelling hopefully, didn't I? Isn't that the kindest thing one can do for anyone?" He walked over to the mantelpiece and played with the model châlet, opening and shutting its front door.

I said, "You'll probably break it if you force it like that."

"O, one can't always wait for the weather." He turned the châlet upside down. "Is it true that women always want to marry men they've slept with?"

I said: "I don't know. I should think some do, some don't. It's probably as true as any of the ideas you can pick up from women's magazines. Does Cynthia want to marry you?"

"She's told me to marry her."

"Do you mean you're going to?"

"Yes."

"O. That does alter things."

"Yes," he said.

"Neale, is all this serious? I mean, it's not just one of those engagements——"

"No, quite serious. I've written to my parents."

"*Why* are you doing it?" I said.

"Cynthia's rather tired of trying to start a career that's obviously not going to get anywhere. She'd like to settle down. And have children."

"Yes, I quite see that. You'll have to get a job, I suppose? A proper job?"

"Yes. When we get back to England. I shall do what's called going into business." He put the châlet down. "This object embodies everything I most hate about life."

I said: "I wonder what life with Cynthia will be like when she hasn't even got the slight glamour of films about her."

"Quiet, I expect," he said. "My quietus."

"Neale, do you mean you've given up the search?"

He turned and smiled at me. "O, but we were searching for Cynthia, weren't we? And now I've found her."

"No," I said. "We were searching long before I told you about her."

"But possibly *you* were searching for her," he said, "without knowing it."

"No, I was searching even before I knew her at school. In fact, that's why I came to know her."

"O well, in that case," he said, "yes. I have given up. Come on, let's go to lunch."

In the trattoria, I said to him: "Now you've sealed yourselves up in an official engagement, this is an unforgivable question. But you're not in love with her, are you?"

He smiled and hesitated. "No. No, I'm not. But at the

back of my mind I have the faintest feeling—as if I had, once, been in love with her."

I said: "You really have adopted my past."

"Have I? What did you want me to adopt—your future?"

"My present."

"Isn't it amusing of English that that should be a pun? But, you see, the things you give people really depend on what they have the power to accept. And I can only take your past." He smiled. "It's your wedding present."

He paid, and we rose to go.

"I'm meeting Cynthia under the Campanile," he said.

"O."

"I'm taking her to the Lido. Coming?"

"No. I'll go back and lie down for a bit."

I slept deeply for two hours. The maid woke me, coming in to turn down the beds. I told her I wouldn't be a moment; she waited outside; I saw her, and she smiled at me, as I went out.

I wandered for a little and went into a church. Someone was in the confessional, and a verger walked up and down staring at me. I came out. Although I was not lost, I panicked at finding myself alone in Venice, and I hurried to Helena's hotel. I was told both she and Philip were out. I went back to the pensione. Philip was waiting in the flowery hall. "I've brought you a note from Helena."

"May I open it now?"

"Yes, do. Please." He turned aside while I read it.

Sorry to be so abrupt, but you know how it is. I'm off this afternoon. I got the wanderlust and I don't want to keep P. hanging around. I'll send you a postcard from the mountains if I get the chance, and in any case I'll write properly when I arrive. Regards to N. Best love— Helena.

262

"So she's off," Philip said. "I hope it will be all right."

"She said she was going to friends."

"Yes. From the old days, you know. She went in a great hurry. She'd hardly let me come down to the garage to say good-bye." He smiled at me. "Well, how are you? It seems a long time since I saw you. I haven't told you about Cynthia's screen test, have I?"

"I gather it was a failure."

"She was upset, I think. Is she all right today, do you know? I haven't seen her today."

I told him about Cynthia and Neale.

He said: "O. Do you mind? Do you mind my asking?"

"I don't mind your asking. I do mind about Neale, rather."

"I thought you did. I'm awfully sorry." After a moment, he added: "One thing I'm sure of. Helena would never have gone off just at this moment, if she'd known."

"No, I'm sure she wouldn't," I said. "But I'm glad she did. I don't want to lean on her too heavily."

"No," he said.

The four of us had coffee together, after dinner, in the Piazza. I gave Cynthia my congratulations. She giggled slightly and said: "Yes, it is rather exciting, isn't it?"

"Very, I should imagine."

She smiled at me frankly. "It's nice to be with friends, at a moment like this. Really old friends, I mean." She glanced over the table. "No offence, Philip. I count you as an old friend."

"Well, old, yes," he said, smiling. "But I was hardly at school with you." He said to Neale: "What are you two—you and Cynthia—thinking of doing? I mean, will you go straight home?"

"Cynthia wants to stay on for a bit."

"Well, now we're here," she said. "We might as well have a holiday. Don't you think, Philip?"

"It seems a first-rate idea."

"One thing," Cynthia said. "If we can find anywhere that can take us, we'll move over to the Lido. It seems silly to have to go over there every day, and then come back again."

Neale said to me: "You can have the room in the pensione to yourself at last."

"Yes," I said. "But I think I'll go home."

Philip turned to me. "Look, I've got an air ticket. A spare one, I mean. Milan London."

"Helena's?"

"Yes. She thought she'd be going to England. I'm sure we could get it transferred to your name."

"O no," I said. "You'd better sell it. The money belongs to Helena."

"She wanted you to have the ticket. She said she knew you weren't looking forward to the journey home. She said I was to try and make you accept it."

I asked when it was for.

"Day after tomorrow," Philip said. "You won't mind travelling with me?"

"No, of course——"

Neale said: "You take it. Then Cynthia can have your railway tickets, and we can come home at our leisure."

I said: "All right. Thank you, Philip. It's very nice of Helena."

"It's all fitted in very neatly," Neale said.

"Yes," Cynthia said, "hasn't it?"

As we lay in our beds that night, Neale said to me: "Shall I tell you the whole tragedy of life? By the time you find out it's mamma you want, she's too old."

I said nothing.

"Don't you agree?" he said.

"Let's try to go to sleep."

We circled, gently losing height. I leaned back in my chair so that Philip, straining at his safety-belt, could lean past me and look down through the window.

"At least it seems to be good weather in London," he said.

We dropped nauseatingly.

Philip said: "O God, I wish she could get better."

"What do you mean?" I said.

We ran along, low above the ground. I felt a touch, a slight rebound; through the window I saw the big rubber tyres begin to spin as we landed. Philip said: "Didn't she tell you she was dying?"

The passengers began to move, taking their coats from the rack, even before the plane stopped. I followed Philip out and across the airfield; through passport control; through the Customs, where the officer questioned Philip and then marked my luggage through with his. We went out, into the bus, and found places on the upper half-deck.

"I don't know whether she told me or not."

"I gather that whether she did or not, you didn't understand?"

"I don't know whether I understood."

We arrived at the air terminal at Waterloo, and collected our luggage. "I'm going to take the tube," Philip said. "Are you?"

"I may as well."

He picked up the two heaviest suit-cases, one of his and one of mine, and led the way. "Is Waterloo quite convenient for you?"

"Fairly, yes."

"I go through on the Northern Line," he said. "I live in Hampstead."

"Philip, could you lend me some money?"

"Yes, of course. How much?"

"I don't know. I was thinking. If I could get a seat on the plane I might fly to Vienna. Straight away."

"I might come with you. Do you think she'd mind if I turned up?"

"I'm sure not."

He carried the cases across the road and set them down on the pavement. "We'd better go back to the air place and fix it up. I can give them a cheque."

Outside the tube station, there were three newsvendors. On a blank sheet of paper, each had chalked himself a headline. Two were about the T.U.C. The third read: Singer Dies on Travels.

Philip said: "They're often misleading, you know. They do it to make you buy——"

"I know." I felt in my handbag for two pennies.

"I'll get it," he said. He bought the paper, and stood looking down the front page. He paused, near the bottom. "I'm afraid it is." He showed me a paragraph of three or four lines, saying Helena had collapsed at a country hotel in the mountains, not many miles short of Vienna; she had been taken to a hospital and had died there.

Philip asked: "Would you like me to stay with you a bit?"

"No, not for me. Would you?"

"No, I think I'll get home, if you're all right. Are you coming on the tube?"

"Not just now. I must ring up Tanya and see if anyone's there to let me in."

"Can you manage your cases?"

"Yes."

We said good-bye.

I carried my luggage into a phone box and rang Tanya. There was no reply. I walked through to the main-line station and put my cases in the left luggage office. I took the tube to Tottenham Court Road. I came out, and walked up the road past the cinemas. At the last one I came to, almost next door to the one that had been shewing it when I left, Tosca was playing. I looked at the stills outside. A notice in the foyer said Last Day. I walked back again to Oxford Street, and took a seventy-three; I sat on top and found I was pressing my finger-nails into the ball of muscle at the base of my thumb. I got off at Marble Arch, went down into the tube and found an empty phone box. I looked up the number, and rang my dentist.

The nurse answered.

I asked if I could have an appointment at once.

"Is it urgent? Are you in actual pain?"

"No. That's the trouble."

"I don't quite see what you mean."

"I haven't been for some time. There's bound to be something that needs doing, isn't there?"

"If it's just a check-up," she said, "I'm afraid I can't book you for at least a week. We're terribly full. I've got a space for next Friday."

"I'll leave it. It was only an idea."

I came out by the exit on the edge of the Park. I walked round the curve, past the bus queues. There were several newsvendors, one with the headline: Singer Dead in Mountains. I bought another copy of the same paper. The paragraph had been moved from the front page. I found it, curtailed, in the centre pages. I went into the Park and put the paper in a rubbish bin.

I crossed the road, walked a little way down Park Lane and turned left. I went up to the d'Arcy Appointments

Bureau. I was not quite sure that it was the same Miss d'Arcy who received me; but she said:

"Yes, I remember. Wait a moment. Didn't we fix you up with a bookseller?"

"That's right."

"Wasn't he satisfactory?"

"He folded up."

"O, I'm sorry to hear that. We'll have to find you something else, won't we."

"I'd like something a bit more serious this time. Something that offers more of a career."

She looked through her card-index box. "You're in luck. I've actually got two publishers who want secretaries."

She began to type. "Aren't we having wonderful weather?"

I looked round. The room was full of sun. "O. Yes."

She gave me the piece of paper. "There you are. I've never heard of the first one, I'm afraid, but the second is a very good firm. I'm sure you'd enjoy working there."

I looked at the two addresses. The first was in E.C.4: the firm which published *The Lady Revealed*. I said: "I'll try the second. I'll go along there now."

"I hope you get fixed up all right," she said.

I carried my luggage in from the taxi and rang Tanya's doorbell.

"Well, well, well," she said. "Fancy seeing you."

"I came rather suddenly. I rang earlier but you weren't in."

She picked up my cases, and took them through. "Lovely to see you at any time."

As I followed her through the hall, I saw a glossy postcard with a photograph of a mountain under snow.

It lay, picture up, on the table. I turned it over. It was for me. Helena had written diagonally across the correspondence square: "All well so far. Will write properly when I arrive."

I followed Tanya into the bedroom.

"Well," she said. "I'm glad you came. I'm going away, and I didn't like to leave because I had your things. I'm all packed up, as you can see." She pointed to the corner. Her suit-cases were standing beside mine.

"I couldn't have your flat, could I?"

"Do you want it? I should think you could have it."

"How much is it?"

"Three pounds a week."

"I could manage that. I've just got a new job," I said.

"Have you? There's not much room here, of course. There's only one bed."

"O, Neale won't be coming."

"Have you split?"

"Yes. He's getting married."

"My poor dear. Still, you've got plenty of other fish to fry. You'll have to start looking out all those old letters you've got and ringing the boys up."

"Yes."

"Will you be responsible for Neale's things?" she asked. "Will you get them back to him?"

"Yes, all right."

"I think everything's okay. I played some of your records. Did you mind?"

"No."

"Well, you could unpack if you'd like. I've emptied the chest of drawers."

"Right. Thank you."

I pulled out the deepest drawer.

"That's right," Tanya said. "Start at the bottom."

I got out the box of letters and put it into the drawer.

Out of my handbag I took the rose from the photographer's in Padua. I dropped it in.

"O, you've brought the rose back," Tanya said.

"No. It's a replacement."

"You've obviously had quite a holiday."

I put Helena's postcard in.

"O, you got your postcard. It came yesterday. It made me wonder if you'd be home soon. Did you see the parcel?"

"What parcel?"

"I put it under the table in the hall. It came this morning. It's a bit dark in there—you probably didn't see."

She went out and came back with a shallow oblong parcel. "Were you expecting it?"

"Yes. It's a present."

"Birthday? Or are you getting married too?"

"No."

"Something for your bottom drawer, then," Tanya said.

I knelt on the floor, with the drawer open beside me, and made no move towards the parcel. Tanya put it down on the bed. "O well. I'll go and make some supper. If I'd known to expect you, I'd have run up something special. I'm quite good, you know," she called from the corridor.

I pulled the parcel down and unwrapped it. Inside there was a cardboard box. I took off the lid. There was a fold of tissue paper with a card lying on it. Above the printed name Helena Buchan, Helena's secretary had typed the words 'with the compliments of'.

I turned back the tissue.

Inside there was something lace. At first I thought it was coffee-coloured; then I saw it was only a little faded, the effect increased by the poor light in Tanya's room.

I pulled it out. I pushed Tanya's bed to one side and spread the lace on the floor. It was a wedding dress, cut in a fashion of the late twenties or early thirties, with a square neck and no waist, and made for a woman much bigger than I was. It lay, front upward, on the floor. The front of the skirt was cut short; I guessed the white stockings must have shown, and the white buttoned shoes. The back hem protruded beyond it. Along its inside edge there was an irregular, thin band which reminded me of the shading we had used to pencil in, in geography lessons at school, to mark the coast on our maps: a narrow line, quite blanched now of any dirtiness, which shewed where the bride had run across the rainy pavement towards the temporary shelter of the bridal car.

☆ AFTERWORD ☆

The King of a Rainy Country is my second novel and third book.

I took its title from the poem by Charles Baudelaire which Neale quotes in the first chapter. The poem is in *Les Fleurs du Mal* and it opens with the line "Je suis comme le roi d'un pays pluvieux".

By choosing to write a work of fiction in the first person I enabled myself to write autobiography or fake-autobiography or, as *The King of a Rainy Country* in fact is, both.

There might easily have been a real-life model for Cynthia or for Philip or for Helena Buchan. There was none. All three are created, sometimes lovingly, by my imagination.

Even Miss Falconbridge, the sympathetic teacher, is invented. She bears the surname of the Bastard in Shakespeare's *King John* because, when she could have been, she isn't in the colloquial sense a bastard.

Neale, however, is a tolerably accurate portrait of a real person. And, in so far as she feels much that I felt towards the original of Neale, Susan is a cut-down version of me.

Indeed, that is why I called her Susan.

My mother brought me up to believe (and my father did not contradict) that my initials were B. A. S. B. and my name was Brigid Antonia Susan Brophy. Only some bureaucracy in connection with my marriage obliged me to ask my mother to find various certificates. From them I discovered that I was registered twelve days after my birth as Brigid Antonia. The Susan was tacked on later, at my baptism.

It seemed therefore an apt name for the rather stunted self-portrait I put into *The King of a Rainy Country*.

My mother, who was born in Chicago, Illinois, and brought up in Liverpool, Merseyside, and who had both U.S. and British nationality until for practical reasons she formally renounced her U.S. citizenship during the 1939–45 war, herself had a forename which few people in England could spell or, if they saw it written, pronounce. Her parents belonged to a Christian sect that designed itself to die out and is now, I think, defunct. Her father became the sect's equivalent of bishop of Liverpool. Each of his four children, of whom there were two of each sex, was called by an English transliteration of a noun in ancient Greek. My mother and her younger sister were Charis and Ion. As Greek nouns "charis" can be translated as a grace and "ion" means a violet, so I imagine that as names Charis and Ion were intended to be equivalents to the English names Grace and Violet.

My father, who was born in Liverpool of parents born in Ireland, was clearly the person who wanted me to be named and spelt Brigid. The spelling is fairly common in Ireland, but in my sixty years' residence in England there has been scarcely a week when I have not received a letter — or worse, a review — calling me by the English spelling Bridget or some Swedish–German–French–Irish hybrid.

My mother taught me and then most of the adults who came into contact with me to spell Brigid correctly.

Which of my parents proposed Antonia I don't know — or why. My mother told me that, while she laboured and suffered on a day in June in London to give me birth, a nurse put some artificial roses on her pillow because it was a flag day called Alexandra Rose Day.

I don't dislike Antonia, but I should have preferred Alexandra. Still, I now have a granddaughter whose second forename is Rose.

I conjecture that to my mother, although she consented

274

to them, my first two forenames seemed to present strangers with much the same difficulties as her own forename. I think it was she who tried to spare me the problems which met her by having me baptized (not in one of the sect's London churches but in an Anglican parish church) by my outlandish names with the addition of Susan — a name, she must have thought, that few people in England would find hard to spell. She, who spoke with the purest lack of accent I have ever heard, which she must have acquired from her Scots-born mother, pronounced the *u* in my third forename as a true and immaculate *u*. I have always wrongly pronounced the first syllable "soo".

My father, John Brophy, was a moderately popular and prolific professional writer of fiction and non-fiction. He was a more subtle and musical stylist than you would guess from his ability to earn enough to support his wife (who seldom needed his help and who herself wrote a novel that was published) and to educate me.

Some of my schooling was at coeducational state schools, some at coeducational or girls-only fee-paying schools, and once at a fee-paying boys-only prep school.

I was bitterly aware that John Brophy felt in honour bound to earn money from his writing, which in Britain is probably the most precarious of professions.

I was glad when, after a weekend of examinations and interviews at the school, I won the top scholarship to a fee-paying, "free-discipline" boarding school in the South of England. A precisely equivalent scholarship was awarded to a boy — with whom I became neither great friends nor great enemies during the five days on which I attended the school. My temperament rebelled against the "freedom" of the discipline, which in practice meant spending all afternoon, every day, weaving at a large loom. Finding I could tempt no instruction from teacher or fellow-pupil, I telephoned my parents and said that I would hitchhike home if they did not want to waste their (wartime) petrol ration on collecting me by car.

AFTERWORD

At the age of fourteen, in 1914, John Brophy gave his age as eighteen and enlisted in the British army. His mother wielded his birth certificate and rescued him once, but he rejoined. He was precocious and had no difficulty in passing for older than he was. The army would not release him a second time but shipped him to France. He served, chiefly in the trenches, on the western front from 1914 until the armistice of 1918. He remained a private soldier.

My mother, too, joined the British army and served in wartime France. The two met in 1919 when they both read English at Liverpool University. He fell deeply and lastingly in love. It took him five years to persuade my mother that he was serious and then to marry him, which she did in the rites of her sect. I think John Brophy was, as I am, a natural, logical and happy atheist, but my mother and her siblings never broke free from the influence of their father, and when the sect petered out they obeyed its instructions by joining surviving sects. John Brophy's novels bear disguised witness to his anxious attempts to find some truth in the mythology my mother continued to stick to.

I was born in June 1929, their second child but the only one who survived to an age reckoned in years rather than months.

When I was six my mother became headmistress of a prep school in a suburb of London. She introduced her pupils, of whom I was one, to John Milton's lyrics and to William Shakespeare's *A Midsummer Night's Dream* and *The Tempest*, which she produced, with me in the cast, as school plays. John Brophy, who was writing a novel about Shakespeare, recognized that I was, as he had been, a precocious child, took me to see professional Shakespeare productions in London and Stratford-on-Avon, and discussed the plays with me as though daughter and father were equals. Any ability I have had as an adult to write English prose I learned from him and from reading the masters he directed me to, Bernard Shaw and Evelyn Waugh.

In the 1940s and 1950s, much was regulated by one's age. I managed, by a special dispensation won by my mother, to

276

join the Girl Guides before I was old enough; I was so tall and so grown-up in manner that I would have made a ludicrous Brownie. But no dispensation was to be had from the rule that I might not take the examination called School Certificate until I was fourteen, or the rule that nobody might take an Oxford or Cambridge entrance examination until the person going up to the university at the beginning of the next academic year in the autumn should be eighteen. I have read that in the 1980s Oxford scrapped that silly rule.

I sat for as few exams as possible, but I evidently impressed examiners as exceptionally able and intelligent. I became afraid that the examiners, not knowing of and therefore not taking into account my physical and intellectual precocity, were judging me clever when I was in fact exceptionally stupid.

This fear did not vanish when I left the last of my schools, St. Paul's Girls' School at Brook Green, Hammersmith, London, at the age of fifteen. I went to Camberwell School of Art and then to a secretarial college where I learned (and acquired some elementary pass certificates in) typing and Pitman's shorthand. Then, as I neared the age when I should be allowed to take the entrance to Oxford, I went to a tutor in Baker Street and then to another in Pimlico lest I had forgotten the Greek I had learnt at the Abbey School, Reading, and later at St. Paul's.

Because it was the first for which I was eligible, I sat for the entrance exam at St. Hugh's College, Oxford. I was given a scholarship that was awarded at irregular intervals when an "exceptional" candidate appeared in no matter what subject.

It was lucky that I had learnt shorthand and typing. That was how I earned my living after Oxford sent me down without a degree at the end of my fourth term.

The name of the man who was the model for Neale is John.

I met him not in London but at an afternoon coffee party in Oxford while we were both undergraduates, I reading classics and he medicine. He played with a wooden duck whose two wheels bore plastic webbed feet. It was attached to a longish wooden pole and John made its feet go *splat splat* across the ceiling.

By the time I met him John no longer lived in college but in a university-approved ground-floor room at the bottom of Longwall. He wrote (good) poetry, took an interest in psychiatry, had taught himself to sing countertenor tolerably, and baffled friends about his identity when he arrived at a coffee party in a beard (which he banished after a fortnight).

Oxford in the late forties and early fifties was a great place for ballroom dancing and (presumably because men vastly outnumbered women) for engagements for marriage. John and I went to dances and balls in the Oxfordshire town where his parents lived, at his public school and at my college, where I once took three men as "my partner", one of them John.

John was also the only person I knew at all well who never asked me to marry him.

About the time I was sent down, John was moved from the Oxford medical school to a large London teaching hospital. We were then both living in London, but not quite together and not as lovers. John had a ground-floor room — presumably, this time, hospital-approved — north of Oxford Street and westward of Tottenham Court Road.

I celebrated my twenty-first birthday, which was then the age of coming of age, at my father's expense but in John's company. We went to a London restaurant to dine and dance.

At John's suggestion we went to free Italian classes at the Italian Institute in Belgrave Square. By day I worked as a shorthand-typist for a firm on an upper floor in Regent Street, but resigned when I found I should not be allowed more than a week's holiday per year. John and I were determined to go to Italy; and we went that summer, though not by the means described in *The King of a Rainy Country*. As we waited on a floating landing-stage for the water-bus along the Grand Canal, John tried to teach me to play three-dimensional chess in our heads. I didn't at that time know the moves even on a flat and visible board. In retaliation I proffered traditional formal logic, but John pronounced it boring.

Although I no longer earned six pounds a week from the firm in Regent Street, I arranged to share a furnished flat in Regent's Park with Sally, a friend whom I had met at Oxford and who loyally was not scandalized by my being sent down.

At Regent's Park I learned that my first book, a volume containing six short stories, only one of which I have ever allowed to be reprinted, was to be published — which it was in 1953, to outstandingly good notices.

I tried to earn enough from working only part-time as a shorthand-typist. The available jobs were often comic and impractical.

From the Regent's Park flat we could hear the lions in the Zoo roar at night and my first novel, *Hackenfeller's Ape*, which is set in the Zoo, began to stir in my imagination.

It, too, was published in 1953 to good notices. Unknown to me, its publishers entered it for a prize for first novels given by the Cheltenham Literary Festival. It won the top prize. My publisher, Rupert Hart-Davis, whom I had then never met (and whose editions of Oscar Wilde's letters I revere) implored me by telephone to go to Cheltenham to collect it. It was a cheque for £50. I went to Cheltenham.

John Brophy, convinced that any literary festival would be pleased to be visited by the more famous Brophy and having telephoned the organizers for confirmation, insisted on coming too.

It was the first visible sign of what I had long dreaded: for all his astonishing generosity he felt a death-blow to himself at my entry to his profession.

My mother, who was the better driver, drove my father, me and my newly married husband to Cheltenham.

I think that J. B. Priestley thought that the second-prize-winner at Cheltenham ought to have been the first. He said in print that my novel was too insubstantial to count as a novel. It is, indeed, brief, spare and without padding.

John Brophy spontaneously invented public lending right (though that was not his name for it and he did not think of public funds as its source) as a just method of rendering writers' incomes a touch less hazardous. He then discovered that it had been devised and was operating in Scandinavia — a point he wisely added to the speeches he made up and down Britain advocating it.

My father died in 1965. In the early 1970s it looked as though the Society of Authors, which had affixed the name P.L.R. to John Brophy's idea, was also going, as he had feared it would, to mishandle the project.

I therefore became co-organizer of the writers' campaign for a just and publicly funded scheme. It must have been then that J. B. Priestley forgave me for Cheltenham. He and his wife, Jacquetta Hawkes, invited my co-organizer and me to lunch at their home near Stratford-on-Avon, and by telegrams to meetings and speeches at open-air demos they generously added their influential voices to those of Graham Greene, John Braine and Angus Wilson in our campaign.

The first Bill introduced by the Labour government was filibustered out. Writers visited James Callaghan at No. 10. The second Bill was steered past the filibuster by the parliamentary expertise of Michael Foot, whom I had long admired as a writer and agreed with as a politician, and who has become a dear friend.

John (or Neale) suddenly married someone I had never met. I expected to be heartbroken and found I had seldom been so glad of anything. For all the instant imaginative sympathy between us, the three matters about which we differed were matters we both considerd crucially important.

I was free now to love, and indeed to marry, the person to whom my second novel is dedicated.

I promised to marry him after three meetings. We married on my twenty-fifth birthday. I became a vegetarian that day. Michael was converted (by our daughter) about a decade later.

John and his wife (whom Michael and I eventually met) moved to New Zealand, where he has charge of a hospital and they have now adult children. He came to see me when he visited Britain in 1984, the year in which I contracted multiple sclerosis. His gestures and tones of voice were still familiar to me.

I wanted to call him Neil in my novel. My English spelling is, however, erratic and not even self-consistent about double consonants and combinations of *e* and *i*. I write rapidly and thought it would be tedious to seek his correct spelling in a dictionary of forenames every time I wanted the narrative to mention the character. So I phoneticized him as Neale. "Kneel" seemed less apt.

My second novel is my only work of fiction to contain sizeable chunks of autobiography.

Brigid Brophy, London, 1990

281

VIRAGO MODERN CLASSICS

The first Virago Modern Classic, *Frost in May* by Antonia White, was published in 1978. It launched a list dedicated to the celebration of women writers and to the rediscovery and reprinting of their works. Its aim was, and is, to demonstrate the existence of a female tradition in fiction which is both enriching and enjoyable. The Leavisite notion of the 'Great Tradition', and the narrow, academic definition of a 'classic', has meant the neglect of a large number of interesting secondary works of fiction. In calling the series 'Modern Classics' we do not necessarily mean 'great' — although this is often the case. Published with new critical and biographical introductions, books are chosen for many reasons: sometimes for their importance in literary history; sometimes because they illuminate particular aspects of womens' lives, both personal and public. They may be classics of comedy or storytelling; their interest can be historical, feminist, political or literary.

Initially the Virago Modern Classics concentrated on English novels and short stories published in the early decades of this century. As the series has grown it has broadened to include works of fiction from different centuries, different countries, cultures and literary traditions. In 1984 the Victorian Classics were launched; there are separate lists of Irish, Scottish, European, American, Australian and other English speaking countries; there are books written by Black women, by Catholic and Jewish women, and a few relevant novels by men. There is, too, a companion series of Non-Fiction Classics constituting biography, autobiography, travel, journalism, essays, poetry, letters and diaries.

By the end of 1990 over 350 titles will have been published in these two series, many of which have been suggested by our readers.